W9-AVM-016

PRESIDIO

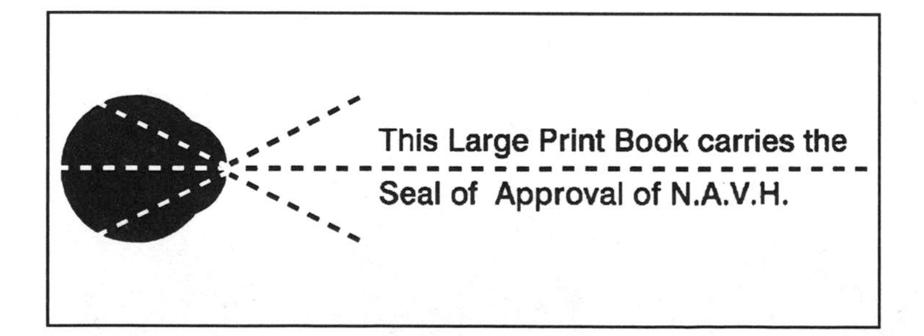
This Large Print Book carries the
Seal of Approval of N.A.V.H.

PRESIDIO

RANDY KENNEDY

THORNDIKE PRESS
A part of Gale, a Cengage Company

Farmington Hills, Mich • San Francisco • New York • Waterville, Maine
Meriden, Conn • Mason, Ohio • Chicago

Map by David Atkinson/Hand Made Maps Ltd.
Permissions are listed on page 421, which is considered a continuation of the copyright page.
Thorndike Press, a part of Gale, a Cengage Company.

Thorndike Press® Large Print Bill's Bookshelf.
The text of this Large Print edition is unabridged.
Other aspects of the book may vary from the original edition.
Set in 16 pt. Plantin.

LIBRARY OF CONGRESS CIP DATA ON FILE.
CATALOGUING IN PUBLICATION FOR THIS BOOK
IS AVAILABLE FROM THE LIBRARY OF CONGRESS

ISBN-13: 978-1-4328-6076-9 (hardcover)

Published in 2019 by arrangement with Touchstone, an imprint of Simon & Schuster, Inc.

Printed in the United States of America
1 2 3 4 5 6 7 23 22 21 20 19

For Janet, my love

Yes, friends, these clouds
pulled along on invisible ropes
Are, as you have guessed,
merely stage machinery,
And the funny thing is
it knows we know
About it and still wants us
to go on believing
In what it so unskillfully imitates,
and wants
To be loved not for that but for itself.

— John Ashbery
"The Wrong Kind of Insurance"

Sincerely I live. Who am I? Well, that's a bit much.

— Clarice Lispector
Near to the Wild Heart

How could one advance on the horizon, if it was already present under the wheels?

— Robert Smithson
"Incidents of Mirror-Travel in the Yucatan"

COLORADO
KANSAS
MISSOURI
OKLAHOMA
ARKANSAS
NEW MEXICO
FORT SUMNER
CLOVIS
LUBBOCK
TAHOKA
CEDAR LAKE
DALLAS

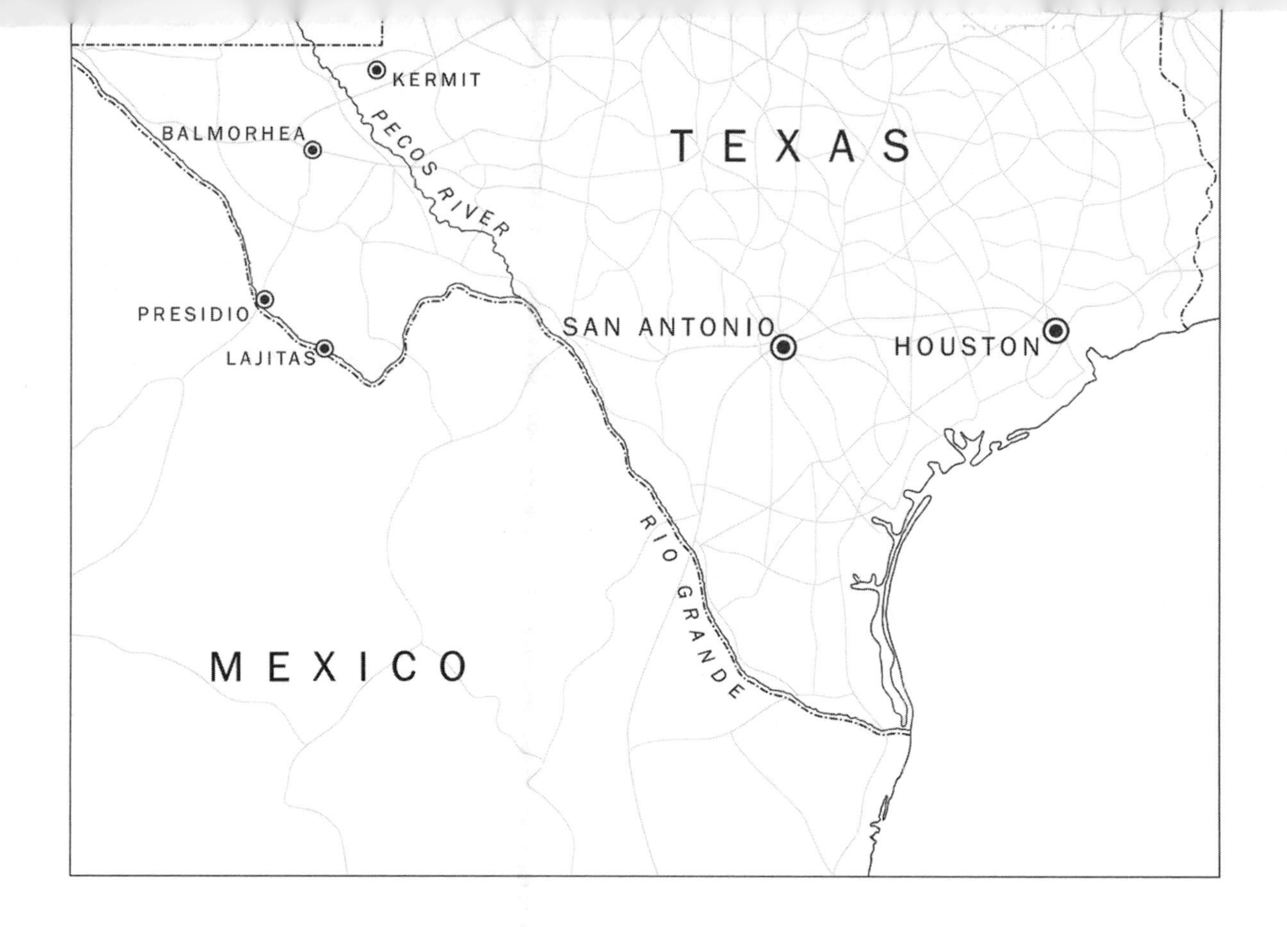
TEXAS
KERMIT
BALMORHEA
PECOS RIVER
PRESIDIO
LAJITAS
SAN ANTONIO
HOUSTON
RIO GRANDE
MEXICO

One

Later, in the glove box, the police found a folder of notes. It said:

Notes for the police:
(Or anybody else who finds this and wants to read it)

My name is Troy Alan Falconer. These are the things I love most: I love checking into a motel room on a hot afternoon, when the cool air inside smells of freon and anonymity. (They always leave the A/C running for you.) I love checking out at dawn, my hair combed wet to meet the world. I love hard-shell luggage and Swiss-made watches. I love black Roper Boots and white dress shirts with pearl snaps, starched so the placket stands up like pasteboard. I love full-size automatic sedans with electric windows and bench seats, upholstered in breathable fabric, not vinyl. I love driving cars like this down empty highways in the middle of the night, listening to the music of sincere-sounding country singers like Wynn Stewart and Jim Reeves.

I love these things for their own sake. But I can enjoy them only when they possess a certain additional quality, a quality that purifies the others — the quality of belonging rightfully and legally to someone other than myself.

If you're lucky in this kind of life, a single motel room can offer up everything you need. Inside the room is a suitcase. Inside the suitcase are the traveling possessions of a man more or less your size, a nonsmoker with passable taste in clothes and aftershave. Inside his billfold — lying right on the bedspread; salesmen like to take a swim before supper — is enough cash to keep you out on the road for two or three weeks. And on the nightstand in the cut-glass ashtray are the keys to his car, parked on the diagonal just outside the door, the windshield making a convex portrait of the afternoon sky.

For me, the instant when I settle down behind the wheel of another man's automobile is the most satisfying part. While the feeling lasts, the earth is full of promise. It's more like getting out of something than into it — like slipping my skin, breaking clean from all the things I need to leave behind (among them the last car in which I've had this same feeling). I check the mirrors, ease the key into the ignition, and idle quietly out onto the road.

The first car I stole solely for my own sake was in Lubbock in the fall of 1970. A brand-new Ford Torino hardtop with hideaway headlights, it belonged to an Air Force second lieutenant who kept a change of civilian clothes on an aluminum tension rod over the backseat, and in the armrest rack a row of neatly maintained eight-track tapes, including a few by the aforementioned singers.

I had never come across a car equipped with an eight-track before. There were only a few good songs to choose from, but I knew I was finally going to get to do the choosing, not some disembodied disc jockey out there in the ether. When I heard the sound of the music coming from the speakers under my command I was so happy I almost forgot to doubt the feeling.

This was past midnight — those empty hours when the highway patrol has nothing better to do than radio in tag numbers — but I cranked up the volume and rolled down the windows and drove straight through to Plainview before I pulled over to take care of the plates.

I'd like you to believe that I started out with some kind of justification, a reason better than anger and want. But that was mostly it — same old story. It wasn't until later that it changed from a profession into a way of life, a calling that felt almost religious if I'd been inclined that way.

If I had, I would have been its reverend, preaching my message of freedom through loss from my pulpit behind the dashboard. But I'd have been delivering the sermons to a congregation of one, a nondescript man whose freshly shaved face could be seen sticking up into the rearview mirror from the driver's side. And believe me, he's heard it all before.

Troy drove back into town on a Friday night in November of 1972 during the final week of the high school football season, when an away game had all but emptied the small grid of graveled streets. He had planned it that way, consulting the schedule in the *Lubbock Avalanche-Journal.* People in small places don't forget their own, particularly the disappointments, and Troy didn't want to be recognized by anybody in town except his brother, who would be where he always was, at home, findable by the light from the television, watching *Gunsmoke* or a fight if he could tune one in.

New Cona wasn't yet a century old. It was one of the farming towns that took root at great intervals on the cheap land formed by the final closing pockets of the American frontier. For those who arrived later, born there, it was never easy to understand why anyone had settled in this particular place in a part of the country that maps had once called the Great American Desert, a place whose previous inhabitants had used mostly as a hunting ground and a near-waterless pass-through in which to strand their enemies.

The town sat halfway down the western edge of a caliche plain formed by the earth that flowed down to the Gulf of Mexico as the Rockies pushed up. The mesa left in the wake was hard and slab-flat, a hundred and fifty miles across, devoid of trees and all but the hardiest brush, covered with low grasses that fed every living creature except coyotes and wolves, which ate the creatures that ate the grass. The Spanish called that part of what would later become Texas the Llano Estacado, the staked plain, maybe because the breaks at its boundaries looked like palisades or because horses' leads, with nothing to tie them to, had to be staked to the ground itself. But the name could have meant something else, orphaned in translation like so many others left over from the Spaniards and the Mexicans.

A few trees could be seen now, in town and clustered in the distance near farmhouses, looking conspicuous, like uninvited guests. Other things rose from the flatness — radio towers, water towers, telephone poles, torqued cedar fence posts in endless rows alongside the roads — but in most visible ways the land had changed little as a result of civilization, and outside town the structures seen from the road all sat low to the ground, obedient to the horizon. The oldest were bleached sere brown, as if the elements were winning a slow war against their intrusion. Looking out past them into the distance, it wasn't hard to imagine the fear a cavalry soldier must have felt here once as he mounted the mesa in pursuit of some enemy he couldn't see. But the land no longer seemed actively hostile. It just seemed like one of the places on the earth that had long ago stopped bothering to hide its indifference.

That night a new moon had left the countryside almost invisible. The only way to gain a bearing beyond the headlights was to look for the distant glow of town drawing a silver bead across the windshield, and this far out the lights remained so faint that Troy's eyes picked them up only when he looked away. The line began to brighten and dissipate into discrete points that spread across his field of vision, and as he drove into them, the outline of a water tower materialized above, dimly visible under a crown of red aircraft beacons pulsing into the dark.

Five miles out he passed a cotton gin, which on long stretches of road in many parts of Texas holds out the first sign of human existence, and it was alive this time of year, even this time of night, casting an orange halo of night-work several hundred yards from the road. A newcomer driving past a working gin for the first time in late fall might mistake its emission for an early snow — alongside it for several hundred yards cotton dust blanketed the road and the bar ditch in dirty white, covering the catenaried telephone wires with strands of cotton lint that hung down like icicles.

About a mile out Troy passed a yard of liquid fertilizer tanks whose vapor lights made them look like phosphorescent pillars hovering just above the ground. The road plunged back into darkness until it reached a rare curve that skirted the bins of a defunct grain elevator and crossed a set of switching tracks not in use since before Troy's birth. Past these tracks the first streetlight cast a silver-green oval onto the asphalt.

As much as he wanted to drive directly through town to see what had happened to it in his absence, he resisted and turned off west of the city limits, taking a service road that cut through a pasture of stubbled buffalo grass and gave over to dirt. Clouds of dust rose into the headlights as the car passed through fence lines and over cattle guards that made the tires thrum with a sound like a kettledrum. The road ended at the back gate of the small county cemetery, where Troy finally stopped and got out of the car and dropped the chain from the gate and knocked the heel of his right boot against the ground to get the blood flowing again after the long drive.

The nights were not yet cool but he could feel the fall in them, the sense that the shadow of the day's heat no longer lay on the land the way it did on summer nights. The only sound he could hear, from somewhere miles in the distance, was the steady metallic keen of a pumpjack. He decided that as long as he was sneaking into town by way of the cemetery he should probably take a detour through the gravel lanes to pay a visit to his family's plot — for the sake of decency, but maybe also for some kind of advance absolution for the reason he had come back here.

The cemetery sat atop a small hummock, the only natural upswell in the land for miles, and Troy looked out from it toward the lights of town as if their arrangement might tell him something. The graves marched up the rise in roughly chronological rows. The oldest, from the teens and twenties, sat at the eastern end. As the ground rose to the west the stones grew newer, larger, and shinier, some decorated with small American and Texas flags and faux-pewter vases filled with plastic floral arrangements. The town wasn't yet old enough for the dead to outnumber the living.

Troy clicked up the headlights and idled along the main path through the cemetery until he came to a gathering of headstones on the southwestern side, edging up against the groundskeeper's cinder-block shed. He killed the motor and stepped out again, but as soon as the quiet surrounded him he regretted his decision and almost got back into the car. Even as a child he had struggled to understand why people looked for comfort in cemeteries, staring at names on squared-off stones. All he had ever felt in a cemetery was a sense of looking for something in the wrong place, worsened by the simple awkwardness of walking upright through fields of the permanently supine.

But he walked up into the headlights, adding another shadow to the ones glancing off the backs of the gravestones. The light shone on the full given names of his father and his mother, buried side by side though separated in death by so many years. He was too young to remember much about his mother's funeral, but he remembered what it felt like on the blistering July day when he had arrived here just after his father's ceremony and hid in his car beneath a ridiculously large cowboy hat and a pair of sunglasses, watching from the road as two county workers mounded the dirt and took down the canvas canopy that had been over the grave, leaving it unprotected against the sun. Out in the fields behind them a tractor was going about its business, raising a cloud of red plow dust against the horizon. Troy remembered it suddenly occurring to him, as he sat there, that if his father had been able to climb up out of the hole and stand on the near side of the opening, he would have had a clear view down the rise and across the wedge of fallow pastureland all the way to the corner of their house, sitting at the northwestern edge of town. The thought of this line of sight brought him a measure of irrational comfort, as if at least one thing would be okay.

In the semidarkness he could make out a half dozen or so gravestones flanking his parents', those of his father's father and mother, who had died before he was old enough to remember them; two cousins — one who had never made it out of the delivery room and another whose body had never returned from Korea, so that his steel casket had been buried with an Army-issued Garand and unworn dress blues inside; a great uncle who died young in a combine accident and another who died at one hundred and one and was buried here against his wishes, having wanted his body to be taken back to Texarkana, where there were trees and civilized bodies of water. Troy stood with his hands in the pockets of his suit pants, looking at the grave markers, feeling as if there was something he should do, though he didn't know what, so he lingered for what felt like a respectful length of time and turned back to the car. As he did a newish-looking grave marker he hadn't noticed caught his eye, several feet to the other side of his father's, and he squinted trying to make out what it said. The tablet was small, a brown granite slab sitting plumb with the ground, and he had to draw up to it to make the light play off the surface so he could see it. When he did he read the name of his younger brother — Harlan Edward Falconer — framed inside a little dogwood oval, cut into the stone in sans-serif letters crowded to fit.

Troy stepped closer to the tablet and crouched down on his calves, studying the letters, trying to figure out what kind of mistake he could be making. It had been more than six years since he had seen his brother in the flesh. But he had spoken to him on the phone only a couple of weeks beforehand to tell him he would come back to help him look for his ex-wife, or the woman who was still legally Harlan's wife but who had walked out on him with all his money that summer after only a few months of marriage.

In that conversation, Troy had omitted at least four pieces of pertinent information — that he knew his brother's wife, Bettie, and had in fact known her before she married Harlan; that it was his fault she had taken the money; that if he'd had the slightest idea where Bettie or the money was, he would never have called his brother in the first place; and that if he had found her or the money, Harlan would never have known. But he had no clue where Bettie had gone. He didn't even know if Bettie was her real name, and he hoped Harlan might have some scrap to go by, a general sense of direction, a town. Among all the untruths Troy had told his brother over the years, he tried to think of those about Bettie as ones that Harlan needed to believe almost as much as he needed them to be believed.

Squatted down in front of the gravestone for a few seconds Troy finally managed to understand what he was seeing: a placeholder. The birth year on the stone sat by itself, followed by a dash — that cruel piece of punctuation standing in for a man's whole life — and on the other side a void of granite awaiting a slightly larger number. The stone was a funeral home special, a layaway installed out here on this sorry flatland excuse for a hill. The deal probably included the mortuary services and casket, Troy thought, maybe even one of the burial suits with the shirtfront and tie sewn into the jacket.

He stood up and took the keys out of his

pocket and let out a low whistle into the night. Harlan was a thirty-two-year-old man, in more or less decent health as far as Troy knew.

"You always did like to be ready for things, didn't you, Harl?" he said.

He got back into the car and dimmed the headlights and drove through the front gate of the cemetery, following the back road into town.

July 19, 1972

Besides the fact that they both provide short-term habitation, hotels and motels have little in common and there are many reasons why I work only motels. The architecture of hotels is designed specifically to encourage temporary communities to form, in the lobby, in the restaurant, the bar, the ballroom, the conference rooms. The rooms face inward, toward halls that lead unavoidably toward and through these communities, where bellhops and clerks and hotel detectives mark the passage of guests. Motels, by contrast, have rooms that face outward, away from each other toward the parking lot and the road, linked only by open landings and stairs that provide multiple, largely anonymous means of exit. There is no central gathering place; the office is never more than functional, just enough room for a desk and a newspaper machine, a little couch that's the last place anyone would want to sit, a rack with outdated magazines. The only real gathering place is the pool, which is big enough to provide a discreet distance, and optional anyway. The café is usually an adjoining building, often run by another proprietor, which frees the diner from being identified necessarily as a motel patron.

The best thing about motels is the way they seem to provide the evidence of human hands without their visible presence, a personal touch completely impersonal because whoever does it does it for everybody and so for nobody in particular — the turned-down coverlet; the drinking glasses with their crenellated paper caps; the sanitary band bisecting the bowl; the tri-corner toilet paper fold, a meaningless act of hospitality and yet I admit I'm disappointed if I return to my room in the afternoon and it's been forgotten.

This morning while I was shaving I noticed the steam building up on the mirror slowly revealing the swirls the cleaning woman had made the day before when she wiped it down. With the hot tap running, the patterns materialized in front of me like vanishing ink becoming visible. I waited until evaporation had cleared the mirror again and with a dry finger I wrote out on the glass, *I WAS HERE BUT I'M ALREADY GONE.*

Few motels around this part of Texas require identification and I know the ones that do. Even the most dutiful clerks never pay enough attention to see that the picture on my license doesn't quite look like me. But I'm prepared to move quickly all the same — if it's a double-decker, I request a room on the ground floor, explaining that I have a fear of heights, which gets a good laugh from behind the desk.

If my luck is working I draw a room with a door connecting to the room occupied by the owner of the vehicle I will later drive away. I watch him closely, taking up positions at the ice machine and the diner, listening through the door for the schedule of his comings and goings.

My liability is that I no longer steal with the objective of converting what I've taken as soon as I can get it off my hands. Instead I keep what I get for as long as I can, in order to live a normal life as free as possible from the strictures of legal possession. On the road, I pass myself off as a farm agent or an oil company representative, one of several traveling professionals whose particulars I've picked up. But my real profession is the careful and highly precarious maintenance of a life almost completely purified of personal property.

It feels like a calling, as I said, or a condition — in either case something I don't have a choice in. When it first came on, I thought I would end up by renouncing all worldly possessions, like a monk, but I knew I didn't have the courage to live the life that required, so I adapted what I already knew and started living this way, having but not owning. I also thought I'd have to disappear, to go away for good from all the people and places I knew, but I had no idea where I'd go besides a monastery or a prison, neither of which sounded appealing. So I decided to disappear right where I lived, to become a ghost in the middle of everybody and everything I knew.

I once ran into a man who said he could help me disappear, legally. He told me he had already done it, that he didn't exist anymore as far as the United States government was concerned.

"I checked into a room at an undisclosed Hiway House motel in an undisclosed

Southwestern state," he told me. "And a few days later, with the help of some undisclosed people, I checked out a dead man. That's who I am right now, as I speak to you. Dead to the law." This required constant maintenance, he said, and constant vigilance. He read to me from a kind of primer he carried, called *How to Disappear in America* by a man named Barry Reid: "You have to keep from depositing traces of yourself. Every place you go you inadvertently leave pieces of yourself. Every article of clothing, every doorknob, every carpet, every telephone, every toilet seat you use will contain pieces of you. Your skin is flaking off all the time."

He sounded far more paranoid than I was, which was a lot.

"You've lost the ability to own anything . . ." he said after listening to me for a while. "Meaning what? You're broke?"

"No, that's not it. I can always get money if I want it. But I don't want it. I don't want to do this anymore."

"Do what anymore?"

"Any of it. The whole thing. So I take what I need to live. And when the stuff starts to feel too much like mine, I dump it and steal everything again from somebody else."

He looked me over and nodded. "I like the way you think. But it sounds like a hell of a lot of work to me."

It's been almost two years now. I worry that when this run comes to an end — it can't go on much longer — people will think I'm some kind of hippie or communist, anti-American in some way and that would be a serious misimpression. If my sin is anything it's being too much of an American — a throwback to the pioneers who settled this great country, always headed somewhere to claim something with little more than a horse and the ragged clothes on their backs. Or before them, back to the Comanche, who made no permanent home in this part of the country and considered most of what he had only temporarily his. His livelihood was based on what he could hunt, what he could take, especially the horses, whose leads he could slip from beneath the hand of a sleeping soldier without causing so much as a rustle in his dreams.

My kind of horses aren't as easy to take or leave behind. After I steal a new car the last one sits where I left it, testifying against me in the parking lot. It's the fatal flaw in an otherwise functional system: the trail that will lead to my numbered door somewhere between Amarillo and Odessa. When it does, these pages will probably be with me, too, notes I've made on nightstand stationery, the only thing I've allowed myself to keep from job to job besides an extra driver's license and a paperback or two. It's my trail back to myself. And the most elaborately detailed confession a jury could hope for. I could say I made it up, but who'd believe me?

For the trip back home he stole a car in Fort Sumner, a 1965 sierra-tan Chevy Nova that he picked over several more attractive options because of its overwhelming inconspicuousness, the kind of car nobody would want to steal or even look at twice. The keys came from the motel room of a professional livestock judge who had registered for the week at the old Bosque Redondo Motor Inn on the south side of the city. The judge was in town for a regional 4-H show, and when he returned from the stock barns he would go out in the early evening for a constitutional around the motel grounds, pulling his dress hat down over his forehead and whistling in a piccolo-like tone that sounded like something he'd practiced. His favorite tune was the old march number "Under the Double Eagle." Smoking a cigarillo, he would make several circuits of the motel before ambling down to the bridge and staring wistfully out over the Pecos, maybe imagining himself in a previous life, fording it with a band of mounted men.

Habit was Troy's chief accomplice; the judge always walked for half an hour. When he returned one night, his car was gone, along with his suitcase, his dopp kit, his wallet, his second hat, and his best suit — a mahogany two-button gabardine with yoke stitching over the pockets, slightly too big for Troy in the shoulders. Besides the clothes the judge was wearing, the only possession he had left was his toothbrush.

Troy parked the Nova well off the road on the pasture side of the house, on a grassed-over strip of caliche alongside the fence, so that if anyone saw it they might mistake it in the shadows for a parts car. He got out and walked to the corner of the fence and stared down the alley, empty except for topless oil drums stationed in pairs beside every picket gate, filled with household garbage now instead of the Texas crude they had once held. He turned and walked close to the fence line, making sure no one was coming up the street before he cut quickly across the yard to the front door.

This house, legally his brother's and

before that his father's, was a low, hip-roofed ranch, repeated with only slight variation up and down the block and for several around, all built in the late 1940s on dropseed prairie at the western edge of town as it neared what no one then knew would be its peak of population.

More than six years had passed since Troy had last set foot on this concrete slab porch. But even by the weak wash of the streetlight he could tell something about the house didn't look right and he paused instinctively to gauge the distance back to the fence corner, trying to remember the type of handle on the Nova's door in case he had no time to waste. The lawn badly needed cutting and the flower beds had been graveled over into rectangular gray moonscapes choked with cocklebur and turpentine weed. Along the half-bricked house front he saw corners chipped off some of the asbestos shingles, exposing the tar paper and nail-heads beneath, giving the place a shot-at look. Then he saw something hanging from the frame of the storm door, a thing that surprised him to recognize so readily in the near-dark — a spirit ribbon, a paper pennant with black and gold silk streamers, a decoration handmade by high school cheerleaders and Scotch-taped to houses up and down the street to commemorate the night's varsity football game, a purely obligatory show of civic pride because the other team, the Morton Indians, a team of poor-town boys, almost always won. The ribbon might as well have been an eviction notice; no one would have thought to put such a thing on the front door of Harlan's house if it still belonged to him. Even in a place this small, he had always managed to keep himself just beyond the boundaries of people's attention, the way a crow in a field intuits the range of a rifle and settles a few feet outside its reach.

No lights were visible in the house or in the houses across the street. Troy walked to the storm door and pulled it open and knocked several times in a hard, purposeful way, with a story arranged in his head in case anyone answered, though he was sure by now that no one would.

He went over and squinted through one of the smoked oval garage-door windows and saw no car inside. Glancing up the street again for car lights, he walked back to the porch and cupped his hands to the kitchen window, letting his vision settle into the darkness while the metallic dust of the window screen stung his nostrils.

Through two panes of glass separated by

a thin metal muntin, the contours of the room where he had spent the mornings and evenings of his childhood and adolescence began to take shape slowly in front of him. They materialized like a diorama in a history museum, manufactured under the direction of memories Troy hardly considered his own anymore: the same gray-flecked Formica countertops, the same panel cabinets still painted canary yellow, the same pipe-legged dinette atop which he and Harlan had eaten for years.

Everything appeared almost the same as he remembered it, making even the smallest differences conspicuous; it reminded him of the kind of dream in which everything presents itself as normal until you realize with a shock that it's not and never was — people's faces are altered, the layout of rooms is reversed, primary colors take on unfamiliar shades.

On the back wall of the kitchen he could make out two framed portraits, both showing a large man in a cowboy hat, a nice-looking woman, and a small straight-banged blond girl. In both pictures they were posed together formally in a lopsided triangle with the man at the apex. The girl was no more than a baby in the first picture and maybe four or five in the second. She and her parents smiled serenely out over the kitchen as if it had belonged to them for years.

On the far end of the counter sat some kind of radio set, a ham or CB with a stand-up microphone, official-looking. The dinette itself was surrounded now by unmatched wooden chairs, heavy, varnished municipal-looking ones, and the surface of the table was half covered with a horde of condiment bottles and containers — ketchup, Tabasco, Worcestershire, salt and pepper, mustard, margarine, grated Parmesan cheese, honey, a yellow plastic lemon juice bottle in the shape of a lemon — a lazy-man's spread he knew his brother would never have created or allowed.

Troy took out his key ring and found the one to the house. It had never occurred to him he would actually need it again. When he found it on whatever ring he had stolen he wondered why it was there, a tarnish familiar in a succession of shiny car keys. But he kept transferring it, motivated less by nostalgia than by stubbornness, a refusal to admit that he couldn't reopen the door to an old life just by wanting to.

He tried the key and it passed into the deadbolt the way old keys do, easy under the pins, the way he had expected — he would have put money against anyone here paying to change a perfectly good tumbler. He pushed the door open and stepped quickly inside, marveling as he had so many times that in a world full of deeds and liens and property rights all you really needed to render something your own was a ten-cent piece of brass with the right kind of ragged edge.

The hallway was black. He remembered where the light switch was by feel and flipped it on. He quickly opened the coat closet, yanked the light string, pushed the closet door almost shut, and turned the hall switch off again, giving himself just enough light to see but not so much that anyone would be able to notice from the street.

He stood completely still and unbreathing in the interior hush, luxuriating in the feeling of being momentarily invisible. He hadn't expected to be worked up by being back here again, even just in this too-narrow entryway, where a cherrywood hat rack had once hung over an old Truetone floor-model, more furniture than radio, rarely able to reel in any of the weak waves ricocheting between the atmosphere and the plains.

Troy had lived in the house with his father and Harlan from the time he was eleven until he was seventeen and began spending most of his nights elsewhere, returning only occasionally for money or to try to avoid paying it to partners in low-level criminal arrangements he had started to make.

Within a year of their mother's death, before Harlan had started school, their father had had the boys start to call him by his name, Bill Ray, a change they accepted for its novelty and its advertisement of their loss. The name didn't stop Bill Ray from being their father, exactly, but over time it seemed to give him permission to settle into a role that suited him better, that of admired older brother, unpredictably attentive, occasionally feared. The arrangement wasn't bad for any of them. It bound the boys more strongly to each other in those first years, and it gave Bill a way to retreat to a time before Ruby, before he'd ever met her and found the happiness that would be so short lived.

His attempts at fatherly responsibility tended to involve teaching the boys things his older brother had taught him in their own father's absence — showy, mostly useless things, like how to wink, how to snap their fingers, how to whistle and spit, to whittle, to catch thrown peanuts in the mouth, to throw a pocketknife to make it plant, to throw a punch, to find arrowheads in the pasture; but sometimes also practical knowledge — how to tell a bullsnake from a rattler by the neck, how to handle a pistol, rifle, and shotgun (though he had a personal aversion to hunting and never let the boys shoot at animals in his presence), and how to drive: first Troy, then Harlan, boosting him up to the steering wheel with a bed pillow. The secret to good driving, Bill Ray had said, was to let your eyes come to rest on the road in the middle distance, not too close to the nose of the hood and not too far out to where it ran up into the horizon.

Bill Ray had been raised on a dryland cotton farm perpetually on the brink of bankruptcy, and as soon as he was old enough to leave home he said goodbye to farming for good. He worked several years as an oilfield equipment driver, but after Ruby died, he lost that job and never held a steady one again, getting by with piecework, mostly driving tractors and checking wells. When the oil companies needed extra hands he roughnecked, earning good cash pay, though it never came often enough, and in late summers, when hailstorms brought business, he roofed for extra money. For a time, because he had no fear of heights, he hired on as a maintainer for a radio tower company, scaling the metal armatures with a bucket of aluminum paint tethered to his waist and a cigarette dangling from his mouth, but that job ended one afternoon when he was caught dozing in the harness at a hundred and fifty feet and handed his severance as soon as he got back to the ground. He told Troy and Harlan he had walked off the job on his own. "I got tired of smelling all that bird ass up there," he said, winking and working a matchstick in his teeth.

His reputation as a drinker wasn't undeserved, but it was exaggerated in the way such things can be in small towns, by people who considered themselves empathetic and thought it was only to be expected. As a practical matter, it meant that whenever work came his way he had to take it. Pulling on his work boots he would tell Troy and Harlan that it was time for them to hold down the old fort again, deputizings that could last for days when he was working on a rig and sleeping at the drill site. As the boys got older, the absences grew longer. Sometimes a week would pass before they heard from him again between jobs, and they made a habit of checking the odometer of his pickup, which indicated that he could have crossed three states in the time he was gone.

While Bill Ray was away Troy, older by three years, did most of the cooking, what he could manage, because he was particular — cowboy supper, pimento cheese, tortillas fried on the burner, Mrs Baird's fruit pies heated in the oven. But it was Harlan who ended up as overseer of almost everything else in the household, to keep it from falling to pieces — the dishes, the trash, eventually the groceries and the bills. Harlan didn't try to conceal their growing parentlessness but people in town, even at the school, seemed not to notice, as if they had reached some private agreement that the Falconer residence was a situation that should be allowed to take care of itself as long as it was able. Harlan was acutely aware of the spectacle of it — of an awkward, overgrown twelve-year-old boy walking up to the window of the county assessor's office to pay the school taxes. In his stolid way, in a voice that had already begun its steep descent into manhood, he would say "yes, ma'am" and "no, ma'am" and "a quarter acre" and "Bill Ray's doing fine, thank you." He rarely complained and when he did his anger seemed to be softened by the satisfaction of knowing that he was the only one in the family capable of taking things in hand.

Just often enough, or during those times

when his attention was absolutely required, Bill Ray would be around. And when he was, he had the ability to inhabit the present with the kind of fierce attention most people lose as children, so that Troy and Harlan would forget he ever had a desire to be elsewhere, just as they feared he would never come back when he was gone.

But he came back, sooner or later, sometimes with a full money clip and a grocery bag of sirloins, like a prospector who had tapped a vein. When a job set him up especially well he would take the boys out of school and drive them to Lubbock to buy new shirts, to see a picture at the State Theater on Texas Avenue, to visit Pinkie's on the strip, where he bought his beer. He'd give each of them a bottle and the three would sit in the pickup drinking like ragged-ass cowboys in town on a ranch furlough. They never did things other families did, never went to school functions together, never went on vacation, rarely visited another family. Once, Troy remembered, Bill Ray took him and Harlan fishing a couple of hours from town at a man-made lake — most lakes in Texas are man-made but this one looked especially artificial, surrounded by a berm of gravel, too square, too near some kind of industrial facility. It was brutally hot but the lake had just been stocked and they caught a decent-size fish in fifteen minutes and put it in a bucket and took it home. The boys wanted Bill Ray to cook it but he said it was a carp and they would have to beat it for three days with a two-by-four to make it tender enough to eat. Instead, he filled the bathtub and left it there for the afternoon. It swam around briefly but then seemed to accept its fate and floated motionless, staring down the length of the tub, as if waiting for an appointment. When the boys woke the next morning the carp was gone, along with Bill Ray.

By the time Troy was old enough to understand how angry he was, he convinced himself that it was mostly on Harlan's behalf, at the injustice of a boy so young having to be his father's father. But he failed to see how much Harlan had to be a father to him, too, or how much of his own pain was caused by his desire to be more like Bill, to inhabit that kind of ease and self-possession, the trick of seeming to float just outside all the places where he was supposed to belong. As it often does, this yearning took the form of competition, a battle of wills made worse by Bill's ignorance of it, or more likely just his refusal to acknowledge its existence.

By ten, Troy had started to light out by himself. Walking to school with Harlan, he would turn off without a backwards glance and hide in the treed bottom across from the county park or the caliche pit west of town, reading library paperbacks by Max Brand and Edward Anderson or sometimes just thinking, watching the shadow line advance slowly over his feet, his knees, his waist, slipping over his head as the sun fell below the far wall. Even at that age, Harlan said, Troy had an uncommon capacity for two things: lying and enjoying his own company.

At fourteen, cleaning windshields on weekends at the Humble gas station near the motel, he was sometimes able to talk passers-through into driving him the distance of a town or two, to Hobbs or Brownfield. One July, an Old Dominion freight driver took him all the way to Artesia before Troy grew bored and made up a story about being due at Fort Bliss for basic training. The driver was young and muscular, with a pencil mustache and high Indian cheekbones. He was duded up like a cowboy movie star, wearing his hat cocked high on his head and a cigarette tucked behind his ear. Troy wondered what someone so good-looking was doing driving a truck and he thought that life was probably just like that, as he had always suspected.

The driver stared absently ahead through the windshield. "Army must be takin' 'em young these days," he said.

Troy had stopped caring whether he was being believed and was talking mostly to himself, addressing the ruler of two-lane road that seemed to extend through eastern New Mexico to the edge of the known universe.

"There's a shortage on," he said finally. "Korea and all."

The truck was coming into Artesia. The driver lit the cigarette and cracked his window.

"Listen, son, I don't mind taking you on," he said, "but I don't appreciate being lied to in my own rig. Why don't you save the bullshit for your next freeload?"

Troy listened to the motor protest as the truck engine-braked at the city limit. He said: "I don't imagine you could spare one of those cigarettes, could you?"

The driver took off his wire-rimmed sunglasses and stowed them beneath a strap on the visor.

"You imagine correct," he said.

While the truck was pulled over at a filling

station and the driver was inside paying, Troy leaned over and spat a prodigious wad of phlegm onto the middle of the spring-shot leather driver's seat and stole the sunglasses and a thermos full of Canadian whiskey and walked away down the road wearing the shades — idly, like someone out for an afternoon stroll. The highway patrol found him within an hour and telephoned Bill, who delayed his arrival until dawn. He waited until they were a few miles outside town before he whipped the pickup off the road, slammed on the brakes, and backhanded Troy in the face, busting his lip. Troy called him a son of a fucking bitch, and Bill hit him again, this time with his fist, bloodying his nose in a gush that made a fantail down the neck of his white undershirt.

It was the only time Bill Ray ever hit him. He understood as if in the bones of his hand how little it would ever accomplish. But for Troy the blows, after a night spent awake in a jail cell, brought a revelation. Riding back to town with his heartbeat pounding in his swollen face and Roy Acuff wailing the "Great Speckle Bird" on the radio, he came to see for the first time that he was not going to grow up to join the world of respectable or even passably decent people — no matter how hard he tried. The truth was that he knew he was never going to feel like trying. He kept the T-shirt he was wearing for many years as a kind of relic, hiding it in the back of a drawer, taking it out from time to time and spreading it across his bed to see how the blood of his youth had darkened to a color as brown as cow shit, crusted and cracking.

Troy stood in the hallway of the house now, staring back into the darkness of the bedrooms. He wondered if Harlan had left the little dresser here, the one where he had hidden his T-shirt. The dresser was nothing, a paltry stick of furniture, made of thinly primered pine, missing three of its knobs, but it was the only dresser he had used until he was an adult so it still seemed strangely significant. He wondered if he would find it as he remembered it, in the northwest corner of his old room. It had sat on an unraveling rope rug, across from a narrow iron bedstead and a box shelf hung on the wall over the bed, a sort of curiosity cabinet filled with things he had found in the pasture across from the house, a natural history of the alien-looking artifacts a hard land like West Texas casts up — a devil's claw, a dead silverfish, the desiccated skin of a horned toad, the carapace of a scorpion half as big as his hand, a collection of severed rattlesnake rattles, and a dozen flint Comanche arrowheads that looked as if they had been carved the day before he found them.

He wondered if these new people, whoever they were, had taken out a mortgage on an entire life he had once lived, container and contents. It wasn't a totally unpleasant thought; maybe their version would turn out better, though signs didn't seem to point in that direction.

He was able to see better now and went into the kitchen, which smelled strongly of cigarettes and cooking grease. The streetlight coming through the window shone on pearl-gray dishwater standing in the sink and illuminated its depths down to forks and knives glinting at the bottom. He pulled out a chair from the table and sat down to take a closer look at the studio portraits on the wall, to see if he recognized the man or wife or little girl. As he sat studying them he felt fairly sure that the wife and daughter were no longer a part of the picture here anymore, if they ever really had been. The house felt the way it always had, like a place without women, but even more so now, useful only for the refrigerator, the bathroom, and the bed, in roughly that order.

The man in the pictures looked big and well fed. He wore a cowboy hat of cream-colored felt and a bolo tie with string-ends weighted down by copper bullet casings. His wide smile beneath a rope of brown mustache gave his face a benignly boyish look, but there was something about the smile that put Troy off; it seemed too satisfied, the type of smile he had grown up seeing at rodeos on the faces of calf ropers as they stood up over the vanquished animal. An unsettled feeling he'd had on first looking into the kitchen returned, a cloud gathering at the back of his brain. And then it came to him with the force of self-evidence: *This was a law enforcement house now.* Harlan had sold it to a sheriff, or maybe to one of the highway patrol stationed in town, though everything about the man in the picture marked him as local, not state. Troy was stunned it had taken him so long to pick up on the signs; there was a time in his life when he would have smelled it instantly, some unbodied presence warding him off before he even touched the doorknob.

On first coming into the house he had felt a strange sense of familiarity, not because it had once been his but because he knew it didn't belong to him anymore, and for years he had spent so much time inside places like it, darkened rooms belonging to other people, in their absence, sock-walking through their undefended possessions. Yet as he continued to look at the picture of the big cowboy it occurred to him that this house felt like a place that still knew him and he had the sinking sensation of returning to it after a long journey to find it ransacked and occupied.

He walked back to his old room, empty except for a stack of cardboard moving boxes in one corner. He coughed and the sound echoed off the sheetrock. He walked into what had been Bill Ray's room and saw that the old matching oak bedroom set was still there, the one Ruby's mother had given them for their wedding. The bed was unmade and mounded with dirty laundry. Troy tried to avoid looking at anything. He turned on the closet light, keeping the door almost closed, and went straight to the bottom drawer of the nightstand, the one he would sneak in to open when he was a boy, mostly for the forbidden thrill of handling Bill Ray's Masonic gear — the carefully folded, starched white apron, the little blue handbook embossed with a caliper enclosing a golden G that he had figured must have something to do with God, though a

God more private than the one he knew from church. He had thought of these things as the visible tip of a vast submerged continent of adult secrets. The drawer had seemed to contain all the talismans of manhood — cuff links, tie clips, money clips, lapel pins, sock garters, pocket watches, penknives, all exotic because so rarely ever taken out and used — along with Bill Ray's olive Army garrison cap and discharge papers and sometimes a bottle of unused aftershave and a box of rubbers. The drawer was empty now except for a scatter of unpaired black socks.

He rose from the floor and saw that a belt and holster had been left looped over the right-hand post at the foot of the bed — the lawman's extra rig. Or maybe he was off duty tonight, Troy thought, although in his experience few men given the right to conspicuously carry firearms ever passed up a chance to do so, especially at public functions like football games. Troy looked at the gun for a minute, then lifted it gingerly from the holster. It was a Colt .38 revolver, standard police-issue with checkered grips, a gun that looked unfired and ceremonial in its polish. He swung the cylinder out and saw that it was empty. It had been so long since Troy had handled a pistol that its deadweight surprised him. He stood up and straightened his left arm slowly toward the dresser mirror, bringing the barrel into line with his eye. He wanted to see what he looked like but it was too dark in the room; his shape was more shadow than reflection. It reminded him how much he hated mirrors, which had caused him more than once during his house burglary days to jump half out of his skin when he caught sight of himself, fearing he wasn't alone.

The idea of taking the gun crossed his mind, just to have something for protection now. But Troy had never worked with a weapon and stealing one from a cop would be the worst way to start, so he eased it back into the holster and wiped down the grips with his coat sleeve.

Back in the kitchen he checked the time and sorted through the mail, learning the man's name, Darryl D. McGuire, deputy county sheriff. He opened the refrigerator but found nothing revealed by its jaundiced light to be worth the risk, so he rummaged around in the cabinets for a can of coffee and rinsed out the percolator and started a pot. Then he sat down at the kitchen table and by the light reaching it from the street began to write on the stationery tablet he had in his coat pocket, trying to clear his mind while he thought about where Harlan could be.

He sat looking toward the hallway where he had just been, which darkened to black from the kitchen to the bedrooms, a distance he estimated to be no more than twenty-five feet, though he remembered it being infinitely longer. As a child he had been terrified of traversing it at night when only he and Harlan were at home and most of the lights were off, per Bill Ray's strict orders to save electricity. The sprint down the hallway to the wall switch in the bedroom he shared with Harlan was a gauntlet that grew agonizingly longer each time he took it. In those five or so seconds he felt as if he was becoming entangled in some unseen web, snatched at by the fingers of thousands of hands trying to get hold of him, to drag him into an even deeper dark from which he would never emerge. The fear tormented him, and to conquer it he made up his mind to plunge into the hallway nightly until it went away, but he gave up after a week and waited until Harlan had gone back to turn on the light before going to the bedroom himself.

Facing the little stretch of painted sheet-rock now, he found it hard to understand how anyone could have suffered so much in such a tiny nothing of a space. And it occurred to him that in some deeply buried way a child's fear of ghosts might just be a substitute for the fear that there isn't anything else out there, larger, unseen, good or evil — that what we see is all there is. And as we get older we accept this, so we stop being afraid of the dark in one way as we begin to fear it in another.

Aug. 18, 1972

I can't account with any accuracy for how I've occupied my time since I started. A lot of it has been spent looking as if I'm busy. I like to show the semblance of industriousness — to be out on the road at dawn, the taste of black coffee and toothpaste in my mouth. I never feel better than when I'm moving.

But many days I just sit in my motel room with the television on, mostly for the sound and motion, watching commercials for products I know I won't have to buy. Or I sit in silence for long stretches listening to passing cars and trucks, to the whine of a vacuum cleaner coming through the walls, to other motel guests shutting and opening their doors, coming and going, talking and talking. Sometimes I sit in a hot bath, one leg crossed over the other, thinking about the world at work while I watch the pulse of my heartbeat in the hollow of my ankle.

To keep myself out of unnecessary trouble, I decided early on to steer clear of hitchhikers, women, and alcohol, and I generally upheld this pledge, which was easy on the alcohol front because I was traveling mostly through counties that had been dry since before Prohibition.

When I met Bettie I wasn't looking for company — but she was, in a manner of speaking, for reasons that became clear. I was in Friona that morning, sitting in a booth near the front of a café, drinking a cup of coffee after the early rush, reading the newspaper. I never come into such places during the rush, never before nine a.m. To do so as an unaccompanied stranger in a small town is like walking onto the stage of a crowded theater with the spotlight on your face. But by nine these cafés are usually almost empty — the farmers and ranchers head out first, before seven, to the fields, then the lingering jobholders, to make their eight o'clocks, followed by the retirees and the profoundly elderly, who go home to watch a little TV before returning at noon for lunch.

This was a nice café, though in its particulars it differed little from any café in any small town in West Texas, probably any town in rural America: the sweet, flat, animal smell of fry grease, not unpleasant but not quite pleasant, either, a kind of limbo smell; a small counter dominated by a Bunn double-tank coffee maker, with a top warmer for a third pot containing no coffee, only steaming water; a chrome three-drawer Toastmaster cabinet, to warm the dinner rolls and the thick, oiled Mexican tortilla chips; Naugahyde-backed booths with chipped Formica woodgrain trim; an Ace Reid cowboy-comics calendar behind the cash register ("Naw, I ain't gittin' throwed off; I ain't got on yet!!") next to a framed piece of crewelwork depicting a windmill against a sunset, above the words "The Eyes of Texas Are Upon You" stitched in Palmer Method script. Next to the cash register a metal toothpick roller and a double courtesy bowl — matchbooks and cellophane-wrapped peppermints. In the vestibule between the two glass doors a newspaper machine, a cigarette machine, a penny shopper rack, and two gumball machines below a row of hat pegs still used by the older farmers and ranchers. On the outside door, facing into the parking lot, a sign that says "Sorry, We're Open" in mock-official red letters on a black background.

I was eating the breakfast I always ate when it was available: a short stack with syrup and a scoop of whipped butter on top; half a cantaloupe; a small glass of milk. The stack was served on a heavy plate decorated around the edge with various cattle brands. The cantaloupe came in a bowl with matching cattle brands. Both sat atop a paper placemat printed with nostalgic frontier scenes from the Old West that had never happened. The milk was served in a short, brown-tinted glass with wavy sides, the same as the ice water.

The only interesting difference about this diner was a pair of high horizontal mirrors that met at a corner above the front window. When you looked into them from my booth you could see the reflection of the road outside and the sight of the occasional car coming from what appeared to be two directions at once, creating an illusion of identical vehicles approaching each other, crashing head-on, and consuming themselves into nothingness in the middle.

In these mirrors I saw the car, an alpine-white 1970 Challenger R/T, slow and pull into the parking lot. She walked through the door at five minutes to ten and paused just inside to survey the room before sliding into my booth across from me, wordlessly, smiling without making eye contact. She was dressed to be someplace other than a town like Friona, Texas — a fancy starched blue-jean dress with a broad white lace collar and blousy sleeves that draped down like wings, half covering slender fingers weighted down with gold and silver and turquoise. Her coal-black hair was arranged on top of her head in a tall complicated braid formation that made me think of Elizabeth Taylor in *Cleopatra* or the Aztec princesses on Mexican nudie calendars. The only thing slightly off about her getup, catching your eye, was the panty hose — white ones, like the kind nurses wear in hospitals.

She looked about twenty-five, though she could have passed for nineteen and I suspected she was at least thirty. Her perfume smelled sweet, like layer cake. She had a confidence-inspiring olive-colored face that only in betraying nothing betrayed her attempt at an appearance of youthful virtue.

I noticed she was a little out of breath. She continued not looking at me and reached over and moved my water glass across to her side of the table and quickly drank down half, then took a menu out of the rack and began to study it, as if we were about to order lunch but she couldn't make up her mind. I finally lowered my paper and looked at her without saying anything. Her back was to the door and I glanced at it — to remind myself where it was, in case I needed to use it in a hurry, but also because I had the feeling that someone would be coming through it any minute now, looking for her.

I was fairly certain I had watched exactly this scene in an old movie, but nothing remotely like it had happened to me. The waitress came over and asked if she wanted to order anything. She continued studying the menu as if it actually offered desirable dining options, then she raised her head and looked into the waitress's eyes and her face became illuminated with the most genuinely delighted smile I had ever seen on someone I knew to be faking it.

"I think I'll have a cup of coffee with my husband here and we'll share a piece of that pie over there under the glass. What kind do y'all have today?"

The waitress returned the smile with

unqualified pleasure. "That's a pecan. Made just this morning."

"Does that sound all right by you, honey?"

I was holding my paper halfway up now, a position of defensive uncertainty. For the first time, she met my eyes, scanning them, trying to figure out if I was really playing along or if I was just stunned into speechlessness. I didn't say anything but I allowed a smile to pass almost imperceptibly over my lips, an acknowledgment of professional admiration.

She looked back at the waitress and winked. "He's always after me about the sweets. But life's short, ain't it?"

"A slice of pie never hurts is what I say."

"You said it. We'll go ahead and split one, then, à la mode."

"All righty, we'll sure get you fixed up," the waitress said and wrote down the order and then made no move whatsoever to go fulfill it, looking up at us again sociably from her pad.

"Now where're y'all from?"

This I wanted to hear. I looked across the table and scanned her face closely for a tell but picked up nothing, not the slightest hint of pause or calculation in her eyes.

"We live over in Longview," she said.

"We're just on our way through to Ruidoso."

This was fine professional work: She had chosen a place in East Texas, the other side of the state, far enough away that the waitress was unlikely to know anyone from there. Friona was a place that people passed through on their way west to the mountains in New Mexico, and Bettie knew not only this but the name of the right mountain town to mention. She had thought it through in half a second, or more likely she'd had it all ready before she sat down.

"It's real pretty up there this time of year — a whole lot prettier than around here, that's for sure," said the waitress, who was probably about a decade out of high school but appeared a decade older than that. Looking at Bettie seemed to make her feel better about herself.

When the front door to the café opened a couple of minutes later I was still, against all judgment, seated at the table, watching this woman who was pretending to be my wife, with whom I still hadn't exchanged a word. The only way I can account for why I hadn't gotten up and walked straight to my car is that I didn't have a sense of myself as a participant in her performance;

it felt more like something I was watching from a great distance, and I wanted to see how it would end. The pie and coffee had arrived; she poured in as much cream as the cup would hold to cool it and quickly drank half, to make it appear as if she had been sitting in the booth longer than she had.

The man who finally came through the door was on the small side but solidly built. He wore a good Western suit and a felt hat with a fan of gray hawk feathers cresting from the front of a woven leather band. His glasses were the brown half-tinted kind that are supposed to go clear indoors but that remain obscured much longer in West Texas because of the ferocity of the sunshine they have been defying. His suit jacket hung away from his paunch and I could make out no holster, though he could have had one on the back of his belt or down under his pants leg. As soon as he took in the room — our waitress; a young farmer; an old rancher in a back booth beneath a sweat-stained hat; a Mexican kid slouched on a counter stool; two other women, retired-teacher-or-church-secretary-types sitting in another booth — I could tell he wasn't sure who he was looking for and I breathed a little easier.

Everyone turned to see who was coming in, staring for longer than would have been polite in a bigger town. She acted as if the door hadn't opened, appraising a piece of pie on the end of her fork. The man went to our waitress where she stood near the cash register and said something quietly to her and she smiled reflexively, then she looked pained and said something back to him and turned her head uncertainly in our direction. The man's head didn't turn to follow. He pushed his hat back and hitched his belt and seated himself at one of the tables along the far wall, almost behind Bettie but where I could see him and he could see me. He didn't look in our direction again. He signaled for the waitress and I heard him order a plate of enchiladas and an iced tea.

I looked across at her, to see how she was taking all of this. She finished her pie calmly and stared back at me, hard, as if a thought had just occurred to her. Then she reached a hand across the table and put it on top of mine in a friendly, married sort of way and said softly: "What do you do for a living?"

I left my hand where it was and smiled a bland domestic smile back at her and answered, more softly: "I think if anyone gets to ask questions, it's probably going to be me, don't you?"

Maybe because she knew the man couldn't see her face, she gave me what I took to be a sincere look, though I had no way of knowing. "It just seems to me like you know what's happening here and you know what you're doing. So I'm starting to think maybe you're not from around here. And that you and I might be in a similar line of work. And that picking this booth was the best luck I've had in a while."

"Why did you pick this booth?"

"It was the closest one to the door. And you were by yourself."

"Maybe I'm a cop. Maybe you picked wrong."

She looked at me in a way that told me not to insult her intelligence.

I fixed her straight in the eye for the first time and slowly retrieved my hand, keeping my filial smile in place for the man's sake: "Lady, I don't know what you've got going, but I'm in no position to be in the middle of anything right now. So I'm going to get up and walk out of here unless that little goat roper over there is someone I need to be afraid of personally."

For a second she seemed happy that I'd gotten the lay of the land so quickly. But then a look of weariness came over her. "I've never seen that sack of shit before today. It's probably the goddamned car. I caught him following me in Hereford and thought I lost him going west but when I got into town, there he was coming around the corner. My windows are tinted so I don't think he got a look at me. He's probably sitting over there trying to figure out if I'm really the one and who the hell are you."

I gave the man another look. "I'd put him at insurance or dealership or private help somebody hired just for your sake. Where'd the car come from?"

The hard look came back into her eyes.

"Where do cars come from? Streets, parking lots, car factories. How the hell do I know? It came with a promise I wouldn't have to worry and here I sit."

I took a sip of coffee and kept up my smile. "Let's say Señor Repo over there decides to make something of it. Would that put you in bigger trouble than a misplaced car?"

"It might."

"Might how much?"

"More than I need."

"Why do you think he hasn't just called the sheriff to help him take care of this?"

She looked annoyed again. "He's working his own line. Or the insurance company is. Or they both are."

Probably just to give herself some business she dug around methodically in her purse and retrieved a piece of gum and unwrapped it and put it in her mouth.

"If you help me get out of here and take me to the bus stop in Hereford, I swear I can make it worth the trouble."

I stirred more cream in my coffee, to give myself some business. "Then he'll take down my plates."

She put up a different kind of smile, one that looked marital and malicious at the same time. "Would that be a problem for you?"

"It might."

She was getting visibly antsy now, starting to lose some of her composure. She tried to keep her voice down without whispering too noticeably. "He wants the car. He's not going to leave it . . . What are you driving? Is it in front?"

I decided to tell her the truth, for the hell of it. "Coronet Brougham. Around back."

"A Brougham? Are you a family man?"

"It helps to look like one sometimes."

"Go get it. Take your time, make him think you've left. Pull around front, and as soon as I see you I'll be out of here before he can make the door."

"Give me a reason. I won't take your money."

"Because I know you don't want that fuckhead to make his quota on me any more than I do."

"Maybe if you'd been careful you wouldn't be in a position for that to happen. Or to put me in the middle of it."

The color ran out of her face. "Believe me, it's not something that's happened before."

I did believe her. And she was right — it would bother me to walk out of there and let a common insurance dick have his day. But what made my mind up wasn't that. It was this: It occurred to me with considerable clarity that as dangerous as it would be to help her, it would be much more so to leave her there and run into her or whoever she worked with somewhere down the road. The fact was that I'd picked the wrong café that morning. And if you don't operate according to facts, facts operate on you. I put down some money for the check and walked out the door. She got in as soon as I rounded the corner, and the little man didn't even make the parking lot before we turned off.

Instead of going to a bus stop, we went to my motel and checked out and drove to Amarillo, where I'd have an easier time picking up a new car. We drove that one to the other side of the Panhandle, stopping at nightfall in Childress (which I'd avoided for a good six months) and took a room at the Trade Winds Motel. During every minute of the next three days, I fully expected the end to come; I could hear the sirens; I could feel the thunder of half a dozen cruisers rolling up and a dozen men with rifles pouring out, the sound of the bathroom window shattering as more came in that way. Or I envisioned myself waking up to two or three strangers, her standing across the room getting dressed, telling them in Spanish what to do with me. I had exposed myself completely and I deserved whatever happened.

But nothing did. She could have rolled me herself — I slept the sleep of the dead for the first time in months — but she didn't even do that. For two days, we barely got out of bed or ate or spoke. On the third, while I was showering, she went through my wallet and started to call me Cliff, laughing when she said it because she knew the name on the license wasn't mine. I said I didn't want to know her name but she told me anyway, so I assumed it was as genuine as mine.

She wasn't much good in bed. She was too selfish for that. But I hadn't been with a woman for almost two years so it seemed to me as if everything she did was a holy miracle. She was generally undemonstrative, but every time she climaxed she made a series of short, sharp squeals, like a coyote's yip at dusk. I was sure everybody in the motel complex could hear. It seemed to be the only time she ever fully forgot herself, and it might have been her only endearing quality — that and the fact that she didn't leave me broke and stranded when I lowered all my defenses.

Of course, what she did after she lulled me into this false sense of security made up for all of that.

New Cona was bisected by a shallow draw that cut roughly northwest to southeast, the same direction as the imperceptible grade of the land to sea level. The draw had once run with seasonal water plentiful enough for horses, and so its course had been the roadway that conveyed the earliest settlers, rugged people who, for reasons lost to history, had chosen this particular declivity dwarfed by this particular immensity of mesaland to end their travels, put down stakes, and spend the rest of their lives. They platted a town on the cardinal points, a mile on each side, a square that hadn't yet been filled out with paved streets. The town lay a hundred miles west of the ninety-eighth meridian — not near enough for the rain that most years fell sufficiently east of that line. A land-sale pamphlet from the turn of the century, coaxing farmers west to the llano, had been artfully equivocal on this point: "The climate here is all that could be expected." Troy didn't know where the name came from. Was there an Old Cona? Probably just a Cona — in Mexico? If there was a Cona, what had made it worth memorializing? The name sounded a little like the one Mexican boys called you in school sometimes, *coño,* laughing when they said it.

Troy had left the house and was driving warily through the draw into town. In his memory the draw had never had water, no more than stood after a rare collected rain, and he still found it hard to envision anything resembling a river running through it.

He felt the familiar plunge as the road dropped down into the bottom, a good paved road, evidence that no more water was expected; the aquifer springs that carved out the land had long since dried up, the water siphoned by irrigation pumps to the endless miles of cotton fields that never had enough.

The bottom of the draw supported what passed on the plains for a wooded patch, with low soapberry and bumelia trees, so the county park had been put there to the east of the road, centered around a little tree-topped man-made hill, an exotic site for children. Rising out of the draw the road passed the county swimming pool, the only place in town where the seasonal return of standing water was guaranteed, closed now, drained until summer. The aquamarine paint from the pool bed reflected upward in the glow of the parking lot lights, giving the impression of daylight being stored just below ground.

Next was the New Cona Motel, one of only a handful of motels in the Panhandle whose layout Troy didn't know by heart. Slowing, he saw the face of an old man in the office window, whitened by a fluorescent lamp. Like most businesses in this part of the state that had once catered to passers-through on their way to the mountains in New Mexico or returning from them, the motel had become a relic; interstate motels and Winnebagos had taken its place and its lifeblood was down to long-haul truckers and migrant farm labor. The street corner nearest the office was fenced in by three eighteen-wheelers, nose to tail, and the parking lot itself was nearly empty, save for a few dirt-covered pickups whose positions indicated the occupied rooms.

Troy took a left at the main road and drove past the squat cinder-brick diner, the feed store, and the one surviving gas station, whose four Exxon pumps sat beneath an orphaned Humble sign. In his absence, the First Baptist Church had built an impressive lighted road sign at the edge of its parking lot, an evangelizing tool many small-town churches had begun using to beam mini-sermons through the windshields of late-night drivers. The vinyl block letters up on the sign read:

You Can't Fall
If You Are Already
On Your Knees
— Genesis 33:3

In his thousands of miles behind the

wheel, Troy had become a connoisseur of these kinds of homilies, and he admired this one, though he felt obliged to observe that whoever coined it must have never suffered the singular indignity of being unable to prevent himself from going all the way to the floor after already finding himself on his knees, as Troy had a couple of times during his drinking days.

For a year or so after their mother died Bill Ray had taken Troy and Harlan to this church, but only during Wednesday-night services. Bill Ray could never bear the social pressure and hollow concern of Sundays. On Wednesdays the pews were usually only about a third full and those who came were either the deeply and openly devout, viewed with a certain wariness by regular churchgoers, or simply people who were lonely and too shy to address Bill and the boys.

Troy remembered being allowed to stretch out on the long, nubby, golden-colored pew cushions, where he would fall into a deep sleep staring sideways at the hymnals in their holders and at the cylindrical receptacles for the miniature grape juice glasses that would be passed along the aisles occasionally for the Lord's Supper. He tried to remember other particulars about the church but he could recall only the baptismal, which was hidden behind a pair of heavy blue-velvet curtains that were drawn apart from a rectangular opening behind the choir seats, revealing the preacher and the suppliant standing together in robes in a sunken fiberglass tub of warm waist-high water. Behind them was a large trompe l'oeil oil painting of a river receding into a coral sunset — a sight never beheld in a waterless country and therefore practically heavenly. He thought about how a single, usually impulsive decision at the age of twelve or thirteen to believe in the Lord and permit oneself to be submerged in water in public was supposed to have the power to change everything for all eternity. After Troy himself had done it, he remembered wondering where the water from the baptismal tank went when it drained away — did it run into the regular sewer?

Troy had no memory of Bill Ray speaking about what he believed but he once said that if church was a place where people gathered under false pretenses at least it was one of the nicer places where they did so. He would sit very still and straight in his good brown suit between his sleeping sons with his arms stretched out on the pew back above them.

Troy drove past the school building, which

like most small schools in West Texas was impressively consolidated. Children entered the low, plain, boxy western end at the age of five, matriculated through the Spanish-mission-style junior high in the middle, and emerged at eighteen — if they were lucky, as Harlan had been and Troy had not — at the larger, boxy eastern end, where the twin civic theaters of the auditorium and the gymnasium sat.

Next came the credit union and the defunct Mac movie theater, missing its marquee since the mid-sixties, not long after it went out of business; the old barbershop, now a CB radio sales and repair store; the Dairy Queen, glassy and still new-looking; and the cream-brick three-story courthouse, constructed in a vaguely modernist style that set it at odds with every other structure in town but conferred its importance.

Like most towns its size, New Cona was a picture of rural America in miniature: Anyone driving along its spine could perceive in less than five minutes the shape of a century's arc — pioneer struggle and its meager, adequate architecture, succeeded by hard work, prosperity, and the ambitious municipal buildings they bequeathed through the fifties, followed by a slow structural and civic retreat in the form of trailer houses, cinder block, Quonset huts, and pastured gaps like a pox in the middle of town. The last time Troy had driven down this road he had been on his way out of town for what turned out to be a very long time. It was a Saturday evening after the rodeo parade and everyone had gone home. The wooden bleachers in front of the courthouse sat empty and the grounds had been cleaned but the pavement along Main Street was still littered with little hillocks of fresh, green horseshit, a fitting token of farewell.

Up ahead to the left shone lights that seemed to be glaring at business brightness, and as he drove closer he saw that they came from an all-night Allsup's convenience store that had not been there when he left. Troy pulled in, looking up and down the street. Except for a cashier stationed behind the counter, there was no one inside, at least no one he could see through the big glass-front window. The top half of the cashier's head was obscured by the hanging cigarette rack, but judging by his posture and the thin gleaning of hair on his face he seemed to be no more than sixteen or seventeen.

Troy got out of the car and walked briskly inside, saying nothing, making no eye contact. He aimed for the milk cases in the back and then lingered in an aisle, pretending to inspect a pegboard hung with Frito-Lay and pork skins while trying instead to get a surreptitious look between the shelving at the boy — not to figure out whether he knew him but to figure out whether the boy resembled anyone he knew, a mother or father his own age who might be able to place him from their son's description.

After a minute his quarry finally shifted into sight, staring slack-mouthed easterly through the store's plate-glass window toward the road out of town, looking as if he would exchange his place behind the counter for any place out there. Troy was half surprised: The boy was Mexican, which reduced the chances of identification sufficiently for him to stand down his guard.

He looked around, picked out a pack of gum, and walked up to the counter, watching the boy take a good look at him as he approached. The boy caught himself and shifted his focus toward the cash register and attempted to put on a professional voice, but it came off like that of most country boys his age in conversation with adults — awkward, pained, half ashamed, as if an indecent subject had been broached. He was taller than Troy but stooped, with narrow delicate shoulders. His face was sallow and pale; his diet probably consisted of too many items from the store's own shelves. He wasn't old enough to grow a mustache but had tried anyway; it looked like a plastic spider on his upper lip, a handful of thin black tendrils headed in different directions.

"You need to fill her up, too, sir?"

"I'm fine for gas, just needed a little something to keep my jawbone busy till I get to Lubbock," Troy said. He put a twenty-dollar bill down on the counter and, wanting to give the boy no time to think, said: "Listen, son, I've got a question for you. I used to come through here every now and then, a few years ago, and I did some business with an old boy named Bill Ray Falconer. You wouldn't happen to know of him, if he's still around here somewhere, would you?"

Color rose into the boy's face and his unease appeared to solidify into something like actual discomfort. He was very still for a moment, causing Troy to become aware of the shining movements of the greasy hot links rolling in the heat-lamp cabinet near the cash register.

"What's the name again, sir?"

"Falconer," Troy said. "Tall, slim, sharp dresser, kind of a cut-up and a rounder when he was young. He had a couple of grown boys if I remember?"

The boy didn't speak right away. "Yes sir, I know him. I mean, I knew him. I'm sorry to say, but he's dead, sir. He passed a few years back, of a heart attack I think."

Troy whistled and looked down at the counter and then up at the tag pinned to the pocket of the boy's paisley-print Western shirt, which said B. JIMENEZ.

"You don't say! I'm sorry to hear that. I sure am."

Troy waited while the boy rang him up. "Didn't he used to live over there near the northwest corner of town, right by the pasture?"

"Yes sir, he did."

"Do either of his boys still live there, as far as you know?"

The boy flushed again on the high bones above his hairless cheeks. He seemed suddenly aware of being in solitary charge of the store at night. Something about Troy unsettled him.

"One of them, name of Harlan, used to," he said, "but . . . well, I don't know. He must've run into some trouble or something because he moved out of there a while back and the county rents it now." The boy appeared to gain a measure of confidence as he heard himself relate verifiable facts.

Troy watched a dirty pickup pull to a stop in front of the store and he suddenly became aware of the unholy fluorescent brightness inside. “Where did this Harlan end up, do you think? Did he move somewhere else?”

He thought he saw the hint of an embarrassed smile move across the boy’s face before it resumed its previous immobility. “Well, he’s still here. But I think he’s outside of town now. He works tending to the big radio tower out east, that one you see over on the Brownfield highway past the Bozart ranch gate. I heard he’s living out there now. But it ain’t exactly a house or anything.”

“And what about the other brother?” Troy asked.

He glanced outside. The man who had pulled up in the pickup, an old man in a feed cap, was filling up with diesel, looking into the store absentmindedly as it pumped.

“I don’t know nothing about him, sir. I ain’t even sure of his name. I think maybe he got into some trouble with the law but I don’t know for sure. He might be dead, too.” The boy paused, maybe wondering if he should have included this final thought but when he saw that it produced no effect he paused and ventured a question:

"What kind of work did y'all used to do with Bill Ray?"

Troy picked up the chewing gum packet and dropped it into his shirt pocket and smiled tightly, fixing the boy for the first time with a good look in the eyes.

"What's your name, son?"

The boy looked at him for a second, then away.

"My name's Brandon."

"Brandon?"

"Yes sir, Brandon Jimenez."

Troy smiled and touched a finger to his brow. "Thank you for your help, Brandon Jimenez. You have a good night now."

Troy wanted to greet Harlan by daylight, so he took the car to the end of a pumpjack road and tried unsuccessfully to sleep. By the time he pulled onto the road to the radio tower, the sun was close enough to the horizon that he could see the outline of the little flat-topped cinder-block shack sitting against the tower base. The shack looked comically small alongside the tower, which rose two hundred feet like a skeletal ladder, stabilized by an array of guy-wires as straight as bicycle spokes running down to the pastureland. The wires pinged as a high morning breeze came in, but when Troy stepped out of the car and began walking toward the shack it was still quiet enough for him to hear clearly, in the near distance, the distinctive metallic chuck of a bolt being shoved forward to chamber a round.

"You come any further and I'll part your goddamned skull."

The voice came from above and when Troy looked up he could see the big cuneiform shape of a head silhouetted just above the parapet that skirted the shack's roof. He instinctively brought his hands away from his sides, turning his palms out and stopping where he was, waiting for the next instruction.

When one didn't come right away, he looked up and asked: "Is that Bill Ray's old Winchester?"

Harlan's head and shoulders came up higher above the parapet, dark against the purplish morning sky.

"That rifle hasn't worked in twenty years, Harlan."

A reply was a long time in coming.

"How do you know I didn't fix it?"

"Because I know you wouldn't."

"Maybe you think that and maybe I'll shoot you anyway."

Troy let his hands drift back down to his sides. "Then do it and get it over with. Or come on down here and let's talk."

Harlan slowly drew the rifle up against his shoulder but didn't seem ready to relinquish his position.

"Where was I calling when I called you last month?" Troy asked.

After another long silence, and the wind picking up: "The phone company let me keep the number. It rings out here now. You shouldn't drive up on a man like that so early in the morning, Troy. You'll get yourself shot."

"Is this where you live?" Troy asked, resuming his walk toward the shack.

"If that's what you want to call it. They don't care if I stay out here. As long as I do my job. It ain't much — hot plate, a cot. No room for a fridge but the tank out there keeps things cool enough."

He fell silent again, seeming to search for something else to recommend his accommodations. "The TV reception's hard to beat. You snake an antenna wire out to the tower leads and you can tune in a Dallas station clear as a bell."

Troy looked around the overgrown tower site, a dry, sorry-looking patch of cleared pasture that the pasture was rapidly taking back. "How did you lose the house?" he asked, beginning to feel the absurdity of conversing with a man crouched on a rooftop in rifle position.

Harlan raised himself slowly, grunting, and walked over to a metal ladder bolted to the side of the shack. He looked out over the horizon, then laid the rifle on the roof against the parapet and wrapped it several times in a thick tarpaulin and swung his weight out over the ladder.

He approached Troy beating the dust from his shirt and pants with his hands and stood looking at him, stopping a good three feet away.

"Lawbreaking always suited you, Troy," he said. "You don't look a day older than last time I saw you. I can't even remember how long ago it was."

Harlan's face was leaner and his eyes more deeply set than the last time Troy had seen him. His features had more of Bill Ray in them than Troy had ever noticed before. He was already beginning to bag at the eyes and elbows and he looked a decade older than he was, due partly to the fact that he now wore a saucer-brimmed felt cowboy hat like the one worn by President Johnson, along with the uniform of the older farmers and ranchers, who preferred heavy khaki work shirts tucked into khaki trousers, never blue jeans. As big as Harlan was, he wore his shirts a size too big, with the sleeves rolled high on his upper arms. His big hands hung down heavily like things he stopped acknowledging when not in use.

"What happened to the house?"

"You asked me that."

"I'm asking you again."

Harlan turned without hurrying toward the shack, through high bluestem grass that nearly fenced it from view on the side facing the road. With each footfall grasshoppers arced out around his boots like splashing water. His voice came from inside the shack, where he had turned on a light:

"She talked me into drawing money against it, as little as it was worth. When she left she took that with her, too. The bank claimed it a couple of months ago. Darryl came over himself and told me he hated to have to do it."

Troy hadn't known about this part. It gave him a momentary sensation of the ground moving underneath him, of ignorance stretching out in every direction. He turned away from the road and looked across the lightening land. The stock tank sat about a hundred yards off at the foot of an old Monitor windmill whose vane had not yet cranked its blades into the wind. A hundred miles further west, carrying the sun, a line of clouds as big as kingdoms marched across the plains and Troy stood watching them, wondering how long it would take Bettie to spend everything.

"What difference does the house make to you? It's been more than ten years since you lived there. Hell, you were barely there when you lived in it. It was mine."

Troy told him about the visit. "It didn't feel half bad being back in there, Harlan, like I thought it would. I just wish you hadn't left the furniture you did. I don't like to think of that deputy bastard using any of it."

"Did you break one of my windows?"

"I didn't need to break anything. I still have the key."

Harlan considered this for a moment. "If the thought had ever occurred to me, I'd have changed the locks a long time ago."

Troy had come up into the doorway. The windowless space that Harlan lived in was no bigger than a modestly proportioned bathroom, except that it had no facilities, not even a sink. Troy had known a few motel rooms only marginally more hospitable. A wooden cot occupied the right-hand wall, made up with a gray horsehair blanket and a caseless pillow. Along the back was a kind of bivouac kitchen with a single-burner hot plate, an electric coffeepot, and a small larder of plates, cups, and boxed goods arranged on a two-by-eight plank raised off the concrete floor on cinder blocks. A heavy black Bakelite wall phone with a braided cord hung near a jack. On a metal television tray to the other side rested a little Philco television set, which looked like an electronic appendage of a large, vaultlike bank of aluminum cabinets, fitted with switches and cooling vents, the housing for the tower's broadcast equipment. The whole place smelled acridly of metal and a weak dome light shone in the middle of the ceiling, brown with bug juice.

"I thought you'd like to know that when I got into town last night I paid my respects at your final resting place," Troy said. "There wasn't anywhere for me to put flowers."

Harlan had taken a small aluminum pot and poured water into it from a canteen and put the pot onto the reddening hot plate coil. He took a rubber band from around a box of Cream of Wheat and sat on the corner of his cot to wait for the water to boil.

"There wasn't anybody else going to take care of it except me, so I thought I might as well get it done. It's a good thing I did, too, while I still had some money. Bettie liked to have killed me for it, but it's pretty much the only thing of value she didn't make off with."

He smiled, looking away from Troy, though Troy was trying just as studiously to evade his gaze. "Only thing of value I have left and I have to be dead to use it. There must be a country song in that somewhere."

Troy took a metal folding chair leaned against the wall, the only other piece of furniture in the shack. There was no room inside for it, so he swung the door out and put the chair across the threshold on the packed caliche and sat just outside facing in, rocking back on the legs. Harlan took a mug down from a hook over the head of his cot.

"Coffee?"

"No thanks. I had a pot of the deputy's last night."

"Whose vehicle is that that you're driving over there?"

"Mine, for the time being."

"You know damned well I'm not putting a foot inside it. The truck's around behind back. I can't promise it's going to get us very far but it's the only thing I'm going to drive."

Troy suddenly noticed a dog almost the same shade of dun as the pasture sand stretched out on its side about a dozen feet from him. The animal was whimpering in its sleep, its feet moving slightly as it ran chasing something along a dream plane perpendicular to the ground. "I thought you didn't like dogs, Harlan. When did you get that?"

"I didn't get him — he got me," Harlan said. "This seems to be where he lives. They call these radio shacks doghouses, so I guess by rights it's his." Harlan rose from the cot and walked to the side of the door, snapping his fingers and whistling. Without stirring its head from the ground the dog opened its eyes to look at him and then longer, suspiciously, at Troy. "He's ancient, old coot. I find him sacked out by his empty water dish. Too old to even whine for it. Just lays there with his head pointed at the dish like a divining rod that tells you where water ain't."

The dog's eyes rolled up and his lids eased shut again. "He's not a bad one when he's awake. I call him Beau Jack. After that one Bill Ray brought home that time."

Troy studied the old dog, which seemed, unaccountably, to be some kind of poodle mutt, greatly overgrown. Troy laughed. "He didn't bring that dog home, Harlan. That damned dog just showed up one day and

Bill Ray kept hauling him out to the country to get rid of him, but he kept finding his way back. So eventually Bill gave up. He named him after some famous colored boxer."

"What ever became of that dog?"

"He liked to run in the pasture at night. He probably started to think those coyotes calling to him were his friends. One morning he didn't come back."

"Sounds like somebody I used to know," Harlan said, meeting Troy's eye for the first time.

He poured coffee and arranged his breakfast on his cot in a way that suggested long-established routine. Harlan had always been maddeningly methodical but the ritual of his movements produced a different effect on Troy this morning, peaceful, almost calming. It made him think of a Benedictine monk he had once watched for an hour in a New Mexico thrift shop carving a pair of sparrows from a piece of evergreen pine.

Harlan began to eat, not looking up from his bowl. "Where've you kept yourself the last few years? You never say where you're calling from."

"Nowhere in particular."

"A wetback I know swore he saw you about a year ago outside a motel in Sweetwater. I told him he was crazy. I said you probably weren't even on this side of the country."

Troy let his gaze climb the tower, hinging his head back to follow its latticework into the sky, where it appeared to undulate like a rope bridge.

"Your wetback was probably right," he said. "A good deal of my work revolves around the West Texas hospitality industry."

Harlan laughed, a noise that managed to sound forced and involuntary at the same time. "Your work my ass. I don't know how you've stayed around here without somebody recognizing you, catching up to you."

"I don't stick around anywhere long enough," Troy said. "But you know what's funny? People don't pay much attention to people in motels. They just assume they're strangers they'll never see again. Maybe wetbacks pay more attention because people never notice them, either."

Harlan ate rapidly, noisily. "Maybe," he said with his mouth full. "And maybe you're just lucky like you always were."

He gathered up the dishes and reflexively turned on the television, which came to life in the middle of some kind of cheap-looking Western movie. On the screen, two men were having a fistfight that ended with one of the men, a lone gunfighter — he looked like a gunfighter, anyway, because of his black gloves and sleeve garters — stumbling across an expanse of desert sand, cradling his bloodied gun hand. The sound was off, so Troy couldn't figure out exactly what was going on.

"When does this thing get powered up?" he asked, looking at the base of the tower, which tapered to a single, almost balletic point, poised on a ceramic insulator that resembled a giant lozenge.

Harlan crowded past Troy, bound for the stock tank with his coffeepot and an armful of dishes. "There ain't been a signal out of here in two years — the little country-and-western station that had it went under. The company hired me to come out here and check on the place because high school kids were busting in at night to drink beer and screw each other, God knows what else, dope I imagine. When I first came it looked like somebody'd slaughtered something in the shack — took me two days to clean it up."

He slowed at the grassless lunette swept out by tires at the head of the dirt road. "As soon as they know I'm gone they'll be back out here like a shot, the shaggy little sons of bitches. But maybe I won't need it by the time we get back."

" *'We'* isn't coming back," Troy said. "If we find her, I'm on my way again, back to regular programming."

A quarter of a mile out a crop duster crossed low in the sky heading east, a single-engine Piper that looked and sounded like a yellow jacket. It was close enough that they could see the head of the pilot inside. The plane momentarily dipped a wing but Harlan just followed it with his eyes and didn't raise a hand to return the greeting. Troy turned to look at the Nova — such a ludicrous lump of shit-brown metal, sitting right out in plain view — and wondered what a crop duster was doing in the sky in November.

"We've got to hit the road today, Harlan," Troy yelled over the receding drone of the airplane's engine.

Harlan headed toward the tank, talking as he walked away. "What else are we going to do, sit around here and play catch-up? I need an hour to break the place down. Stow your things — whoever's things they are — in the truck bed. Then you can follow me out into the pasture. We'll put that car down behind a windbreak and pull off the plates, cover it with brush . . . That's how you and your boys would handle it, ain't it?"

"No boys, Harlan," Troy said. "Only me. And that's what I'd do."

Sept. 5, 1972

The first time I stole a vehicle it was just an old tractor, a dirt-red Allis-Chalmers diesel. I was seventeen. It was so easy I think it ruined me. Nobody locks a tractor, there's no key. Just a soot-blackened starter button and a choke and it shudders to life like an earthquake, like it was planning to all along.

I took it one night to get to the state line bar west of Bronco, to work out a bootlegging run I had planned for rodeo weekend with two older boys. (We lived in a dry county bordered closely by a wet state, a piece of geographic luck that presented moneymaking opportunities.) Nobody could come get me and I wasn't about to walk the two miles from my uncle's, where I was plowing that summer. So I took the tractor and parked it behind a windbreak ridge a hundred yards from the bar and then drove it back to the spot behind the old hand's trailer where he was keeping it.

It wasn't his tractor anyway — the bank had been trying to repossess it for a month. But I treated it as if it were my very own, I think mostly because I'd already anticipated how satisfying it would feel to take something with impunity, to be in sole possession of the knowledge of my act. I guess I always knew I would be good at it.

I left Texas in my early twenties to see if I could make it somewhere else, learn something about the world. I bumped through Tucson and San Diego, then Sacramento and up north as far as Spokane and Seattle. I found legitimate work here and there but I ended up mostly robbing houses until my nerves couldn't take it anymore; I understood why so many house burglars became drunks and drug addicts. Automobiles were easier and the money was better. From the beginning I liked everything about the business of stealing them.

Almost as much as horses were in previous centuries, automobiles are essential for livelihood in the West, and when I consider the comparison I focus gratefully on the fact that progress has led to the discontinuation of capital punishment for the act of stealing something so vital.

When I first got into the business I apprenticed the way people in legal occupations do. My first job was a body shop in Hobbs, New Mexico, working for a man who had been pointed out to me as someone in need of specialized automotive work. By my mid-twenties I ran in the kinds of circles where I heard about openings like that. As you might expect, this one required no automotive skill beyond taking a car apart, though I ended up doing little of that. I was the go-getter, the night man.

The station was owned by an ex-cowhand named Jim Quaintance, who had run cattle and then hired on with a sheriff's department before realizing that his temperament favored the other side of the law. His violent days were mostly behind him, but he kept a short-barreled shotgun on hooks beneath the cash register just in case.

He worked me like a sighthound. I'd come into the station in the evening, and by nightfall I was roaming the streets with a rider to take my car when I found another. Those were the golden years — so many doors so innocently unlocked, so many keys in the ignition for the turning. My only adversaries were dogs and insomniacs, but even at that age I had a second sense for them, lying in wait for me out in the darkness.

Two

Harlan changed into a new set of khakis identical to the ones he had been wearing before, except these were washed and pressed. Before padlocking the shack he placed all his remaining food into a bucket for the dog, which didn't wake to watch them leave. They set out before noon, headed toward Brownfield on their way to Tahoka, picking out a route on the empty farm-to-market roads that faintly grid the Panhandle before unraveling into capillary irregularity as the plains break up south of Midland.

A final fall heat wave had set in. The warmth spawned dust devils that rose from the harvested fields in spectral columns, drafting up a hundred feet toward low-pressure thermals, changing color as they wandered from red farmland to caliche to sandy loam. On the hot asphalt before the pickup, light lakes materialized like mercury pools, draining upon approach, refilling a mile down the road.

Troy looked out the window toward the bobbing black pumpjacks, dozens upon dozens, diminishing toward the horizon, some working in tandem, some out of rhythm, dancing their own dance. It seemed like some kind of a joke that the machines built to suck prehistoric sludge from the depths of the earth looked like mechanical dinosaurs.

Even with the gas pedal flush against the floor the pickup could no longer manage more than thirty. Sitting shotgun uncomfortably as the wind whistled through the window frames, Troy found it hard to believe this was the same truck he had known, the one in which he and Harlan had spent so many thousands of circuitous miles, in which they had learned the featureless geography of West Texas and how to drive through it. A black Diamond T, the pickup had been the pride of Bill Ray's young life, the first vehicle he ever bought brand-new, in 1938, the year of Troy's birth. In light of that event, the purchase had been an even more reckless financial extravagance than it would have been under normal circumstances. Fully loaded, the pickup had cost twelve hundred dollars, to the eight he would have paid for a new Chevy or Ford. He drove his old Packard all the way to Las Cruces to get it, returning after midnight to find that Ruby had locked him out of the house and that several of the neighbors seemed to know because their kitchen lights still burned brightly at such a late hour. Bill Ray slept in the pickup that night, luxuriating in the factory perfume of virgin upholstery. Ruby wouldn't speak to him for a week, but she was eventually worn down by the simple sight of the truck, a one-ton apotheosis of American power — Lockheed hydraulic brakes; six-cylinder flathead Hercules; a hundred-thousand-mile guarantee. Advertisements called it "The Handsomest Truck in America" and it delivered on that unpoetic promise with a broad silver grille burnished like a bank teller's window.

Thirty-two years later, that vehicle was almost impossible to bring back to mind. The odometer had zeroed over too many times to count and the digits behind the milked glass had lodged permanently at four nines and an eight. The factory black lay buried beneath several coats of beige latex house paint that Harlan applied semiannually with a brush. To check the rust he had painted over the chromework, too, chrome that Bill Ray had babied with a chamois, but rust had run rampant in the bed walls, which wore so thin that Harlan had to torch them and put up pine running boards. The boards fenced in a ragged wooden toolbox that stuck up two feet over the top of the cab, and behind the toolbox lay remnants of old chicken-wire coops that Harlan had built during years when he had sold hens and eggs door-to-door. For drivers passing it, the ramshackle pile of moving parts seemed like an apparition from the road's past, an Okie rig finally repatriated from the California fruit fields.

Harlan's one attempt at improvement had been to install a combination AM/FM and CB unit in a bracket under the dashboard, but the truck had rejected it like an unsuccessful transplant; the receiver worked for a month and the CB remained off because Harlan didn't like talking to people on it. He filled the silence by singing country songs to himself, along with half-remembered, half-tuneless bits of doggerel that Bill Ray had sung, drawn from sources mysterious to his sons, perhaps lost to history:

Sy and I went to the circus
Sy got hit with a bucket of shit

But Sy got even with that damned old
circus
He bought a ticket and didn't go in.

Georgie was a-shaving one fine day
And sliced the nose right off-a his face
Well the doctor he sewed it on
Upside down
Now ever time it rains
George damn near drowns.

Oh I knew an old fellow from Boston
Who drove a little red Austin
There was room for his ass and a gallon of
gas
But his balls fell out and he lost 'em.

One bright day in the middle of the night,
Two dead boys got up to fight
Back to back they faced each other
Drew their swords and shot each other
A deaf policeman heard this noise
And came to arrest those two dead boys.

Troy and Harlan had each spent so many years driving alone that the shells of their respective solitudes remained intact as they sat together in the pickup. But eventually Harlan's voice penetrated Troy's and Troy leaned forward to open his side of the windshield, finding that the crank was jammed. He reached to roll down his window but the handle turned loosely in his hand without disturbing the glass in the least, so he sat back and resigned himself, staring westerly at the combine-cut furrows of a sorghum field, whose long parallel lines began to create the illusion of a sweeping broom as the truck passed them. The sun was well up now in a cloudless pale sky and Troy remembered something someone had told him about this part of the Great Plains — that the only way the sky could get bigger was if the earth got smaller. Stretching out before him was a piece of earth that looked eventless even for the plains, as if nothing more consequential than breaking and planting had occurred there in all human history. Harlan sometimes knew stories about these patches of nothing county, stories not inscribed on historical markers because their particulars were either too trivial or too grim. He had always been an amateur student of history — intelligence gathered from newspaper articles and television shows, overheard conversations of settler-family ranchers — but his interest had deepened with age, in a way that tends to happen with much older men who suddenly feel the need to understand their place in the order of things.

"What about here, Harlan?" Troy asked, breaking the silence as the truck labored along a dirt farm road five miles west of Tahoka. "Did anything ever happen here?"

Harlan spat a length of tobacco juice into an empty tomato can he was holding between his legs and looked to his left for a long while.

"Right back yonder," he said, easing off the gas and scanning the flatland over his shoulder. "There's an old playa out there called the Double Lakes, a big salt lick now. About ten years after the Civil War this cavalry captain named Nolan staged a bunch of buffalo soldiers from San Angelo to find some Kwahadi Comanche that'd been raiding camps. But it was the dead of summer and a drought was on and those boys didn't know what the hell they were doing. A bunch of 'em rode around for days and got lost on the plains and couldn't find a drop of water — they ended up drinking their own piss, and then the piss of their horses, then the blood of the horses after they died. A few of the men died, too, if I remember."

Troy looked out at the bleached flatness where Harlan had pointed and saw nothing remotely resembling a lake. "Right out there?"

"It started there," Harlan said. "And that's where those that survived returned. The funny thing — not funny to them, naturally — was that while they were out there dying, old chief Quanah Parker had already come in and talked the Comanche raiders into going peaceably with him back to the reservation."

Harlan leaned forward and folded the bottoms of his forearms on top of the steering wheel the way someone would rest on a tabletop, his customary posture on the road. He turned partway toward Troy and laughed, baring teeth that were, like those of most people who had grown up in the area, permanently discolored with brownish-yellow striations caused by the natural fluoridation of the plains groundwater. Troy's teeth had once looked just like this but several years earlier he had paid a dentist in Seagraves to bleach them, partly out of vanity but mostly to enhance an impression that he came from elsewhere.

Harlan had noticed Troy looking at his teeth.

"You know what they say about spending your life drinking this llano water?"

Troy didn't want to know but he waited

for the answer he knew would come.

"That if you dig up people's remains, those that have lived here all their life, their bones will be the same shit-brown as their teeth. In other words, the place brands you right down to the skeleton. You might be able to fool people with your shiny white teeth now, but when you die your bones will tell the truth."

Troy shifted his ass on the hard leather bench seat, seeking a more forgiving spot. "Thank you for adding that to my storehouse of knowledge, Harlan. Truly. Where in the hell do you get this stuff?"

"It's all bone, ain't it? Stands to reason!"

They drove on, coming to pavement and passing a small state rest area with a pair of low unshaded concrete tables, the least hospitable place to rest that Troy could imagine. Harlan continued talking, mostly to himself: "You know, the thing we're barely able to understand around here anymore — and we ain't even removed from it by all that many years — is the kind of time it took to get around this country back when you got around on horseback. Anywhere. *Days* in the saddle just to go the hundred miles from Lubbock down to Midland. How godawful huge this land must have been back then."

Troy looked down the road at the pale blue water tower visible over the town of Tahoka, a landmark that seemed to be getting no closer, seemed in fact to be receding as the truck plodded heavily toward it. "I'd pay good money for a horse right now — it feels like we're on the back of an old smoothmouth mule," he said. As he did the pickup's engine made a hard sound, as if something in it had bottomed out and was struggling to regain the surface. Harlan eased off the gas and let the truck coast almost to a stop as a big propane tanker blew past them, shaking the pickup with its wake. Troy looked over, alarmed at the thought of having to walk in broad daylight, but Harlan's face registered no sign of concern. He took the pickup out of gear and gassed it aggressively, then rammed the stick into second. Slowly, almost imperceptibly, like one of the mile-long freight trains that stop-started on the West Texas flatness bound for elsewhere, the truck began to regain momentum.

They had started out east instead of due south because a cotton farmer in Tahoka owed Harlan fifty dollars for a welding job, and before having to accept any of Troy's ill-gotten money he insisted on making an attempt to get the little that was still his.

They pulled in to a Shurfine grocery store, where a phone booth sat to the side of the building, next to a bagged-ice freezer. It was early afternoon and only one other car sat in front of the store, at the far corner of a lot in which hundreds of pop-tops had been embedded over the years by tires and summer heat, giving the asphalt the appearance of a lake filled with minnows swimming just beneath the surface.

Harlan got out and went to the phone booth, leaving the folding door open as he pushed back his hat and put a dime in the slot. Troy stayed in the truck and couldn't hear the conversation but he didn't need to; it was short and concluded with Harlan returning the receiver slowly to the hook and walking back to the pickup, scanning the sky reflexively. He said nothing by way of explanation except, "You need to piss before we go on?"

Troy didn't answer and Harlan reached to start the truck. But when he turned the key this time, after so many thousands of times of turning it with hope and trepidation, it produced no effect beyond the faint electric report of the starter, which Harlan allowed to spin ineffectually for several seconds before taking his hand off the key and putting it with the other one on the steering wheel. He sat still like this, looking toward the plate-glass front of the store, where the honey-colored light caught the face of a blond grocery clerk leaned against a row of shopping carts, shouldering them slowly toward the door.

"Well, that's that," he announced.

"That's what?"

"That's it, for the truck."

"What do you mean?"

"I mean she's gone. She ain't moving from here. Ain't moving anywhere again."

"Get out and pop the hood. I'll try starting it again."

"I'm telling you it's done for, Troy. There ain't no use."

"What're you talking about? How do you know that?"

"Because I know this pickup as well as I know anything in this world. I'd say we were lucky we made it into town."

Troy stared at the side of Harlan's head, at the sweat stains extending out onto the brim of his hat.

"Get out and look under the goddamned hood, Harlan. See what we need to do to fix it. We can't just sit here."

"That's all it's made of, is fixes, Troy. And they've done all they're going to do. It'd take a whole new engine to get it going again. And they stopped making new engines for this pickup when they stopped making the pickup. Which was a long time ago." He continued to sit with both hands on the steering wheel, staring ahead as if he was still driving. He took his hat off and wiped his forehead and put the hat back on and made a chuckling sound. "Who would've thought it would be you and me sitting here again in this old son of a bitch when it finally gave up the ghost?"

Troy shouldered open his door and stomped out onto the pavement and turned and leaned back in threateningly. "Goddamn it, Harlan! *We've made it thirty fucking miles.* What the hell are we going to do now?"

Harlan reached over and opened his door and got out, too. "I don't know about you, but I'm going inside to get myself something cool to drink. You want anything?" He looked Troy straight in the eye and walked unhurriedly into the store, taking the pickup key with him and dropping it and its old diamond-shaped leather key chain ceremonially into the outdoor trash can.

Troy watched him go and stalked up to the truck and smashed the heel of his hand as hard as he could against the high arch of the fender, which received the blow with the solidity of stone despite all the years of rust and bodywork. He hadn't expected the pickup to get them very far, but he had hoped at least to Midland, maybe Fort Stockton. If they had made it to a motel, he might have been able to do something. But not here in the middle of town on a Saturday afternoon in screaming daylight, with witnesses idling by, finger-waving from their steering wheels, nothing better to do than gape and try to place the two strangers they saw in the parking lot of the Shurfine.

Troy looked into the store, which was almost empty, save for two women cashiers conversing across their registers. He looked up and down the street and he could taste the familiar taste of fear in his mouth as he walked briskly over to the passenger side of the car on the far corner of the lot, a nicely kept purple Chrysler Newport that probably belonged to the owner of the store. Keeping his head upright, he cast his eyes down through the window at the steering shaft. No key in the ignition. All doors locked, incomprehensibly.

He went back to the truck and sat crossways on the seat, staring at the Newport, trying to think. After a few minutes a car pulled into the space next to him, a big Ford Country Squire station wagon, powder blue with wood-panel side detail, driven by a woman with a pretty face whose blond hair was pinned up inside a chiffon scarf against the wind. Troy nodded to her as she got out and walked into the store, leaving two little boys behind in the front seat, brothers or even twins who seemed to be Mennonite, though the woman, in a nice pantsuit, did not. The boys, maybe seven or eight years old, had pale complexions and close-cropped white-blond hair. They wore the same, plain Western-pattern shirts worn by other small-town boys their age but their shirts were somehow instantly recognizable as being homemade, marking the boys as members of their sect.

The woman left the station wagon running but the driver's-side window was rolled down and over the motor Troy could hear the two boys, up on their knees on the passenger side of the bench seat, peering over the wide dashboard into the store:

"Hey, Jacob, I've a question for you: Which one came first, the chicken or the egg?" asked the nearest of the boys, the bigger of the two, who had a high forehead and wore cheap oval plastic-framed glasses that looked as if they had been made for a girl.

The other boy, a slightly smaller version of the first except that he was plump, with a cushiony freckled face, ignored the question at first, pointedly, but then he seemed unable to resist playing his part in a ritual he knew would end badly.

"Chicken."

"Nope."

"The egg?"

"Nuh-uh."

"Well which one, then?"

"Neither one, you dumbass, God came first!" And as the boy said it he swiftly and viciously punched the other boy with a closed fist on the hard, lean stretch of his upper left arm, setting off an ear-piercing wail.

"You frogged me, you bastard!" the aggrieved brother screamed. "You four-eyed fucking bastard!" The two of them plunged from sight as they wrestled down into the footwell, where their shrieks tailed off into desperate grunts and pants and the sounds of blows that caused the station wagon to wobble on its tires. Then the driver's-side door burst open and the one with no glasses flew out in a blur, running low to the ground like a quail. He circled the back of the car and broke toward the store, pursued closely by his attacker, who stumbled on some loose gravel but righted himself and then began to apologize loudly, pleading for silence as the first boy struggled to enter the store, hauling back on the heavy glass-and-metal door, whose hydraulic closers seemed to be conspiring to keep him from the arms of justice.

Troy looked again into the store and saw Harlan standing at one of the cash register counters with his hat in his hand, talking to the woman checking him out. Before the second boy had passed fully through the door, Troy stood up and walked in rapid but measured strides to the back of the pickup and swung his suitcase out of the bed and grabbed Harlan's canvas rucksack and transferred it into the same hand and then with his free hand he opened the back door of the station wagon and threw both bags onto the seats. He pushed the door shut without slamming it and executed a series of swift, gracefully choreographed movements that would have impressed anyone if anyone had been looking outside to see them. He opened the driver's-side door and slipped down into the front seat behind the wheel, pulling the door shut gently beside him and dropping the gearshift into reverse. He backed out rapidly, taking the wagon in a right-hand crescent across the empty parking lot and then pulling it forward just past the rear of the pickup into the meager camouflage it provided between himself and the store windows. Harlan had taken two steps out of the store when he saw Troy sprawled across the wide front seat of the station wagon holding the passenger door open for him.

"Get in, Harlan."

Harlan stopped on the sidewalk, holding a Dr. Pepper bottle in each hand by the neck and a bag of Fritos under his left armpit. He bent down slowly and set both bottles on the concrete.

"*Christ, Troy.* What in the hell're you doing?"

"We can't stay here to talk it over this time, Harlan. Get in the car, goddamn it. Hurry now." He was looking up at his brother almost penitently from the awkward posture into which he had contorted himself in order to keep the passenger door pushed partway open.

"Troy Alan! Jesus, you can't do this here, in the middle of Tahoka. I probably know that lady in there or know people who do."

"That lady's gonna have her car back just as soon as I can find another one, no harm, no foul. She'll have a hell of a story to tell people."

"I'm gonna go in there and tell her right now," Harlan said but he didn't move from the place where he stood between the two full cola bottles, like someone about to perform a carnival trick with them.

"Your bag's in the backseat of this car with me, and if I get stopped before we get out of here the first thing I'm going to say is you and I did this together and you went chickenshit and your ass will end up in jail just like mine."

Harlan seemed to think about this. "Not for as long."

"Long enough."

"I guess that's a chance I'll take."

Troy looked wildly behind Harlan into the store and gritted his words down into his teeth. "You know, Harlan, that Boy Scout uniform you've been wearing your *whole goddamned life* is getting pretty small on you, don't you think? Have you got any better ideas? Do you want to keep losing everything in your life?"

A new-model two-tone Dodge pickup rolled slowly into the parking lot, driven by an elderly man hunched under a silver felt cowboy hat, alongside a hunched woman who was clearly his wife. As older couples in small towns sometimes do, they pulled into a parking space and stopped and sat with the engine idling and the windows rolled up, showing no signs of speaking to each other or preparing to go into the store. The air-conditioned pickup cab seemed to serve as an extension of the seating arrangement in their living room, where they probably sat most of the day in the same proximity, rarely speaking there, either.

The man looked across toward Harlan standing in the parking lot and the wife looked, too. They both nodded at him and turned to face placidly forward again, either failing to notice Troy in the car or being unable to make immediate sense of the scene that presented itself to them.

Harlan nodded back to them instinctively. Keeping his feet planted as if they were wedged down inside a hole, he turned his upper body awkwardly to look behind him into the store. He heard Troy's voice again over the station wagon motor. *"You've got about ten seconds before she looks out here and sees her car with somebody else driving it and starts to scream. And you've got five seconds before I drive off and leave you here to explain it all."*

A sound nearby caused Harlan to start. The old man had finally opened his door and stepped down from his pickup and was making his way slowly to the front of it while his wife remained inside. Except for the addition of a khaki zippered windbreaker, the man wore clothes identical to Harlan's — khaki pants, khaki work shirt, black belt, black boots. But his clothes looked new and his hat was a dress Stetson, crisply blocked, straight and high on his head. He was very old but something about the way he carried himself, about the pitch of the hat, conveyed an air of authority that announced him as a rancher. Ranchers exuded this kind of imperious air in West Texas because they knew the land had once belonged to them, before it was fenced and parceled out by plow hands. They still spent their lives having to answer to almost no one but themselves and the land — to God also, presumably; maybe to their wives and children, but not often, and not necessarily; maybe to cattle buyers, though in good years it was the other way around; and to the sheriff if they got into trouble, though that was a rite of manhood. Looking at the old man as he ambled slowly forward, fixing Harlan with an implacable gaze, Troy thought: *You're the one, aren't you? I come from farm people. It was always going to be one of you fucking ranchers. You'll get me caught, won't you, you arrogant old horse-riding prick?*

"How y'all?" the man called out loudly to Harlan as he rounded the pickup and headed in his direction, a vacant friendly look on his face.

Harlan stared back at the old man with a look of mounting panic in his eyes.

"Just fine and you?" he replied.

"Oh fine, just fine."

The man had thick green-tinted eyeglasses, the kind worn by old men with glaucoma, and large flesh-colored hearing aids looped over his ears. He stood rigidly erect but took careful little child's steps in his polished riding-heeled boots.

"This heat get y'all yet? Sure is something, ain't it?"

"It sure is," Harlan replied, hearing himself say things he had said his whole life except the words seemed to come from a script now. "Never seen anything like it."

"Boy howdy," said the old man, approaching.

Every platitude landed like a bullet fired at close range, just missing. The man stopped to look at Troy and nodded to him but he continued to address Harlan, as if he was uncertain how to converse with a grown man lying across a station wagon seat. "Your buddy over there looks like he's in a hurry." Troy stared at Harlan without moving or displaying any acknowledgment of the old man's presence.

Harlan couldn't believe what was happening to him. He couldn't believe what he knew he had to do. He bent down suddenly and retrieved both Dr. Peppers and carried them at an awkward loping clip across the parking lot toward the open station wagon door.

"Yes sir, we are in kind of a hurry. We was supposed to be all the way down to Big Spring by now. Got a late start."

Putting his hands on his hips, the old man shook his head warily. "Well, you watch. Highway patrol's real bad down there, just a-layin' in wait," he said. "Don't you get yourself no ticket."

Harlan answered without looking back at the old man. "We'll sure watch. You take care now."

He tried to hand one of the bottles to Troy but Troy had already put the car in gear and started it rolling toward the road and Harlan had to jump in, holding the bottles in one hand and pulling his legs in, swinging the door closed while somehow keeping the bag of Fritos clamped against his body. The tires of the station wagon momentarily lost traction on the gravel and kicked up a caliche cloud that rolled around the legs of the old man. The man didn't wave but just stood and watched the station wagon wonderingly as it tore away.

Troy goosed the gas and looked over at Harlan to make sure he was really in the car.

"Okay!" he said. *"Okay now!"*

Harlan's breath heaved as if he had been sprinting. He looked out the window, watching the old man recede. "*Jesus Christ.* What's okay? You tell me what's okay. Where the hell are we going to go now?"

Troy reached up to adjust the rearview mirror and looked behind him. "Not through Big Spring, for damned sure. That old man will have us pegged around there. We need to double back to a place where I left something we need. Look behind us, Harlan. Tell me what you see."

Harlan's heart thundered in his ears. His brain swam in fury and exhilaration, the exhilaration intensifying the fury. He turned around on the seat and scoured what was visible through the big back window, onto which his mind projected scenes from movies he remembered, scenes that never ended well. But out the window he saw only what he had seen his whole life, wherever he had been in West Texas: a flat, straight road leading between scattered buildings into a featureless plain, with a single traffic light flashing yellow at the edge of town, cautioning nobody because there was nobody around.

Sept. 17, 1972

AAA-approved vacancy welcome clean rooms clean beds reasonable rates Route 66 weekly quiet color TV by RCA cable 100 percent refrigerated air heated pool thermostat-controlled direct dial phones free local calls coffee shop open late steaks chops Mastercard and Diner's Club sleepers longboy beds cribs kitchenettes guest laundry truck and U-Haul parking in rear left turn okay welcome senior citizens no pets!!!

In Amarillo, the Arrow and the Plainsman, with its big fenced pool and pink-and-yellow doors like pastel piano keys; the True Rest, the Town House, the Skyline, the Palo Duro. In Dalhart the Texas. In Lubbock the Koko Inn and the 89'er, with fond memories of the Western Ways and the Astro now gone, blown away by the big tornado in '70. The Rambler and the Ranger in Shamrock. The Plainsman in Lamesa. The Westerner and the Imperial in Odessa. The Catalina in Wichita Falls. In Monahans, the Sunset and the Cowboy. In Happy the Hitching Post. In Tucumcari, the Blue Swallow. In Sweetwater the

Palomino. And in Cummings the Starlight Motor Hotel with its monogrammed hand towels and bedside lamps in the shape of bronze cowgirls on horseback forever twirling their little bronze lariats.

I'm in room number 38 of the Lamplighter in Hobbs, N.M., where I've been for the last three days under the name of Nolan Sackett, a character from a Louis L'Amour Western. It's been six months since I last stayed here and those months seem to have given my face a new lease. I can probably manage at least a few more days before people start getting too friendly, the way they always do.

I'll give you a brief physical description: I'm of medium height. I have a medium-size rounded face on which my unexceptional features seem to take up no definitive positions. My hair is light brown but in pictures it sometimes looks dark brown, sometimes blond. I'm agreeable-looking but just short enough of handsome that people tend to forget my face because it doesn't turn out to be what they expected. My voice is mild and as easy to tune out as an accountant's. I've escaped two near-arrests in my life, the only times I've ever been taken in, because the victims weren't able to pick me out of a lineup.

Sometimes I realize I've been by myself for too long, locked up in my own head. I drive through a thunderstorm and find myself thinking every lightning bolt forking down into the fields has my name on it. I worry about being tracked down not by the police or somebody I've robbed but by somebody I've never met, somebody I can't even imagine. I try to ease my mind by going to the movies or walking the aisles of variety stores, just to be around people. Sometimes I go into post offices and leaf through the state posters, looking to see if there's a sketch resembling me, a description of what I've done — but there never is.

I used to spend many afternoons in county libraries, reading at the public tables, using aliases to check out books that I would mail back anonymously from other towns. I loved the democratic quiet of libraries — the sound absorbed by all the paper and buckram and dust — but eventually I had to give them up because librarians began to spook me; they're as bored as bartenders and remember faces just as well.

I became a reader less from a love of books than from the love of how an open book in your hand seems to cause people to leave you alone. I still read anything that passes through my hands: magazines, Western novels, dime novels, thrillers, detective mysteries, romances, science fiction, history novels, small-town newspapers, *TV Guides,* sales catalogues, instructional manuals — even an instructional manual can be satisfying if someone has put some time into it — penny shoppers, road maps, dictionaries and textbooks, cookbooks, hymnals, and the Bible, the only book regularly available in the rooms where I live, always found in the second drawer of the nightstand.

In libraries I especially liked reading old newspapers. My interest followed a kind of formula: The papers couldn't be too old, from World War II or the Depression, because that information had already been filtered and pressed down into history and newspapers seemed like just the scattered leavings. But if the news was too recent it felt too close; I couldn't get a perspective on it and the lies and exaggerations seemed too apparent. Somewhere in the middle — anywhere from a couple of years to ten or fifteen — was the sweet spot. I could spend hours at a polished wood library table paging through the big books of old municipal newspapers, reading them with the pleasure of a good novel.

My travel pattern carves an erratic crosshatch across the Texas Panhandle. If you took pen to map to track my path — as some district attorney will — the resulting figure would look like an elaborate Jacob's ladder or a cat's cradle, the lines radiating from multiple convergences and ricocheting back out again, no line left too short or retraced too often. The lines pass mostly through small towns with small sheriff's departments, sometimes through towns that no longer exist, uninhabited, un-post-officed, two or three brick shells against the road to show that an attempt was made — Lahey, Bronco, Sligo, Allred, Hud, Goodnight, Tascosa, Nara Visa, N.M.

Early on I made the decision to confine myself to the wide open of the High Plains because it was the place I knew best and because it has always given me the comforting illusion that I can see whatever's coming at me from forty miles. But the longer this goes on the further I need to range off the llano, to put greater distances between myself and the jobs; I have to keep my motels, my stories, and my aliases in constant tripartite rotation, preventing any from congregating too closely in time or space in a way that might lead a man whose face I only dimly recall to spot me across a café floor and stare covertly in my direction over the top of his laminated menu, leaning in to whisper to his booth mates: "I'm telling y'all: That's the same son of a bitch!"

The clothes I'm wearing tonight belonged to a personal injury lawyer from Oklahoma City. I hit a little jackpot with him: pigskin suede jacket, single-breasted, center vent, Bert Paley label; dark brown Dacron dress slacks by Corbin; baby-blue dress shirt, Van Heusen Vanopress; rust-colored tie embroidered with a crosshatch pattern of Conestoga wagons; gold-plated winding watch, Benrus; polished shell cordovan wingtips, Florsheim Imperial, nearly brand-new, still stiff. I robbed his room at the Black Gold Motel in Pampa while he was in the shower.

He was traveling with all the signifiers of his prosperity and belonging: wedding band; watch; fountain pen; dress Stetson; wallet with driver's license, family pictures, BankAmericard. I never take a man's wedding ring, his toothbrush, or his family pictures, though in this case his two young sons vaguely resembled me so I kept a snapshot of them, figuring it might come in handy. He had ninety-seven dollars and fifty cents in cash, and a pair of brown-tinted sunglasses, lying here on the bedside table, next to a paperback spy novel dog-eared at pg. 117, the part where it was starting to get good. I'm wearing his socks; his belt; his undershirt; his boxer undershorts, laundered bright white for him by someone; his aftershave, Corral Pour Homme, expensive-looking, with aromas of pine needles and soap. Accuse me of what you want to, but not seeing things through has never been one of my shortcomings.

I know you must want to understand how a person could come to this — to the point where he can't tolerate calling even an article of clothing his own, much less a television set or a car or, God forbid, a house — to the point where even the thought of belongings fills him with a kind of dread.

I can't tell you what happened. I just know I woke up one morning and the world wasn't the same and I couldn't find a way back to the way it was before. I think everyone has that kind of door in his mind, that if allowed to open even an inch is very hard to get closed again.

Sometimes I think back to something that happened two summers ago, after I'd worked my way into a car-theft ring in the Dallas area with a catchment extending south to Waco and west to Abilene. The money was good and there was something about belonging to an organized outfit that gave me a feeling of pride, a feeling I later came to recognize as one of the more dangerous a professional thief can have.

My first job, a kind of audition, was to boost a car straight from a lot, a trophy — a pristine new-model Plymouth Barracuda, cobalt blue, shaker hood, rally dash, six-pack 440. I took it with no trouble on a Sunday morning in Wichita Falls, when the dealership was closed and a church quiet of the kind only West Texas knows had descended on the city. I ran it onto State Highway 81 from Bowie toward Dallas, and I don't mind telling you I was proud of myself that morning — this was a bread-winner of a car. I could already feel the grudging respect coming my way when I brought it in.

But I wanted to pass some personal time inside this all-American internal-combustion cocoon. So I took it off onto the empty farm roads south of Bowie and blew it out for a couple of hours, floating on the sound of the pistons shivering the needle past 120.

Late in the afternoon I pulled off alongside a stand of dryland corn with a notch in the rows about a third of the way down one side. I knew what this notch would be harboring and as I pulled in I quickly found the patch of ripe watermelons, nestled down in the furrows like fat green babies.

I popped the trunk of the Barracuda and walked around thumping rinds. As I moved along the rows I caught sight of a weathered pine signboard speared into the dirt on a garden stake, the kind you see in nurseries labeling the plants, except this one was too big and had too many words for that. I had almost expected to see such a sign nestled somewhere down there among the melons. If you aren't from the country you might not know the story behind this sign — a funny story, rooted in the lore of farmland almost as deeply as farmers' daughters and apple pies cooling on windowsills. It goes something like this: Boys, mostly boys, raid watermelon patches, a birthright, rite of summer; farmers hew and cry and sit on their porches at night with shotguns across their knees, scanning the corn stalks for headlights; one day, an ingenious farmer gets an idea; he hammers a sign into his patch that says: "WARNING: ONE OF THESE WATER

MELONS IS POISONED!" This works until the night when an even more ingenious melon bandit, calling his bluff, takes some paint and adds a postscript to the sign — "NOW TWO ARE!" — before carting off his share.

Maybe because of the way the story turned on the power of words, it found its natural home in church sermons, for which it was probably invented, and it was often used to teach farmland people something they already knew deep in their bones — you reap what you sow.

I thought about getting a pen and adding the coda to the sign, out of a sense of tradition. But I decided I couldn't risk the low comedy of getting arrested for stealing produce, so I helped myself quickly to a small melon the color of a jadestone, and later, at a motel in Denton, I took a pocketknife and carved a big slice and ate it while I watched an episode of *Bonanza.*

I understood what was happening almost immediately. I threw it all up, but whatever poison the melon contained was so noxious it must have instantly infiltrated my system because for the next three days I lay in bed barely able to move — my hands and feet painfully distended, my head and face so swollen I could barely open my eyes to see how terrifying and near-dead I must have looked. In my delirium I began to imagine that my head was slowly denaturing into a watermelon and that this was the intended effect of the toxin I had ingested, some alchemical compound engineered by a pesticide company as a terrifying deterrent to watermelon theft.

As the days went by, the room kept threatening to rupture at the seams. Even the light leaking in around the curtain edges was unbearable. A painting on the wall depicting a beautiful woman seated beneath a tree staring out at a river turned out to be a jigsaw puzzle held behind glass. This seemed like a joke someone was playing on me, as did the Japanese-looking wallpaper with a pattern of tree branches that keep changing into live snakes.

By the first morning I was struggling to get breath around my tongue, which felt like a slab of uncooked meat lodged in my mouth. Ideas drifted up into consciousness that had no coherence in and of themselves except that some seemed to be buoyant and keep me afloat while others sank as soon as I grabbed them, pulling me beneath the surface. Besides respiration the only thing I could hold in my mind for any length of time was the image of the gleaming Barracuda sitting out in the parking lot, begging to get made. I also thought about the farmer — a man likely to become my murderer, a man who might well have been a pillar of his community, a churchgoer, yet a man who had taken considerable time and effort to syringe actual poison into his near-worthless watermelons. How many had he poisoned? Or did I pick the one winner out of them all?

I kept the maids at bay by bellowing when they knocked. Around the evening of the second day, the motel owner used the passkey to let herself in. She was middle-aged, tough-looking, broad-hipped, dressed in a turquoise pantsuit. I managed to veil myself partially with the sheet.

Probably for specific legal reasons she remained with her feet just behind the threshold of the door. She asked me in an abnormally loud voice: "Sir, is there something the matter with you? Sir, do you need someone to take you to a hospital?" I heard myself answer, telling her I had the flu. I asked if she could get me a glass of water, maybe something to eat. But the voice that came from my mouth sounded nothing like me. It sounded vaguely like

Harlan but more like a wounded animal that had acquired powers of speech to articulate its dying. I was afraid she couldn't understand me. But she went away and came back with a plastic gallon milk jug of cold water and another empty jug cut in half, for me to vomit into. Much later — I had no idea whether it was a day or a week — she returned and left an unplugged crockpot full of beef broth.

She wore strong perfume that smelled like potpourri and the untanned tops of her breasts rose up out of her blouse like crescent rolls. She parted the drapes to bring a little light into the room and stood disapprovingly over what it illuminated. "Now you eat this for me and I'll check back in a few hours," she said. She turned up the A/C and put the television on for me with the sound low.

I watched the small black-and-white screen without being able to focus my eyes. When I did I saw images of an immense crowd of soldiers somewhere, clapping and whooping, laughing, gathered around three tall highline poles. Each of the poles seemed to have three or four men dangling from it. I watched with mounting horror, thinking it was news footage showing soldiers who had killed some men, probably Vietcong, and strung their corpses up on poles in front of a jeering crowd. I couldn't understand why we would be allowed to see such a horrifying scene on network television. But after a while I realized it was only a USO program and the men on the highline poles were still alive. They were just GIs who had climbed up there to get a better view of the dancing girls in Bob Hope's show.

I had no memory of eating but the cooker was empty when the woman returned to take it. She came back with it full and lingered this time, talking, trying to lighten the mood. She stopped calling me sir and seemed to have formed a maternal feeling toward me.

"I think you might pull through, sugar. And that's good for me, because when somebody checks out of here toes up it does a number on my motel association rating."

The whole time, she never asked a single personal question, never threatened to call an ambulance. She seemed to understand I was in no position to present myself to a doctor — motel proprietors can be that way sometimes, as complicit as fences.

I'm fairly certain now that this kind-hearted woman never existed but was a figment of my contaminated brain, conjured up as an embodiment of my will to survive, to sweat the poison from my blood.

There's an aspect of a high fever that's magnificent, as if you've been freed from all physical encumbrance, floating on a cloud lighted from within by unearthly light. Then you realize this must be what a man feels near death as his body begins to surrender itself, so you lie there torn by a strange mix of euphoria and dread.

I had a dream in the middle of it. I was riding in the passenger seat of a car whose make I couldn't determine, driven by a man I'd known during my first days stealing cars in New Mexico. He had been paired with me as a kind of mentor, but he didn't particularly like me and I didn't care much for him, either. He was an alcoholic and wore a suit jacket with the lining sagging below the hem like an old woman's slip showing beneath her dress. He always called me hombre.

Finding myself in a car with him was clearly a dream because he was already dead. We were in the middle of nowhere, in front of a little white-shingled farmhouse. I didn't know the house but I had the distinct feeling it knew me, that I must have lived in it at some point and forgotten about it.

The man said he had an important piece of information to share before he dropped me off. We sat in front of the house for a long time and I became aware that he was fumbling with something in his lap, which turned out to be the scraps of a twenty-dollar bill he was diligently trying to tape back together with Scotch tape. I realized that he would continue trying to tape it back together for eternity and I felt bad for him.

What he ultimately told me turned out not to be important at all; it was something a high school football coach once said to me after I'd missed a tackle on purpose because I didn't care for the game of football. The man repeated the exact words the coach had screamed on the practice field that day, gripping the center bar of my facemask, yanking me around like a wrestled steer:

"Son, I don't care if you fuck up. But if you do I want you to fuck up going a hundred and ten miles an hour. Do you understand me? This isn't about football, son. This is about life! This is the goddamned United States of America!"

Near dead in the noonday twilight of a cheap motel room, it occurred to me that I'd ended up following his advice.

The two brothers, her second cousins, had woken Martha in their native state, savaging each other, and she had been within seconds of loosing an ear-splitting scream when they suddenly bolted from the station wagon and the strange man opened the back door and threw something onto the seat and got into the car.

Martha saw him for a split second but he didn't seem to have seen her. She thought he must have mistaken her aunt's car for his own and she was about to sit up, but then something made her stop. She clamped her eyes shut and lay very still in the berth behind the backseat of the station wagon, where she had sought refuge from the boys on the way into town, stretched out along the seam formed by the carpeted floorboard and the angled seat back, a protected place she often claimed, staring up through the side window into blue sky, imagining herself rising out into the open air.

After a lot of yelling another man had gotten into the car and it had pulled out and Martha thought a panic sound she heard in her throat would escape from her mouth but it didn't. The men had stopped talking now and all she could hear besides her heart pumping was the violent sound being made by the engine, not anything like the station wagon's regular sound, and the thunder of the tires pounding gravel up against the floorboard below her head. She had never known anyone in her life who had been the victim of a car theft, because for most of her life she had not known anyone who owned a car. But she knew a car was being stolen now and knew she needed to do something, though every instinct in her body told her that if she did nothing, if she remained absolutely still and absolutely silent, it would be better. She would ride to wherever they took the car, which would probably be far from Tahoka; when they finally stopped she would wait for them to get out and then sneak away and hitch a ride and no one would be able to catch her.

In the year since they had brought her here to West Texas she had tried to run away three times but had never made it further than town, where too many people already knew why she was there and who she was: a Mennonite, or once one, from a family of Old Colony Mennonites, descendants of families that had migrated in the twenties from Manitoba and Saskatchewan through the Great Plains into the Chihuahuan desert, seeking freedom from state interference in their affairs and finally finding it in northern Mexico, along with persistent drought and deprivation.

Martha was one of eleven, a family of nine girls and two boys. Three years earlier, her father, an oat farmer on the brink of ruin, had set in motion events that had brought her to this place with what seemed like a negligible act of disobedience: He had shod the wheels of his ancient two-cylinder tractor with rubber tires. It was a modest concession to modernity, made to save badly needed money on gasoline and upkeep on the tractor — there were men even in conservative colonies who had done it years before. But in his colony rubber tires remained prohibited by ecclesiastical law because it was possible that a tractor with tires could be driven on public roads, could conceivably be driven all the way to Cuauhtémoc City. Such use of tractors for transportation could lead to an inevitable acceptance of the automobile — and once the automobile entered Mennonite life the struggle to keep worldliness at bay would be all but lost. Aron Zacharias knew men would come and eventually they did. He dug in his heels and they went away and others came, accompanied by concession-seeking groups of cousins and family friends, in whose presence he steadfastly refused each request to remove the tires. After almost a year of deliberation the elders finally excommunicated him and six months later Martha's mother, under pressure from her family, who had expected some disgrace like this from him, formally shunned him — the worst punishment possible in a society defined by belonging. His church and livelihood had already been taken away from him and finally his children were, too.

But on the dark winter morning that he left for Cuauhtémoc City, he drove a neighbor's borrowed pickup to the tiny cinder-block-and-plywood farmhouse he had built with his own hands and, by the light of a Coleman lantern, found Martha on a mattress sleeping between two of her younger sisters and pulled her up in her nightgown and told her to be quiet and took her with him. The pickup was pulling away before Martha saw her mother, Anna, coming through the door onto the swept dirt yard in front of the house. Children filed wonderingly out into the yard behind her, seemingly more children than lived in the house. Martha remembered seeing her mother standing there in her own white nightgown, barely visible, the whole scene made dream-like by the reddish glow of the taillights over the yard. She remembered her mother making no attempt to run after her or scream for her father to stop. She seemed to have come outside only to witness her daughter's leaving.

Martha and her father shared one half of a trailer house with running water and gas but no electricity on the eastern edge of Cuauhtémoc City in a lot behind a small roadside hotel. The hotel was attached to a two-story stucco restaurant that sold hamburgers and tacos to truckers and workers from a livestock feed elevator down the road. The trailer came furnished, meagerly, and had an old swing set in front, indicating that a family had once lived there, but one of the set's pipe legs was now broken, causing it to lean over like a statue of a horse in perpetual stumble. The trailer was divided in half, the rear occupied by two Mennonite men in their early twenties who had also left the Old Colony church, by choice, and had come to the city to learn automotive work. The two living quarters were separated in the hallway by a curtain made from a child's blanket decorated with an image of a huge, idiotic-looking cartoon rooster Martha had never seen before but that the men told her was an American creation named Foghorn Leghorn. The men helped Aron get a job at a service station patching truck tires, a job he considered to be biblical retribution but he took it because he had no choice.

He had never been a man of many words and after they moved into their new home Aron said even fewer, speaking to Martha only to tell her what to cook or what he needed, though what he seemed to need most was her simple presence, as if she stood for everything he had lost and the remote but still conceivable possibility of getting it back. In the way a nine-year-old does, Martha understood this, and it gave her a feeling of usefulness that tempered her fear of him and what might happen to them. She accepted the fact that it was just the two of them now without a second thought, the way she accepted most things in a life over which she had never had the least control. She missed her mother sometimes, but she missed nothing else about the farm or the colony and she truthfully didn't care if she ever saw it or anyone from it again, not her sisters or her brothers, her house or her few friends.

She had turned nine not long after they arrived, but Aron didn't remember it was her birthday and she didn't tell him. She slept by herself in the living room of the trailer house on a spavined, mustard-striped couch, the first time she had ever slept without other bodies, hot or heat-seeking, crowded up against her. She had to rise at dawn to make breakfast — the way she had for as long as she could remember — by herself now, instead of helping her mother. But after Aron and the two men had gobbled it down and left for work, a solitude unlike any Martha had known descended inside the ramshackle daylit trailer. At first the time alone frightened her. It felt so good she was convinced it must belong to some category of sin that nobody had told her about, but after a couple of weeks she stopped worrying about indulging in it. The only sounds that managed to reach the trailer house were those made by the occasional truck pulling into the rear parking lot of the café and a nest of mourning doves roosted somewhere in the trailer's rain gutter, loudest in the couple of hours after dawn. Without electricity there was no possibility of a television set, as she had dearly hoped, but one of the men owned a silver-and-black Sanyo Channel Master transistor radio and she would sneak it from his room and put it back after she had listened to it.

Mennonites in Chihuahua spoke Plautdietsch, Low German, and the men and boys were allowed to learn Spanish, but Martha knew more Spanish than she let on and she and her siblings all learned English from their mother, who had been born in Texas. So sitting with the radio at the kitchen table, she always tuned it to one of the X stations to hear country-and-western music and the American news, which seemed at that time to be mostly about a war and about a general unhappiness spreading across the United States.

She was allowed to walk across the alleyway to the café, where the women would sell her hamburger meat, eggs, butter, tortillas, and coffee from the kitchen, on credit Aron would settle at the end of the month. After a few weeks the women let Martha stay and keep them company after the lunch rush. Cuauhtémoc, a town then of about ten thousand people, had been all but built by the Mennonites since their arrival in Chihuahua in the early twenties, but even in those years almost none lived in the city. The prosperous ones from the more liberal colonies drove down in pickups before dawn to run their businesses and buy their supplies, then headed north again before sundown. The Old Colony men came on weekends in their covered buggies, parking their horses between cars. The café workers regarded Martha with a kind of wary curiosity, realizing that she and her father were exiles but unsure whether this came about through choice or banishment. Some of the younger women — subscribing to the belief in the area that Mennonites were forced to wander the world in order to protect the terrible secret that they kept family relations far too close — reached the same conclusion about both possibilities.

The long summer days spent by herself grew oppressive sooner than she had expected, emboldening Martha to venture further from the trailer after Aron and the men had eaten lunch and headed back to work in their shared pickup. She would walk in the opposite direction along Avenida General Sepúlveda, the main conduit leading into the city from the apple orchards and cheese factories that lay east toward Chihuahua City. Sometimes she went as far as the big plaza, where the trunks of the trees had been painted waist high with slaked lime to protect them from leafcutter ants. Amid these short irregular white columns old men sat on benches, breathing through their teeth and speaking to each other very rarely, stirring only to throw little rocks when stray dogs wandered too close. Sometimes a small group of soldiers came for marching drills on the swept dirt. Their uniforms didn't all match and some wore canvas puttees on their legs that resembled the white-trunked trees and reminded Martha of pictures of soldiers she had seen in a book about the First World War.

Four loudspeakers stood at the corners of the plaza, sometimes playing scratchy recordings of polka marches and sometimes broadcasting official municipal announcements nearly impossible to understand. Tarahumara Indian women squatted on the grass at the edge of the main path with their babies, selling ollas and pine needle baskets, the women inexplicably wrapped in heavy woolen rebozos in the towering heat. The Indian women and girls covered their heads with scarves the same way the Mennonite women did and Martha wondered if it was for similar reasons. Not long after they came to the city she had stopped wearing her scarf but she still wore the dark-print calico dresses her mother had made for her, the only clothes she owned, and with those and her hair and her face no one in Cuauhtémoc could mistake her for anything other than what she was. Walking down the streets, peering into the windows of panaderías and dress shops, she was careful to keep her distance from passing Mennonites who might be able to identify her. By the third month in the city she even dared to take the municipal bus, riding it to a long street on the edge of town with the strange-sounding name of Sin Nombre — Nameless. She wondered if this was its real name or if the mapmaker just helpfully labeled places no one had gotten around to naming yet. Sometimes she got off at the mirador, whose steps she would mount to look out from the high viewing platform over the state of Chihuahua, wondering why anyone would go to the trouble to build a scenic lookout in a place like this, too flat and far away from the Sierra Madre for them to look very impressive. But from the top you were able to see a pretty little waterfall, a thin stream that tumbled down about fifty feet during the rainy season from a cleft in the rocky terrain on that side of town, and this year uncommonly good rain made the San Antonio Valley just to the north, where she had spent her entire life, spread out like a deep green carpet with its grazing pastures and fields of oats and corn. She had never been to Cuauhtémoc City before her father had brought her to live here, but she and her sisters and brothers had heard about it since they were babies and had tried to imagine the sumptuous streets its mystical Aztec name had been coined to describe. Looking out toward the valley from the platform, it stunned her to see just how near the city had been all along. She could have walked here from the campo in a day's time, though doing such a thing would have been inconceivable to her then.

Life in Cuauhtémoc settled into an unvarying routine of housework, tedium, and ministering to Aron and the two men, broken up only by the trips into the city that she feared her father would discover but came to see as her right. So many things about the years she had lived in the colony began to feel like memories from someone else's life, while the life she was living now in the little trailer house seemed as if it could go on indefinitely, as long as the work kept bringing in enough money for food and rent.

The end came before they had been in the city a year, one afternoon in October. It was gray and raining. Martha had stayed in to make a caldo for Aron for his birthday, with good beef she had saved up for, cooked according to a Mennonite recipe handed down since Russia but almost fully Mexicanized now, flavored with chilis and epazote. While she was browning the beef Jonas, one of the two young men who shared the trailer, came in loudly through the screen door, startling her because neither he nor his friend Isaac ever came back to the house in the afternoon before quitting time. The larger of the two and older by a year at twenty or twenty-one, Jonas was the only one who had paid any attention to Martha, addressing her dismissively on the rare occasions when he found her by herself. He displayed his arrogance during these encounters by speaking to her in Spanish, as if it was a secret language they shared. Jonas was built straight and solid but had an unusually thick neck and a big moon face that cast an undeserved impression of plumpness over the rest of his body. He told her to call him Joey, the name he used at work and the one his friend Isaac now used, but she refused and went out of her way to pronounce his given name clearly.

Martha had borrowed Jonas's transistor radio from the top of the dresser in his room and when he barged into the trailer she turned to the kitchen table to try to grab it and hide it, but she couldn't reach it before he came into view. Jonas didn't take off his wet straw cowboy hat and hang it on the peg near the door but walked straight into the kitchen and dropped heavily into one of the chairs.

He didn't say anything for a while, listening to the music from the radio and looking at Martha, who was turned half toward him uncomfortably at the sink. "You like this radio of mine?" he finally said in Spanish, picking it up off the table and turning it around to admire it. He moved the dial to static and then back and thumbed up the volume knob until the chorus of an old ballad —

He went up to her mother's house,
Between the hours of eight and nine
And asked her for to walk with him
Down near the foaming brine

— blasted harshly and metallically through the narrow rooms of the trailer.

She didn't answer him.

"You like all the batteries I'm always having to buy for it, too?" he asked.

She wiped a film of grease and flour from the countertop and didn't turn to look at him. "Why are you home so early?" she asked finally over the racket of the radio.

"I'm sick. Even a strong man can get sick sometimes, you know?"

But she knew he wasn't sick — she could smell the sourness of beer and cigarettes on him through the heaviness of his damp clothes. She worried he might have lost his job. "Where's Isaac?"

Jonas stared down at the expanse of the unset table and looked as if he might go to sleep there. But he hoisted himself up from his chair and began swaying rhythmically to the song on the radio, looking like an overgrown child learning to dance. "You ask a lot of questions," he said, and waltzed clumsily up to her, waving a hand in the air, scuffling his boots on the buckled linoleum.

He grabbed her before she could turn around to ward him off. He wrapped his arms around her in a way that seemed almost gentle, except that his arms were heavy and hers were pinned down to her sides. She didn't make a sound as he started in but she tried to stiffen her body and tuck her face down into her chest to avoid his attempts at kisses, which landed on her neck and the side of her head.

Without seeming to exert himself in the least, he lifted Martha so her feet weren't touching the floor and walked with her the five steps out of the kitchen into the living room and fell bodily with her, atop her, onto the yellow couch where she slept, flattening the breath out of her when they landed. As it was all happening, Martha didn't feel anything that seemed like fear and she couldn't decide what to feel besides painful embarrassment. Jonas had his head buried in the couch cushion over her right shoulder and his wet hat had fallen onto the carpet. His breath was starting to heave. Up close like this the sharp odors of axle grease and sweat from the garage mixed with those of the beer and smoke, but beneath everything she also thought she smelled something unfamiliar, sweet and musky, some cologne he must have put on.

He might have been able to accomplish what he started but when he reached down for his pants he realized he was wearing his overalls and as he struggled heroically at his chest to undo the brass fasteners, Martha felt him shudder and heard him let out a quiet whining sound, as if he was about to cry. He stopped shifting on top of her and lay panting for several seconds as she began to get her breath back underneath him. He pushed himself off her and bent down, still huffing hard, and retrieved his hat and clamped it down onto his head and stood next to her, looking at her lying on the couch. His face beneath his hat was blazing, flushed with the kind of embarrassing blood-red that only fair-skinned Germanic people can get. He didn't speak. He simply lumbered back to the kitchen, where he retrieved his blaring radio and turned it off and walked back toward his room, putting his hand against the wood paneling to steady himself. Martha sat up and pulled her dress back down over her pale legs and looked at it carefully to see if there was anything on it. Then she got up and went to the screen door and looked out to see if anyone walking by might have heard what happened, but no one was around and it wouldn't have mattered anyway because in truth the two of them had made no more noise than the birds in the nest on the top of the trailer.

The rest of that day and the next passed without incident, a normalcy that seemed unreal to Martha given what had happened, until she made up her mind that this was what normal felt like now. She thought hard about everything and decided that she didn't hold against Jonas what he had tried to do, though she wondered how she would feel if he had succeeded. Even now she liked him more than she liked Isaac, who was silent and passive and ate with his mouth hanging open like a cow. That evening the two of them emerged glumly from their room as they always did and crowded into the kitchen, taking their places around the little dinner table, lighted at night with a battery-powered lamp. With a mound of zwieback in a wicker basket there was barely room for the caldo, which sent up a column of steam from a speckled Granite-Ware roasting pan, the trailer's only cooking vessel besides an old iron skillet.

After grace Aron said nothing to Martha about the dish she had labored over for him, but he made a point of ladling himself a much larger helping than anyone else got and he smiled as he ate it, a rare sight. As usual, nobody spoke during the meal. Jonas kept his eyes meticulously away from Martha's but every now and then she would catch him looking at her with a mixture of menace and fear. Martha avoided his gaze, too, not because she was afraid of him but because she already resented the fact that she would have to worry about his fear of what she would do, a fear she probably could not diminish even if she swore to him on a Bible that she wouldn't tell anyone what had happened.

As they were finishing their dessert, Aron abruptly broke the silence at the table.

"So where were you today?" he said to Jonas in Spanish, not looking at him, staring down into his bowl of pudding.

Jonas didn't raise his head or the spoon he had just buried in his bowl.

"Estaba enfermo," he said finally, and then slowly lifted the load of pudding to his mouth.

"No you weren't," Aron said and after a long silence added: "You don't like to work. And you drink too much. Te despidieron."

"They didn't, either," Jonas shot back, looking around the table at the accusing eyes on him. "Those *cabrones.* I quit."

"Either way, you don't have a paycheck now," Aron said. "And you don't talk like that in front of the girl."

As she always did when men spoke Spanish around her Martha wore an exaggeratedly blank face, but she knew that Aron knew she understood everything, so she was especially careful not to look in his direction. She looked instead at Jonas, whose face had begun to color. He made as if to talk back but thought better of it and furiously shoveled two more heaping spoonfuls of raisin pudding into his mouth before bolting from his chair, struggling to unwedge his bulk from the table before stomping back to his room, shaking the flimsy trailer floor.

Martha saw him only once more after

that. In the dark of their shared bedroom that night, with several bottles of beer in him, Jonas bragged to Isaac about what had happened on the couch the previous afternoon. The girl had been asking for it for weeks, he told him, and so he finally gave it to her.

"You're so full of shit, Joey," Isaac said. "I'm tired to death of your shit. Shut up and go to sleep now."

"Hand to God, I'm not lying to you," Jonas said and cast about in his mind for something to lend the power of authenticity to his account: "Let me tell you, brother, she had the prettiest pussy you ever saw."

The next morning Martha left for the café and Jonas drove away early to the garage to beg for his job back. Isaac found Aron behind the trailer hoeing at a stand of weeds and related the night's conversation to him, terrified at the thought of what he was saying but far more terrified that Aron would find out and suspect he knew. Aron waited inside for Martha to come back home and the moment she entered he grabbed her and flung her to the floor and clamped a hand around her throat and ordered her to tell him the truth, which she did between convulsions of terrified sobbing, choking on her tears.

Aron stood up and fetched his toolbox calmly, as if he were only on his way to work, and went to find a neighbor woman who sometimes drove him. He surprised Jonas in the parking lot and ran him down before he could reach the pickup. For the better part of an hour, until the police and the ambulance finally arrived, Aron waited next to Jonas's heavy, heaving, bleeding body, surrounded by milling Mexican garage hands uncertain what their responsibilities should be after such an incident, so they just stood close by in case he tried to run.

Jonas remained in the hospital for three days. Aron spent two weeks in a close, noxious jail cell with fourteen other men, two of them young Mennonites he didn't know and never addressed. After the incident, Martha was taken in by the family that ran the hotel and restaurant, and a few days after Aron's release, back at the trailer by herself, she saw Jonas for the last time, when he came to pick up his possessions, left outside in a cardboard box.

He climbed slowly out of the passenger side of a pickup driven by a small Mexican man she didn't recognize and walked up the driveway, limping with his right leg, looking nervously up and down the street.

He came close to the kitchen window, behind which Martha was watching, fairly sure he knew she was there, though he never looked in her direction. A few times in her life Martha had seen boys' faces and hands battered and swollen after fights but she had never seen anyone beaten as badly as Jonas had been. The middle of his face was covered with a knot of gauze that concealed what had happened to his nose. Both of his swollen brows were shaved clean and dabbed with Mercurochrome and the left one had been sewn up along the length of its ridge, with black stitch-ends that poked out like porcupine quills. The welts on his cheeks had turned the sickly color of verdigris, and even his eyelids looked raw and pink, like a rabbit's. Martha watched him, frightened but electrified, barely moving or breathing. He was almost unrecognizable, not simply because of his face but because of the way he carried himself now, with a kind of gravity she had never seen him display, like that of a much older man, though it also looked as if he had been crying. The man who had driven him leaned out of the window and said something and Jonas slowly picked up his box, containing everything he owned in the world, and carried it to the truck without ever looking back toward the trailer.

After Cuauhtémoc, Aron and Martha never stayed in another place again for more than a few months. They lived in Chihuahua City in a motel room with a kitchenette until some misunderstanding unknown to Martha caused them to have to leave. They went up the federal highway to Juan Aldama for a time and then all the way back to Nuevo Casas Grandes, but it was too close to the colonias and Aron worried that they had been spotted, so they quickly packed and went as far north as possible, to Juárez.

In each place Aron mostly took farmhand work, the easiest to get. But farming other men's land was hateful to him, especially on the big sprawling corn and milo operations where he said it felt as if they were mulching money itself to fertilize land being overfarmed into sterility.

One morning in the summer of 1971, after they had been in Juárez for two weeks paying for a room they couldn't afford, Aron told Martha to stay put and wait for him and he took a bus into El Paso to find a man he had met several years earlier at a grain elevator in Cuauhtémoc. The man, Preston Salas, was white but had a Spanish surname and looked strangely almost Mexican, with straight black hair and dark brown eyes. He was from the Texas Panhandle but for many years had conducted business along the border and into Chihuahua. In Mennonite parlance he was known as a coyote, though too many Mennonites had come to know this too late. Salas and a silent man he introduced as his younger brother had shown up under the names of Ed and Bill McConnell at various colonias just before harvest time in 1969, toward the end of a long drought that had pushed many families to the breaking point. Carrying cash and presenting themselves as independent commodities buyers trying to establish a beachhead in the valley, the two had paid above-market prices for corn and beans and pigs, and came back writing checks for more. The checks cleared, buying Salas and his partner entrée to dozens of family kitchens and council offices, where they struck the kinds of deals they had been pressing for. This time they brought in a fleet of produce trucks and livestock trailers and cut checks for astonishing amounts that turned out to be as worthless as Preston Salas and his so-called brother, who were never heard from again.

Aron had avoided becoming a victim only because his spread of oats, half eaten by crown rust, was too meager to attract Salas's attention. Later, in Cuauhtémoc, he had learned Salas's real name and discovered that after Chihuahua he had ended up serving prison time in El Paso in connection with a hospital bid-rigging scheme. Tracking him down was easier than Aron had thought it would be: He simply looked him up in the residential directory of the telephone book, which had three densely populous agate pages of Salases, Abelardo to Zarita, but only one named Preston. Aron dialed the number and they had a brief telephone conversation before Salas agreed to see him, in a tiny vinyl-sided ranch house in Ysleta where he lived alone, nine months out of jail and still on probation.

The difference between the man Aron remembered and the man who opened the door was so striking he thought he had come to the wrong address. The Salas he met in Mexico had looked like a middle-aged lawyer in a pearl-gray Stetson. This one was dressed in cutoff shorts and a yellow T-shirt with a picture of a woman in a skimpy bathing suit on it. He looked a decade younger and much thinner, with a weedy mustache hanging over an irresolute mouth. He still wore a good hat but a ponytail hung beneath it now. He ushered Aron into a living room unfurnished except for a brown velour love seat and a small television set on the floor whose power cord snaked across the carpet. He lit a cigarette and held out a plastic bowl of corn chips, which Aron, holding his own hat in both of his hands, declined. They conversed in Spanish, which Salas seemed to understand better than he let on. Aron spoke in a measured, businesslike manner, using no more words than he needed, laying out his circumstances with the colonia and stating his offer plainly: If Salas could stake an intermediary, one who wouldn't be recognized in Cuauhtémoc, to return and set up as a buyer, Aron could supply him with more than enough private information about debts and market arrangements among Mennonite cheese makers that he could easily go back in and make big check-buys from several of them.

"How much does that mean for you?" Salas asked, picking a piece of tobacco off his tongue, looking Aron in the eye.

"Forty percent," Aron said.

Salas smoked and considered the proposition before saying that he found at least two things hard to take on faith in such a scenario — one, Aron's willingness to sell his own people down the river; and even more, his people's collective susceptibility to getting cleaned out again so soon in exactly the same way they'd been cleaned out before. But Salas's look didn't corroborate the doubts coming out of his mouth; the look told Aron how much he needed the money, too.

"They took my family away from me, everything I had — so I'm owed, that's why," Aron told him, standing while Salas sat. "The other thing is something you already know: They all believe too much in the goodness of man ever to be able to guard themselves very well against somebody like you."

Salas kept his gaze leveled on Aron, exhaling smoke without turning his head.

"Somebody like you, too," he said, grinning.

After several more minutes of useless talk Salas said he would mull it over and get back in touch, but Aron knew what the answer would be. He walked up the hallway toward the front door. Salas called out sarcastically after him: "God be with you, my brother."

Aron put his hat on his head and opened the door and walked out without looking back.

"And you."

Aron ended up agreeing to thirty percent,

and the arrangement would have worked except that he entered into it with someone whose luck was even worse than his own. He learned later from a lawyer what Salas hadn't known, that the U.S. Customs Service had put a tap on his phone and started to sift through his mail because they suspected — erroneously, as they were to discover, to their annoyance — that he had been hired by a still-incarcerated cellmate to shepherd a shipment of marijuana from Ojinaga into the Big Bend. Customs investigators had made no progress in the case, so they waited a few weeks, transcribing Salas's calls to Chihuahua setting up the check fraud and then they took him in for violation of his parole. As a courtesy, the agents reported the arrest to their counterparts in Juárez, who cursed at them in English over the phone for making work. But when the Mexican agents typed Aron's name into the system, they turned up the kidnapping warrant that had been outstanding against him since not long after he had taken Martha from the colonia.

She was alone the next morning when three Juárez municipal officers with unholstered pistols came to the door of the cinder-block apartment house in Libertad to which they had traced Aron. Martha opened the door. The men stood speechless for a few seconds, having never seen a Mennonite girl except in pictures in the newspaper and, even then, not expecting a face so alabaster pale, hair so blond it manifested as silver in the morning sun. The men looked at her and then at each other for several moments until one of them broke the silence by taking out a piece of paper and reading a formal-sounding statement. Like a lot of Mexican police in the area, the three seemed less like officers than like regular people who had shown up out of curiosity to see what the actual police were doing.

In uncertain circumstances with Mexicans, Martha never revealed that she knew Spanish. But that morning in fear she forgot herself and told the officers that she was alone and that her father had left for his field job and that she didn't know when he would be back. She said she didn't know what the word secuestro meant, though she did, and then, fumbling wildly, she told them that they had come to the wrong apartment because there was no Aron Zacharias here. One of them dutifully read the arrest order again and a look of flushed panic spread across Martha's face. She began speaking in rapid, guttural Low German and tried to shut the door but the biggest cop stuck his shoe almost casually against the jamb. Martha backed away from the door and began to weep with her mouth closed as they filed one by one into the sparse little room, which contained a sink, a two-burner stovetop in one corner, a rollaway bed folded in two, an aluminum lawn chair, and a small chest of drawers, atop which sat a small black-and-white television with a hoop antenna. The youngest of the three cops, who was rail thin and looked no older than sixteen or seventeen, whispered to his superior: *"This is the first time I've ever seen an albino in person."* The older cop opened the bathroom door cautiously and peered inside. "She's not albino, *pendejo,* she's menonita." The three began awkwardly gathering the clothes and the few other things that seemed to be the girl's — a purple plastic hand mirror, a faded crocheted blanket, an unclothed rag doll of indeterminate gender that Martha had become ashamed to be seen with but could not bring herself to leave behind — and put it all into a clear plastic bag they had brought with them. Martha squatted down on her bare heels near the door and began to wail openly, a keening that sounded more terrible because of the way she tried unsuccessfully to keep it under control.

She reverted to speaking to the men in Spanish again, insisting that they had come to the wrong address.

"Nobody's done anything wrong here," she said. "We are Mennonite. We follow our own laws, higher laws, not your laws." The men, who were used to conducting their business in far worse circumstances, ignored her. She stood up and started to yell now. "If my papa comes back and I'm not here, he won't know what to do! He'll go out of his mind!"

The senior-most-looking officer, who had a large paunch and mustaches like two old gray mops, paused in his efforts to stuff Martha's possessions into the bag and told her with an unusual degree of kindness in his voice: "Niña, don't worry, he's not ever coming back here again." To get her into the car, he and the others had to carry her by the arms down the narrow metal staircase in front of the apartment house, as old women and children and a handful of teenaged boys emerged down the landing to see the cause of the noise.

The children stared and the women shook their heads and crossed themselves. When the officers were far enough away from the building one of the teenaged boys yelled out, *"Pinches* oinkers! Why don't you go find some girls your own age? *Comemierdas!"* Then he laughed a high-pitched whinny and the other boys threw punches at him and everyone shuffled back inside as the police car pulled away.

Martha was taken to the police station, then to a small municipal clinic where two stout, stolid nurses had to hold her down to force her to undergo the examination they needed to give her. She was registered into a Catholic home for orphaned girls in downtown Juárez, where she refused to speak and barely ate or slept for two weeks. Numerous attempts during that time to contact her mother through the colonia met with no success until word finally came from an elder of the campo that her family had given permission for her to be handed over to an aunt, a woman named Johanna Bonner, in Texas, who had agreed to pick her up at the border bridge. Martha remembered seeing Johanna only once, an occasion when her aunt had passed through the campo on her way to Cuauhtémoc and a great effort had been made to keep the children from her, which transformed her visit into a momentous event talked about for years afterward by those who were young at the time.

Anyone listening to accounts of that visit would have thought Johanna had murdered her husband and children or left the church for a life of prostitution. But her only offense had been to flee a hard life and a loveless marriage at sixteen to head north to the United States, to a settlement of more progressive Mennonites who had also left the strictures of Mexico and bought several sections of cotton land around Seminole, Texas. She began to go by JoAnne instead of Johanna. A few years later she married again, a Southern Baptist minister, and settled down to a respectable, reasonably happy life as an itinerant small-town preacher's wife. She hadn't heard from anyone in her family in more than two years, and it had been even longer since she and Anna, her sister closest in age, had spoken. When her uncle Cornelius asked her to take in Martha, Johanna told him that she barely remembered the girl but she didn't object or ask for an explanation that she knew would not have been forthcoming. He conveyed the basic facts of Martha's life since she had been taken from the campo and said simply that Anna had asked him personally to make the request, which he did with great misgivings. Johanna and her husband prayed for guidance together that night kneeling in their bedroom, but there was never a serious question of a choice.

Johanna drove to El Paso by herself before sunup one Saturday morning, smoking the whole way. She had had her hair done and she wore a teal-colored pantsuit she had picked out in advance. She told her husband that it scared her to think about being in Mexico again, even if only just over the threshold, and that she wanted to look as little as possible like the woman she had been when she lived there. She drove past the U.S. Customs checkpoint and across the Good Neighbor International Bridge down to a narrow parking lot alongside the anchorage of the crossing, a newly built bridge into her old country, still gleaming and festooned with bright American and Mexican flags. She saw the girl standing outside the aduana with two federales, one of whom held a small canvas bag with her things. The officers looked Johanna over boldly and appreciatively as she got out of the car and started to walk toward them. She threw the half-gone cigarette she was smoking onto the asphalt and tried to put it out with the toe of her high heel but it kept smoking behind her as she covered the length of the parking lot toward her niece.

The federales didn't ask her to produce any identification or sign any documents but they seemed to be under some kind of specific orders to accompany Martha all the way to Johanna's station wagon with their hands on her narrow shoulders and watch her safely into the passenger seat. If Martha had leapt from the car and bolted just after they passed the boundary of the parking lot, the men probably would have just stood there and watched her disappear into the salt cedar along the river. They handed Johanna a newly issued forest-green Mexican passport in Martha's name. She thanked them in Spanish and asked the one who seemed to be in charge if there was anything she needed to know, besides the facts she had already been given.

"Señora, we saw the girl for the first time this morning about an hour before you did," the man replied in good English. "Buena suerte. Drive safely."

Johanna stood outside the car looking in at Martha, who sat expressionless in the passenger seat, staring straight ahead. Martha's cornsilk hair had not been washed in days and she was thin in the cheeks, dark-lidded, dressed in a navy-blue flower-print dress that sagged around her shoulders and made her look sallow even for a Mennonite.

They rode in complete silence to Whites City near the turnoff to Carlsbad Caverns, where Martha spoke for the first time, in Plautdietsch, saying she needed to go to the bathroom. Johanna stopped at a curio shop–diner and made a point of going inside with her.

Martha refused to have anything to eat. Johanna bought herself a hamburger and a Coke, and after she ate, Martha watched her fix her makeup and lipstick in the rearview mirror. "I bet you've never been in a car like this before, have you?" Johanna told her. "It's new. It's the first brand-new car we've ever had." Martha made no response and after a few miles back on the road she climbed over the front seat and curled up around her bag in the backseat, mostly to get away from the powerful lingering aroma of the burger. It made her so hungry she was afraid she might be sick, until Johanna lit a cigarette and the smell of tobacco took its place. She fell asleep within minutes, listening to Johanna humming along with a country song on the radio. When she woke it was late afternoon and she was very hot and the sun rainbowed into her eyes through the side window of the car. For a few seconds she couldn't remember where she was and thought she must be back in Chihuahua, waiting for her father to come home from work. But she sat up to the slowly passing procession of a small, tidy municipal downtown, with a church and a courthouse and a post office and a gas station, all of whose signs were written in English, and she put her head back down and pressed her face into her bag and started to cry for the first time since she'd been taken away.

THREE

Sept. 20, 1972

This was back in December 1970, the winter of the year it happened. I drove into a heavy snow outside of Los Ojos, N.M., in a dealership car, a pristine Canadian-nameplate Pontiac Parisienne that I had stolen off a lot in Albuquerque and realized too late was sitting near empty. I decided to find a place to stop for the night, but by then I could no longer see more than a few feet beyond the hood.

Something about the way the snowflakes streamed into the cones of the headlights created the sensation that I was moving backward and then it felt like I had lifted off the road and floated up into the low clouds. It was a nice feeling at first, with the heater pumping and the radio picking up a station strong and clear. The windshield wipers thumped, keeping time with the song that was playing, then falling out of rhythm with it, then slowly falling back in:

I know this time, it's really over
For there's no happiness in store.
And I will never be the fool I was
before.
No one can call me Mr. Fool no more.
My tears were scattered, with all the
shattered
Dreams that faded in the past.
Vows were spoken, vows were broken
But the last one was the last . . .

I cracked the window to get some cold air on my face, but I must have drifted off for a second anyway and let the tires wander. The wheel yanked hard to the right and the Pontiac barreled at a precarious angle down into the bar ditch and the tires pounded up in the wells as I plowed through a bank of heavy snow almost as high as the tops of the windows.

For the better part of an hour I tried to get myself out, rocking it back and forth — D and R, R and D, D and R — a blind game, gaining a little more traction with each try until I could feel the wheels about to grab and haul me back up onto the asphalt. But near the top of one arc I got too eager and gunned it and it fishtailed and fell back. The engine raised a mournful whine and the car settled into a part of the ditch that made the place where I'd been before seem like a tropical paradise. The wheels just spun helplessly now and as I kept trying, the burnt-detergent stench of transmission fluid began to register in my nose; if I didn't stop I was going to ruin any chance I had of getting it out later.

I sat still for a while beneath the blanket of snow, listening to the muffled sound of the engine, staring at the red needle lying against the corner of the capital E, wondering how long it would be before I'd have no heat. Earlier that week at the El Don Motel in Albuquerque I'd burgled the room of a farm pesticide salesman from Tucson, who was in town for a convention. The only coat he had packed was a lightweight corduroy dress jacket, which I reached for now, knowing it was seriously unequal to the weather outside the car. I opened his hatbox and took out his hat, a beautiful gray-felt Stetson half a size too big, and clamped it down over my ears. Both doors were packed shut, so I rolled down the window and dug with my bare hands until I had room to squirm out on top of the snow, which swallowed me in great gulps up to my armpits as I fought to get to the road. The snow was still coming down hard and the flurries were heavy. But when I topped the ditch into knee-deep drifts I could see by the orange glow of a roadside light that I'd run off the pavement just short of a rest stop. In the distance I made out a pair of picnic shelters and two garbage cans up on pivot poles, the tops of the cans covered with untouched cylinders of snow that looked like frosted wedding cakes.

A gust took my hat and I watched it skitter away across the surface of the snow leaving tracks like a small animal. I found it hard to believe that this was the place where I was going to die, out in the snow, like a goddamned Laplander, not back in Texas where I belonged but in a state that couldn't even come up with an original name for itself.

Past the rest stop near the tree line I saw something else through the blur — lines of red pinpoints glowing like coals, a pattern my mind recognized but was unable to reveal to me until I thought of the words themselves: cab lights.

I pulled my chin down into my coat and aimed in their direction. The truck was a red cabover Peterbilt with New Mexico plates and an Oklahoma City address on the passenger side door beneath the legend I.T. ENTERPRISES, SOLE PROPRIETOR. It was idling, pumping a warm diesel smell out into the snow, a wonderful smell, the smell of humanity. I banged hard on the door with the flat of my palm and scooted to the side in case I was dealing with someone who kept a weapon at hand. I waited for what seemed like a week and then I knocked again. Before I had banged twice the door flew open, almost knocking me into the snow, and the beam of a powerful flashlight caught me in the eyes.

"Where did you come from?" a voice boomed. "Why are you here?"

I was going to answer the first question but the second one sounded odd and I didn't know exactly how to respond. I was blinded and the snow was gusting hard into my left ear. The voice repeated itself with greater urgency.

"Why are you here?"

"I'm really sorry to bother you, mister," I said. "But I've got myself in a bit of trouble. I ran my car off the road over —"

The voice cut in, threatening: "Are you a friend or an enemy?"

I raised a hand to deflect the light, and to demonstrate the purity of my intentions. "Well . . . I'm a . . . I'm not a . . . Listen, I don't mean you any harm. I'm really sorry to've come up on you like this in the middle of the night but I just ran my damned car off the road, over past the picnic tables, and it's stuck down in the gully and I'm nearly out of gas."

The flashlight's brightness caused me to be able to see the veins inside my eyes, which looked like a road map for a place I would never be able to navigate. The beam of the light flickered momentarily past me out into the night, as if the man was searching for my car, or for someone else hiding out in the snow, and then it returned to my face.

"In other words you're in need of shelter for the night?"

"Now, just until the sun comes up. If I could trouble you until then I think I'd be able to get down there and put something under the tires and get it out."

I switched hands blocking the glare from the flashlight. "I'm a quiet sort, I promise you. I travel by myself just like you do, you won't even know I'm in the truck. I've got a little money I can give you for your trouble."

The flashlight stayed aimed into my eyes during a glacial silence and then the voice said: "Letter to the Hebrews 13, verse 1:

'Let brotherly love continue.' And for those in need of a little incentive, there's verse 2: 'Be not forgetful to entertain strangers, for thereby some have entertained angels unawares.'

"I won't take your money," he said. "Come inside. Pull the door behind you."

He switched off the flashlight and through the dazzle still blinding my eyes I saw the vague form of a man withdraw into the darkness of the sleeper cab behind the seats. I beat the snow off my jacket and pulled myself up into the cab and hauled the door shut against the wind.

"Lord almighty damn, am I grateful to you," I said, settling into the passenger seat still shivering, smelling the marvelous metallic heat inside the cab. "That storm was on top of me before I knew it. I'm not much of a mountain driver."

I breathed into my numbed hands and shoved them into my pockets. "Like I said, you won't remember I was here as soon as there's enough daylight to see. I don't even snore." He didn't say anything for a while and I decided I'd said too much already, but he finally cleared his throat and spoke again.

"Where do you come from, friend?"

"Over in the Panhandle. Near Lubbock.

Where you can see a storm like this coming a month off."

"Out in the sticks."

"So far out in the sticks there aren't any sticks."

I looked over and saw that he had pulled a pair of pleated curtains partway between us. A radio in the sleeper that had been playing a soft broadcast of a talk show or a soap opera fell silent and I could hear rustling and heavy nose-breathing behind me. I couldn't make up my mind whether etiquette would be to turn around to address him or if doing so would be a violation of his sanctum. So I just unbuttoned my jacket and sat awkwardly facing the dashboard, looking at a watery reflection of myself in the windshield, past which the world was slowly emptying itself of all color and form.

"I'd like to apologize for my welcome," the driver said after a moment. "I'm a little wound up out here tonight." He spoke in the same polished-quartz tone I'd first heard, a voice that reminded me of a television commercial except for a rough edge to it, a feeling that it had once sounded better.

He fell silent again and I could hear more huffing and moving around, as if he was wrestling with the bedsheets, struggling to get settled again. Considering the close quarters, I probably should have been more wary of him, but I was still overcome with gratitude, like a man plucked from the surface of the moon.

"I think I should warn you before you get settled in," he said, "that I won't be doing a whole lot of sleeping back here tonight."

The direction of his voice seemed to indicate that he wasn't lying down but had taken up a seated position in his bunk slightly to my left. I imagined him perched there like a Buddha, gazing past the side of my head out the windshield, though it was too dark for me to see any reflection of him in it.

"I'm not here to rob you," I said. "I swear I'm not. You don't have to worry about me."

He coughed sharply and suddenly, causing me to jump. "No, it's not that," he said. "The problem isn't you, it's me. I've got a trailer of patio doors that were supposed to be in Las Cruces tomorrow morning, so I availed myself of a little trucker's help and now I'm sitting here snowed in and it's holding me captive in its cruel and vigilant grip."

Jesus, listen to the way this guy talks, I thought.

I asked what he had taken.

"Dexedrine. Four spansules at five-thirty this afternoon. I won't sleep again until tomorrow night, nor eat. If you get me talking, I'll take you right into next week. But the devils do more than keep me awake — they lay my senses bare, work a ferocious number on my imagination. I start to feel like my heart's coming out of my chest. Sometimes I'm filled with fear and sometimes with an unreasonable love for the world."

"I don't need you to go feeling any love for me, you understand?" I told him.

He made a baritone laugh that dropped down into harmony with the hum of the engine. "What I'm speaking of is a purely spiritual phenomenon, chemically achieved. You're safe with me. You can relax."

"I haven't relaxed in so long I don't think I could even remember how," I told him.

As he talked I tried to form a mental picture of the driver, my accidental innkeeper, but nothing took shape. From his voice I could rough out his age, probably late fifties, early sixties. He asked my name and I told him the first one that came to mind. When I asked his, he said it was probably better if I didn't know it — a reversal of the role I customarily played as the cipher in most of these passing acquaintances on the road. He said I should think of him simply as a benefactor that fate had placed in my path.

He asked my permission to smoke.

"Can I offer you one, Bob?" This was the name I had given him.

"I'm trying to quit," I said, lying for no reason.

I saw the glow of an electric lighter and little ropes of smoke began to twirl past me and flatten out and fall against the cold of the windshield. In the reflection the end of his cigarette flared and faded, giving me the odd sensation of being able to see someone without being able to see anything.

I wanted to sleep but I felt I should probably try to be sociable if he was. "Has anybody ever told you you'd make a good preacher?" I asked.

"As a matter of fact, Bob, I made a pretty bad one — fifteen and a half years in the pulpit, Southern Baptist," he said, as if reciting rank and serial number.

"How's that for calling it?" I said.

He didn't elaborate so I decided to ask the obvious next question: "How'd you get behind the wheel of a rig? That's not the regular career path for the clergy, from what I've read."

He exhaled audibly, a bit dramatically. "It's a sad story, but commonplace, I guess. Maybe sadder because it's so commonplace."

"Listen, I don't want to stir up any memories for you," I said — which was true, because I didn't want to hear any.

"If you spend as many hours alone as you do in this profession, they stir up all by themselves," he said. "They're the only things that help you pass the time — good, bad, neutral, no matter."

I told him: "I'm a salesman myself, so I know the feeling."

"It's a lonely life on the road, but a life in the pastorship is lonelier. You wouldn't think it, would you? You're surrounded by people. They come to you — smiling, crying, worried, guilty, none of them ever telling you the truth because, God forbid, you might find out who they really are — when who they are rarely turns out to be very damnable, or interesting — and of course none of them have the slightest genuine desire to really know you. You're just a conduit to something that might mean they're not going to cease to exist after all. And so when someone comes along who shows the faintest glimmer of interest in you as a person, you latch on like a drowning man."

He paused and lit another cigarette. "Are you a religious man?" he asked me.

"I suppose I'm as religious as most people who make a point of saying they are, which is not particularly."

"Considering the fact that I don't know you from Adam, would you mind if I made a confession?" he asked.

"Adam who?" I said.

"Okay, then."

He went into a story about a friend he had met in the Army, a man who had also thought about going into the ministry but instead had become a high school ag teacher. The two men had lost touch but eventually ended up in the same western New Mexico town, where the pastor, my truck driver, had taken charge of a seen-better-days Second Baptist Church and set about trying to turn it around. His friend Mickey married and became involved in the church, serving as a deacon, and the two became close. But then Mickey had some kind of crisis of faith, maybe more of a general breakdown in his life, and he started showing up on Sundays less and less and finally stopped coming to church altogether. His wife, Charlene, a good-looking blond girl from Dallas several years his junior, continued to come, teaching Sunday school, bringing covered dishes for funerals and revivals. Sometimes she would visit the pastor's office and the two would commiserate about her husband. She would cry and tell him she didn't know what was happening to Mickey, and he didn't, either, because Mickey wouldn't talk to him about it. And then, as if the diagnosis was just the physical confirmation of a horrible fact all three had known for a long time, Mickey found out he was dying of lung cancer; he wasn't going to make it to forty-five.

The decline was slow and agonizing. The pastor visited the house every day toward the end, talking to Mickey until Mickey couldn't hear him anymore. And then one sunny afternoon, while Mickey lay in the other room dying, unhearing, the pastor and Mickey's wife went to bed together.

"If I'm going to be honest with you, I'll tell you that I didn't feel bad in the least right then. In fact, I had the same kind of feeling I'd always had when I was absolutely sure I was doing something right."

They waited six months before they let

anyone know they had feelings for each other. They married and had a baby right away. "I could feel the relief in the church, where bachelor pastors are held to be some kind of latent infection," he said. "Everyone was so happy for us, especially for her."

But it all went south inside of a year. They fought every night. She never said it, but he knew she hated him for what he had done to his friend, as if she had played no role. He realized what a horrible mistake he'd made throwing his life in with hers and it shocked him to realize how little a person could actually know about another. He had been blinded to anything he might have known because of the grief he had felt for his friend and what he had done to him.

"She was one of those people who could walk between raindrops, never a hair out of place, always the right thing to say. But when it came to happiness she was a zero-summer. If I was feeling good, then I'd somehow subtracted that precise measure of joy from her side of the ledger, and the only way for her to get it back was to exchange it for some of her misery. She was smart enough to know what sort of image she needed to keep up for company. She'd save it all for me. Nobody would have believed it if I'd told them with my hand on a Bible."

He laughed in a way that didn't sound rehearsed anymore. It sounded painful. "I remember how her body looked after she had the baby, how her cheeks stayed fat and her tits collapsed like the tents coming down after the circus — you'll have to excuse me. I remember it because it made me so happy. Her body had been such a sight to see and it was a shame — but it meant she couldn't hold her beauty on me like a knife anymore."

He was really warming up now. I was even starting to enjoy listening to him. It had been months since I'd been in a conversation with anyone for this long.

"During the worst days I had myself convinced that she wasn't human at all but an instrument of divine purpose dispatched by God to test me, to see whether I would fall, and when I fell so far the first time I was ever tested, she was transformed into the means of my punishment. Of course I don't believe any of that now. I believe in sin and I believe in bad luck and I think that sometimes the second doesn't have anything to do with the first.

"You can't see me," he went on, "but I'm

not an attractive man, Bob. I'm fat. I'm the kind of man who can shave in the morning and have a five-o'clock shadow by the time I finish the toast. If you ran into me on the street, you wouldn't ask me for directions to the church. I could have saved myself a lot of trouble if I'd taken a good look in the mirror a long time ago."

I could smell that he had gotten into something to even himself out. He passed it over my shoulder, a little hip flask, maybe vodka. It tasted harsh and metallic, the way I imagined the truck would taste if it was rendered into a liquid.

"There are people like me — maybe like you, Bob — who drag the past behind them like a big plow that picks up more dirt every day. And there are people the past just seals up behind — zip! — without a trace as they move ahead. After Mickey died, I don't think she ever thought about him again, except as an excuse to hate me."

A cloud bank of smoke encircled my head. "I started to fall apart. I was as shaky as an old man. One morning I woke up thinking I was going to die right there. My heart was flopping around inside my chest like a winged animal. I remember getting down on my hands and knees on the living room floor and digging through my daughter's toy box to find the little plastic stethoscope she had in there, hunching over on the carpet so I could get this tiny ridiculous thing into my ears and down onto my chest at the same time. Can you picture it, Bob? A grown man?"

I said I couldn't, but I could.

"That morning she was out at the grocery and I made up my mind to leave her and set things right once and for all. I wrote a note telling her I was going to make a confession to the deacons and step down. I put it on the kitchen table, but then with all my things in the trunk I lost my nerve. I had Easter service to preach. I convinced myself I owed it to the church to wait until after that.

"Charlene came across the note the next morning in my pants pocket in the dryer. She put it on the ironing board and smoothed it out and drove down to the church and Scotch-taped it to the front door in broad daylight, like goddamned Martin Luther himself. On the bottom she wrote in her own hand: 'Too much of a chickenshit to tell you himself. Now you know the truth about what you were whispering behind our backs. P.S. You can all go to hell.'

"I didn't think she had it in her, in a small town like that, where they're just waiting to judge you, but damned if she didn't. She packed up the car and went back to her folks in Dallas and I haven't seen her or my little girl since — she'll be eight in April."

He paused. I was afraid he might start to cry but he didn't. He was the kind of guy who had practiced keeping it together telling stories like this, stories much worse.

"I bounced around for a while, until I put away enough money to finance a rig and this is where I've been since. I don't even have a house anymore. I live back here and up there. It's not a bad life."

He left off, the first sustained silence of the night. The snow had let up outside and the parking lights shone into a stand of pines in front of the truck. Back in the deepest part I caught the flank of something flash, seem to come forward and then retreat — maybe a black bear, but probably just a doe eyeing the trash cans.

"Sometimes I struggle now even to bring her face and voice back to mind," he said. "But I do, because I know what she really wants is to steal a whole part of my life — years! — by making me want to forget everything: about her, about Mickey, all those years before her and during. But I don't let her. I remember her to save part of my own life. The more I do, the more kindly and loving she becomes in my memory. Then I think: Maybe I'm wrong. Maybe she was a better person than I thought she was, and I start to miss her, and I get sad because I know it's not really her I'm remembering anymore. But everything in our memory is half made up anyway, so what does it really matter, right?"

He yawned and let out a weary breath.

"Thus endeth the reading."

He passed back the bottle, almost gone. I heard him shift heavily behind me, stretching out, as if he'd spent himself bringing his story across the finish line.

I was at a loss as to what to say. I liked him well enough not to say something cheap, especially not that I was sorry. So I just sat for a while, which felt like the most honest thing to do. After a few minutes I decided to ask him a question his story had brought to my mind, a question I'd wanted to ask of a preacher since I was a boy — realizing it was a little late for both of us.

It concerned a passage in the Bible I had never been able to get past, somewhere in the Old Testament near the beginning, maybe Leviticus or Deuteronomy. This was one of those stories about the Israelites hauling the Ark of the Covenant — they always seemed to be having to haul it somewhere — and an ox pulling the wagon loses its footing. A poor drover named Uzzah reaches out to steady the Ark to keep it from falling into the dirt. And maybe because he wasn't one of the Levites who were specially appointed to take care of the Ark or because nobody was supposed to actually touch it, I can't remember, God strikes him dead on the spot.

"Ever since I first read it," I said, "I've kept trying to make sense of it. Once I thought maybe the real reason God killed Uzzah was because Uzzah didn't trust God, that God would never allow the Ark to fall in the first place. Or maybe Uzzah did trust God but it occurred to him: Hey, I'm right here, God put me here! I'm the one he's chosen to save the Ark from falling. But of course he realized his mistake pretty quickly as he hit the ground dying. God put him there within reach of the thing, all right, but not to save it. He put him there so Uzzah would presume in all his human pride to know what God was thinking, which would give God the great instructive opportunity of making Uzzah an example of what happens when human beings start thinking they know what God is thinking. And I thought: Maybe in the seconds before he died Uzzah figured this out and he said to himself: Okay, so that's what God decided to do with me! He decided to accord me this highest honor of sacrificing my life in such a manner to teach my people this important lesson!

"But you know what I think's a lot more likely? Uzzah lying there, drawing in the last breaths of his life, thinking: All I tried to do was the right thing, the right thing — which is so hard, the hardest thing in this world — and now God has made me the asshole of history for it."

It shocked me to hear myself talking like this. What was my question supposed to be, anyway? I trailed off but then I realized there was no reason to be embarrassed: From behind me came the heavy measured rhythms of sleep breathing and I knew that whatever was in the flask had done its job.

I pulled off my jacket and balled it up against the window but I couldn't sleep. By sunup, the snow had stopped. For the first time I looked back into the sleeper through the curtains but I could see only the top of the man's graying head facing away from me beneath a gray blanket. His large body all but consumed his tiny quarters. I put on the jacket and climbed out of the truck to find a place to piss, walking into the thicker pines where the snow wasn't as deep and a little ice-choked stream trickled through, looking as if it had found its way into the woods to die.

When I came back, I saw that the trucker had woken up and driven on, leaving a rectangle of snowless asphalt — a negative image of the truck, black on white — with tire tracks leading from it to the road.

Thinking about it now, I'm pretty sure I never actually asked him about the story from the Bible. But it was something I'd wanted to talk to somebody about for a long time and still do.

Martha had long since lost track of direction. She had no idea how far they would drive with her before they decided to stop long enough for her to get away. She told herself to keep calm, to push down the waves of panic that kept mounting, the feeling that she wouldn't be able to prevent herself from hurdling over the seat to grab for the door. Over the noise of the engine she tried again to listen to their talk, but it was lower and calmer now than before, so that she could catch only fragments, words and half words that sounded like Spanish or Plautdietsch, though she knew they couldn't be. The more she tried to clear her mind to extract language from the air the more her mind wandered. She thought about her aunt Johanna, whom she had never liked, though she knew her dislike didn't really have anything to do with Johanna herself and Martha felt bad about that. She thought about what Johanna's pretty, round, made-up face must look like now as she sat in the police station or on a pew in her husband's church, her pale Mennonite cheeks red and puffy from so much crying, blaming herself for leaving Martha and the boys and the keys in the car, even though everyone in America left their children and their keys alone together in their cars. She wondered how hard it could possibly be — in a place with such long empty roads, with so few automobiles and most of those pickups, with what seemed like a ratio of police all out of proportion to actual criminals — to track down a huge blue station wagon with fake wood paneling and two men up front. She wondered mostly why anyone would want to steal a car like this, so ridiculously big that even people with herds of children seemed to own one only under duress, an embarrassment forced on them by the immense piles of crap that came along with baby making in the United States.

Martha was one of the rare children from a religious background who took literally the admonition to count one's blessings, though it often seemed to her that the only purpose of the exercise — in a hard and unforgiving life like hers — was to scrounge up the one or maybe two good things that could qualify so unhappiness didn't go completely unchecked. As she lay there, feeling the road knock beneath her, she considered it a blessing akin to a miracle that her bladder wasn't pressing on her, at least not yet. The second blessing was that the two men had somehow failed to discover her when they made a rapid stop about an hour before, down a dirt road. She had known from snatches of their conversation that the stop was coming. Then the ride became rougher and she could smell raised dust. They slowed and the one who was driving told the other one that he kept clean license plates hidden across the countryside for emergency situations and this was their lucky day because he had just buried a pair outside the town of Seagraves. After the car had turned off onto the dirt, Martha snaked her hand slowly across the carpet of the station wagon to a corner near the tailgate and grabbed hold of a bunched-up canvas hunting coat belonging to Brother Ted, Johanna's husband, and drew it slowly across her body and tried to tuck her legs and feet under it. The car pulled over and came to a hard stop on the caliche, jamming her up against the seatback. She heard both men get out and she turned her head into the darkness of the carpet beneath the coat and shut her eyes. The silence that had fallen with the engine off made her feel as if as a floodlight had been turned on her. Every shallow breath sounded like a shriek.

"Get up on the bumper and keep your eyes down the road — if you see anything, a pickup, a trail of dust, a goddamn cottontail, you whistle at me and take the wheel and I'll jump in. Can you do that?"

"What're you gonna dig with?"

"My own two hands. I don't put 'em deep. Nobody else is going to be out here in a cow pasture looking for buried license plates."

The car dipped in the back as the second man — the one she knew to be named Harlan — climbed on the bumper to be the lookout. She heard the footfalls of the other one, the driver, Troy or possibly Roy, recede in a trot on the packed dirt. She turned her head as slowly, as imperceptibly, as she could manage and peered with one eye through a buttonhole of the canvas coat and saw the wide thighs and crotch of the second man, his belted khaki trousers pressed against the back window, his chest and head out of sight above the top of the car.

She considered lifting herself to see how far the first man was from the car but she was unable to will her body to make the movement. Martha had not prayed in more than two years but she prayed now; she struggled desperately to remember something, anything, that she had once committed to memory from the *Ernsthafte Christenpflicht,* the old Palatine primer whose dagger-pointed medieval letters, blackening the page with text, had always caused her to think not of God, as she was supposed to, but of hellsmoke and Beelzebub.

The only passage she could summon whole from the book was completely wrong, she knew, but she recited it in her mind anyway, as devoutly as she could, trying to release any power that might be latent in the words despite their meaning:

> O heavenly Father, be merciful to me and protect me from the gross sins of adultery, fornication, impurity, lasciviousness, idolatry, witchcraft, malice, quarreling, jealousy, anger, strife, dissension, reveling, drunkenness, and such like, which would separate me from Thy great love.

She heard the first man's trotting footsteps approaching the car and waited to feel the bounce of the suspension as the big one stepped off the bumper, but he seemed to remain motionless, dutiful at his post. In the shrouded light in which she lay she anticipated the shadow of the second man, who was probably standing no more than a foot from her now, with only the back window of the car between them. He was the more alert one, more suspicious, the one she was sure had stolen the car — he would look through the window and see her so easily. But his shadow didn't fall and Martha heard nothing, no voices or movement, until faint metallic scraping sounds began to register from the back, echoing through the chassis.

She heard the wind start to pick up, slapping raggedly at the side of the car.

"Nothing out there . . . nobody."

"Just a minute," came the reply from below.

"You keep a screwdriver on you for things like this?"

Nothing except the metal noises, now tapering off.

"Bury it with the plates. You never have tools when you need them." Then footsteps again and the metal sounds, fainter, this time from the front of the car.

Gusts of wind landing harder. Snort. Guffaw.

"It's no wonder they haven't caught you yet."

The noises stopped.

"Okay, let's haul ass."

She felt the bounce of the second man climbing down from the bumper and she clamped her eyes and her fists tight and thought: *Now. Now. Now. And now. And now. And now. How will they come in?* She thought about her teeth, the only part of her body that felt remotely like a weapon, though she knew if she were close enough to get teeth into either one of them it would already be all over, except for whatever blood she could draw.

A door slammed shut and then another, compressing the air inside the station wagon like a thunderclap. The engine jumped back to life and they were moving again. It occurred to her that it was possible they were going to wait until they were off the main road a little farther into the combine-emptied cotton fields and the second one would climb quietly back for her while the first one kept driving. Martha pulled the coat aside slowly and peered up the carpeted seatback as if up the side of a battlement, waiting with her body tensed against the breach, but it didn't come and she felt the tires swim up off the dirt and back onto smooth asphalt.

It seemed like hours had passed since then, but she knew it was unlikely even one had gone by. The car slowed and turned and she held her breath. A little later it turned again and then twice more, back in the direction they seemed to have been going in the first place, and she guessed they must be trying to stay clear of towns or maybe they were moving in circles because the troopers would expect a straight line. She had listened for cars passing against them and had counted only three since they came back up on the paved road. The men barely talked now. She heard the one driving say that they needed to get off the road again.

"The law's on the hunt right now. Their blood is pumping the way it does when you think you have a bird in your sights. But let a day pass and it'll be a different story, they'll start to lose interest."

Lying up against the seat, Martha thought: *Except that neither one of you have any idea what kind of bird you really are. The only person in this car who knows is me. And we're the kind of bird they're never going to stop looking for, high and low, night and day.* For a minute the thought made her feel slightly less desperate, as if she shared a small measure of power over her fate with this pair of American Texas dumbasses who didn't know they were kidnapping a Mennonite girl on top of stealing a pastor's wife's station wagon.

They'd have to stop for gas eventually and when they did, if they both got out, she'd have time to run. Maybe they wouldn't see her. But who would pick up a hitchhiker as young as she was, and if she made it to a bus terminal, where could she afford to go? She had five one-dollar bills and two fifty-cent pieces in the pocket of her jeans, her entire holdings, accumulated from Johanna's purse over great duration.

After maybe another half hour on the road she felt the wheels go back onto rocky dirt and her chest tightened again. A right-hand turn and more dirt and this stretch lasted a good while before she finally felt the car begin to slow and pull off onto some kind of shallow incline that tilted her feet higher than her head and then the back of the car started to bounce violently, telling her that they had left the roadway altogether. She clutched the hunting coat to her body and pushed at sharp angles with the sides of her feet to keep herself up against the seatback, before feeling the car stop again.

Neither man got out immediately. The second one, with the deeper voice, spoke first: "You remember this place? That time?"

"The last time I ever hunted," the other one said.

They didn't talk again for a while and just sat. But then they turned off the motor and Martha froze and opened her mouth wide to breathe as quietly as she could. Her heart didn't race as fiercely this time, maybe only because her body had become too tired to respond. The doors opened, one by one, and then a back door opened, inches above her head. They were getting their bags out and then they shut the doors and one of the front ones opened.

"I had a good new tarp in the back of the pickup but I guess you didn't think to take that when you were packing us up."

"I didn't exactly have time to make an

inventory, Harlan. I believe you've been acquainted with scrub-grass before."

The door slammed shut again, hushing everything. She could hear them shuffling away from the car but the wind had finally died down and their voices remained clear amid the short scraping calls of killdeer, the only other sound on the stretch of plain.

"Nobody can see the car down here. We'll get ourselves up on the flat, against that lip there, where we can see out over the road but we still have a view of the car. If we have to hightail it, it'll be a straight shot back down, thirty seconds."

"Thirty seconds hell."

"You'd be surprised how fast you can move when you need to, Harlan. You just haven't needed to in a long time."

"What do you propose we're going to find to eat out here?"

The answer, if there was one — and Martha suddenly realized her own stomach felt hollowed-out and hard — was lost to the sky as the two men walked further from the car and she was left alone for the first time since it had all started. She listened hard for several minutes for their voices, holding her breath to be able to hear better. She counted to sixty in her head ten times, to make sure she wasn't misjudging time, and then, keeping the hunting coat draped most of the way over her head, she raised herself slowly on her stiff arms and looked through the back window closest to her head, on the passenger side. She could tell she was looking west because the sun sat almost directly in her line of vision, low in the sky but not low enough to keep from blinding her as she tried to pick out the men's forms on a risc that swept upward just past the car, covered with sand sage and salt cedar shrubs. She squinted and after her eyes adjusted she was able to see their silhouettes against the sky at the crest of the ridge. She froze, momentarily terrified that they might be looking back toward the car, watching something moving inside it. Their parallel shadows stretched out forty feet on the dirt toward her, reaching halfway to the car. She closed her eyes and a blazing orange disc filled her field of vision and the tiny outlines of the men flashed like a broken filmstrip behind her eyelids.

On the backs of her hands and her calves sticking out from the coat she could feel the fresh air that had come into the car, and every part of her body told her to jump up now and run, open the back door, go as silently and as quickly as she could. But she had no idea which way to go to get to the road. From their high vantage point they would see her as her feet raised dust against the prairie, and they would catch her even if she made it to the road, because the chances of finding a car to flag down were next to nothing. She pushed herself up an inch more and twisted her torso to look up the length of the car toward the steering column, hoping to see keys hanging there, for whatever that would be worth — she'd never driven a car; she had no idea if she could reach the pedals in one this big. But the men knew better than to leave a set of keys in an open car, even one in the middle of nowhere. She listened to the lonely ticking of the car roof as the heat of the day dissipated and then she eased herself down again and drew her feet up under the coat as far as she could manage. She told herself that as long as she remained motionless, all but invisible under the coat, her mind scoured of thought, she would be protected and able to figure something out later. As she lay there, she tried to make herself believe that if she exerted enough effort pretending she wasn't there then the two men would become powerless to find her. She thought of a disembodied feeling that came upon her sometimes as she grew older: the sudden conviction of the utter strangeness of being inside her skin, of looking the way she looked, of the sound of her voice when she spoke, of her limbs moving when she willed them to, of living at this particular time in the history of the world, in this particular place in the universe — how not a single part of it seemed to be the result of necessity, and the thought that the mere act of changing her mind might unmoor her instantly from it all. Sometimes the possibility seemed so real it terrified her and the fear was followed by a rushing sensation of leaving her body. Sometimes this feeling made her consider that there might be such a thing as a soul after all, except that the *she* she felt herself to be — the *her* of herself, the self that went past words — felt like something different than a soul. She lay under the coat concentrating all her thoughts on the infinitesimal point of that self, picturing herself vanishing physically inside it.

Unmoving, she watched the night come in the reflection on the window to the east. The hard, colorless afternoon light that had been exploding in began to soften to a distinct yellow as the sun bent itself over the lip of the land. Within the space of ten minutes it dropped several registers, from bright orange-yellow to purest orange to blood red and down to purple, followed by a long descent into a barely perceptible blue before the dark consumed it completely. She tried to match the colors in her mind to the names of color-wheel hues she had had to learn at school in Tahoka, the first real school she had ever attended: red, scarlet red, scarlet, crimson, magenta (she liked the sound of that one, though she always picked the wrong shade when the teacher asked her to identify it), purple magenta, purple, purple violet, violet, blue violet, blue, bluish cyan, cyan blue. Dropping there into black instead of making its clockwise ascent into the greens and back up to yellow again. She thought of all the individual colors that had to exist between the ones she had learned — thousands, *millions*? — and she wondered if each of them had names, too.

She had never understood why people spoke of the loveliness of sunsets — weren't they just forerunners of darkness, ushering away the light that was the symbol of God and all we were supposed to glory in? She found herself thinking that this particular sunset was beautiful even so. She thought maybe she felt that way because she had seen only its reflection, and reflected light — the sun on a pond, the light of a lamp in a mirror, the light of the moon — always seemed more beautiful than when it was shining right at you.

Four

Sept. 26, 1972

For the sake of convenience I'll try to keep the legally relevant information together, so here is most of it:

This was all about a sum of twenty-five thousand dollars. Minus maybe a thousand that Bill Ray spent before he died and that Harlan spent before it disappeared.

Bill Ray came into the money the old-fashioned American way — through sheer dumb luck, on the second pull of a nickel slot machine at the Ruidoso Downs race-track in Ruidoso, New Mexico. The best part was that Bill Ray never played the slots — hated slots, in fact. He bet only the quarter horses and he lost more than he ever won.

He died three months later. I learned about it by accident, at a motel in Clovis, the closest I had been to home in a while. Calling Harlan was something I risked from time to time, to let him know I was alive; it had been six months since I had made the last call. But the voice that answered on the other end of the phone wasn't his, it was the voice of an older man, measured, practiced. He said, "Hello. Falconer residence." I didn't say a thing, put my hand over the phone. "Hello? May I help you? Is anyone there?" I had heard the voice somewhere before, like a family voice, but it wasn't family, and then I knew. It was the retired pastor of the First Baptist Church, a voice from my youth. I had liked him well enough, but he'd had my number from early on and I stayed clear of him, to the degree you could in a small town. There was only one reason he would be there answering the phone, a phone only Harlan answered, in a house nobody visited.

I put the phone in the cradle and looked out the window past the railing into the motel parking lot. He hadn't been sick as far as I knew. But Harlan had told me he was drinking more. For almost two years he had been all but gone from town and the house, living with a woman he had met, in a trailer home outside of Hobbs. I had reached him there only once. The woman picked up. At first she pretended she didn't know who I was talking about, then she stopped and put him on the phone.

I sat in the room in Clovis for a long time thinking about what to do. Sometime after midnight I called the house again and listened to it ring. I kept calling and on the third try, Harlan finally picked up. He said they'd found the pickup beside the road outside of Bronco. It didn't seem to have run into anything but just eased off the road alongside the barbed wire fence and rolled gingerly to a stop up against a telephone pole. He was at the wheel. His head was resting back against the gun rack. His hat had pushed down over his brow. The farmhand who found him said he thought maybe he had just fallen asleep. He said that when he raised his hat Bill Ray's eyes were wide open and he was smiling. He didn't even look dead. He looked absolutely fine, the way he always had.

There was no will. But sometime after Bill Ray came into the money he wrote a letter that was ruled dispositive by the county judge. The letter said that if anything happened to him Harlan should have the money and the house. Harlan felt the need to tell me this, but he didn't broach the idea of giving me any of the money. If he had at that moment, I wouldn't have taken a dime. If he'd handed it to me in new bills lined up inside a suitcase, I would have waited until he left and hauled the suitcase right out to the motel dumpster.

But over the next few months I started to think about the money in a different way. At first it was only the conviction that some of it was rightfully mine, but I knew this was nothing more than jealousy and hurt and I couldn't let myself go on like that. Then it started working on me for another reason — as a way out, maybe the only way. It occurred to me that the money didn't belong to Harlan any more than it had belonged to Bill Ray. He'd gotten it the way someone finds money lying on the street. What would I do if I robbed a motel room and came across that kind of cash in a man's luggage? A couple hundred dollars was the biggest score I'd ever made but what if I came across a bundle? What would it mean (besides the fear about how badly someone would want that kind of money back)? What would it be possible to do with it? I don't speak of things in terms of rules, but in this case: What would be permitted? Could I spend it? Could I allow myself to keep the things I bought with it? Would they feel like someone else's? I began to think they might. I thought about using my half of the money to rent a little furnished place somewhere, a trailer outside of a town where no one knew me. If people got too nosy I could make up an awful story about the war so they'd stop asking questions. I'd get a used car — legit, for the first time in years — and a change of clothes. I'd stop turning over rooms and suitcases and give myself some time not to be looked for, maybe long enough for it to blow over, as unlikely as I knew that would be. It was a dream of a little vacation, as funny as that must sound to you.

I wrote a postcard to Harlan asking for my half. The words were so painful to write I almost couldn't go through with it. It put me back in a place of wanting, of laying something on the line, a place I never wanted to be in again.

He answered the way I knew he would: "Bill Ray said it would just go to bad use. Can you tell me honestly that it wouldn't?" I hung up on him.

After Bill Ray moved out, Harlan hadn't ended up living alone. Companionship had come to him probably the only way it was ever going to. He told me that he tore a small advertisement, half in English, half Spanish, out of the Lubbock newspaper and sent off for a package. It arrived a month later with a Nuevo León, Mexico, postmark, containing a sheaf of mimeographed papers and half a dozen Polaroid pictures of the faces of reasonably attractive women who appeared to be in their late teens or early twenties. Harlan filled out the forms and mailed a check. A week later he received a call from a man who spoke perfect English and invited him to bring a bigger check to Del Rio to meet a woman who had agreed to become his bride. She wasn't the woman in the picture he had chosen; she wasn't any of the women in any of the pictures he had seen, but Harlan hadn't been naive enough to expect this. They told him her name was Inés and that she was twenty-two, which might have been low by as much as a decade but she was pretty, with high Indian cheekbones and long glossy black hair in a braid down the middle of her back. She was short, coming only halfway up Harlan's chest, but she had a dignified, straight-backed way of walking and wide shapely hips that made her seem taller. He told me that the man who drove her to the meeting place in a parking lot behind a fast-food restaurant seemed to be waiting for him to haggle, but Harlan didn't have any intention of doing something so vulgar. He wrote out a check for five hundred dollars on the hood of the pickup, most of the money he had to his name at the time.

She knew almost no English except for basic greetings and a handful of ridiculous phrases — "I find you very attractive." — "Allow me to make your house a home." — "Do you like steak? I sure do." — that some other non-English speaker had probably taught her to keep things from going bad too quickly, which might lead to a demand for a refund.

They stayed in Del Rio for a week, until the marriage license could be arranged. An ancient-looking man with decaying teeth married them in a hallway of the hotel where they were staying, with two hotel maids as witnesses.

She moved into the house and stayed for six months. He told me he loved her almost from the beginning and she seemed happy, cooking for him, watching television during the day, sitting with him in the backyard in the evenings. I'm sure she never saw or spoke to anyone except Harlan. She had never been away from home this long and she was probably homesick. Or maybe she just wanted the green card and gave him more time than most women would have. Either way, one morning when he was on a welding job the neighbors saw an ancient Studebaker driven by a young Mexican man no one knew pull up in front of the house and she ran out with her suitcase. Harlan never heard from her again. He had to divorce her ex parte by placing a notice in the newspaper.

The idea that Bettie take her place was Bettie's alone. If you don't believe this I don't know how to convince you except by pointing out its simple brilliance, the kind you know right away because it's so hard to tell from insanity.

She said: "You want your money? I'll get you your goddamned money. I'll marry your brother and get it back for you."

This was later, in another motel, in Dalhart. I was washing my face in the bathroom. I walked out and looked at her.

"I'll be her cousin. Distant — like second, third. Or her friend, you know, from la escuela, from a long time ago. I'm the one she tells about it — how good he was to her, how it broke her heart to leave him, but she just couldn't live away from her mama and her papa, her país, for so long, et cetera, et cetera. You can take some snapshots of me. Not too sexy. Enough to whet his appetite. And I'll write a letter, very formal, to ask if he can find it in his heart to accept me in her place, to give me the happy life Inés should have had, if only it had been God's will. Gracias a Dios."

She laughed. I didn't laugh or even smile. I had known her all of — what? — a month, but I knew her well enough to know she didn't really have a sense of humor. If she was saying she would go through with something like that, she would: She'd meet him at the border with a suitcase; she'd marry him legally; she'd go back to live with him; she would probably even sleep with him, I had no doubt, until she figured out how to get the money. She was better at the long game than anybody I'd ever known.

How I ever believed she'd leave Harlan his half or bring me mine is another matter. After working for so long to live a life with my eyes open, I let myself fall into the kind of delusion where you don't just get a few things wrong. You flip and lose the ability to judge anything. Of course, it's possible I knew what would happen all along and decided to allow it, so that if I couldn't have any of the money Harlan wouldn't, either. But when I found out, it didn't make me want to kill her any less.

Harlan called the number she sent the day he got her letter. She drove down to Del Rio and met him by herself, in an embroidered puebla dress she picked out at a Salvation Army that morning. She pretended to struggle with English, though her Spanish was so bad she worried he might figure it out.

He wouldn't have figured it out if she had started to speak Russian, Chinese, Esperanto. He was out of his mind with happiness. After he married her and took her back, he even ventured into town to show her off — to high school games, the café at lunchtime, where people stopped eating to look at them. She nearly blew it when a family across the street invited her to a children's birthday and she accepted, to appear sociable. She offered to bring a piñata and bought one at the Gibson's variety store in Denver City. But she didn't know anything about piñatas — her mother had shunned everything Mexican like it was the plague — so she didn't realize you had to fill it with candy yourself. The party ended with a dozen six-year-olds hacking a paper mule to pieces on the ground, wailing in anguish when they realized there was nothing inside.

I called one morning and she answered. Harlan was out on a job. She said, "¿Hola?" in a weak tentative voice and then said, "Oh," and laughed and I could hear her lighting up a cigarette. I pictured her sitting there in the kitchen I knew so well and I wondered what she was wearing. She sounded happier than I thought she would, but now I know that was just her perverse pleasure in talking to me while she was getting ready to do what she was going to do.

He kept the money in cash, in a fireproof box beneath the floorboards of the work shed in the backyard. He was as careful as he should have been, but he never really mistrusted her; she said she watched him one night through the window of the extra bedroom when he thought she was sleeping. He opened the shed door and turned on a flashlight and set the light upright on the floor and got down on his knees and extracted the box from its hole. The beam shone up at his face, making it look as if a treasure chest was gleaming into his eyes the way it does in children's books. For a minute, she said, she felt sorry for him. And maybe she did. She might even have felt sorry for me when she disappeared. I don't deny the possibility. But if she had such feelings she never confused them with work.

As the dark came on Martha fell asleep and had a short, powerfully realistic dream in which she was back in Cuauhtémoc, riding in a city bus. The rattle inside the bus was deafening and the air smelled like gasoline fumes, as it always did inside the municipal buses. She was sitting a few rows from the back. The interior metal curving above the windows on either side of her had been painted, as such buses often are, this one in pinks and greens, depicting a beach scene of waves rolling ashore on a moonlit night, flanked by palm trees that leaned inward from the sides to frame the composition. The ceiling of the bus was dominated by its own painting, a bright red sacred heart of Jesus, encircled by three strands of thorn and pierced by seven arrows atop a field of flame, against which the blood seeping from the bottom of the heart looked real enough to drip down onto Martha's lap.

The bus seemed to be moving aimlessly through the city at night, somewhere on the outskirts, where she could make out only the occasional light coming from a store sign or shining weakly through the lace curtains in the windows of houses. At first, she thought she was completely alone but then she looked over and saw her mother sitting in the seat across the aisle from her, staring out the opposite window. Martha looked ahead to see who was at the wheel but the interior of the bus was so dim she couldn't make out a face in the wide convex rearview mirror above the driver's seat. She looked back toward her mother, understanding implicitly that she would not be allowed to talk to her. When the bus came to a halt at an intersection in the bluish glare of a streetlight, she could see that her mother was wearing one of her best Sunday dresses, one that Martha herself had helped sew: dark plum cotton drill with a sprigged rose pattern and crisp pleats falling from the waist. Her braids had been plaited up elaborately beneath her scarf. She had on her heavy stockings and her Sunday shoes and the kind of pressed black apron that Mennonite women wear on formal occasions, which conceals almost all of the beautiful pleats on the fronts of their dresses. Martha looked down at her mother's hands to see if she was carrying her Bible, though she knew it wouldn't be there because it was clear that her mother was on her way to a funeral, not a worship service.

When the bus stopped, Martha expected to see a church or a funeral home but instead she saw the empty parking lot of the mirador, a place she had never been at night. Bare bulbs hanging from sawed-off telephone poles lighted the entry to the swept dirt path that switched back and forth in diminishing Zs to the top of the rise and the big viewing platform, constructed from cedar plank and heavy pipe painted municipal Mexican green. The construction of the platform reminded her of playground equipment, a playground built for adults, though whenever she'd visited the mirador during the day it was usually full of teenagers who had cut school and went there to smoke and grope at each other's bodies while they stared out despondently toward the horizon.

She wondered whether her mother would get out here. But when she turned back to look she saw that her seat was already empty. Martha stood and wrapped her arms around herself and walked through the empty aisle out into the cold night, looking up the rise for her mother and the bus driver but seeing no one ahead of her. She had no memory of going up the path but suddenly found herself at the end of it where the viewing platform should have been. It was completely gone now, after so many years, and on top of the hill there was only a ragged field of dark teosinte grass that smelled like corn and came up as high as her waist. She had to push it out of the way with her hands to get through to the edge of the rise. Near the edge the grass gave way to rocky soil and when she finally emerged to get a look out over the land, she was terrified by what she saw. The entire valley stretching below her northward to the horizon seemed to be on fire. A sea of orange undulated beyond the range of her vision as if a volcano had erupted and the lava had flowed all the way to the city. But as she waited to feel the heat of the fire on her face she realized it was not flame. It was the lights of an immense city that had overtaken the fields and orchards and spread to cover every square mile of Chihuahua. As the realization took hold, the blazing light briefly seemed beautiful to her and her breath was taken away by the thought of a city so immense. But just as quickly the thought became more terrifying than fire. The colonias and the campos and the crops and the trees and the barns and the queserías and all the people who had lived apart from the world down there must be gone now, forced to root up and move again as they had had to move from the Old Country to Russia, then to Canada, then down through the United States to Chihuahua. Where were they all now and why did they leave her behind?

In the dream she heard someone start to cry and then wail into the night over the endless city and she realized it was herself. She woke up in the back of the car whimpering and saw that it was still night.

After his release, Aron was taken in by a Baptist benevolence society that found temporary lodging in Juárez for ex-prisoners who professed religious convictions. Interviewed by the minister who came to the visiting room, Aron would say nothing beyond confirming his name, age, and birthplace, but because he was the only Mennonite coming from the jail, he was automatically given a bed. He was placed in a shabby adobe-and-cinder-block boardinghouse in Felipe Ángeles, a poor neighborhood near the river. The winding dirt street where the house sat ran end-on toward a berm that hid the river, beyond which lay El Paso and the United States, marked at that point by two towering concrete smokestacks of a copper-smelting plant, taller than anything on either side of the river, painted with red and white stripes that gave them the appearance of having something to do with candy or Christmas or some other kind of American abundance.

Aron served only fourteen months of his sentence, after Martha's mother and her family refused to cooperate fully in court during the course of the case against him. He had been sent to the municipal jail in Juárez rather than the state prison; the old file clerk who served as his legal representative argued that sending him to the prison would mean signing his death warrant. But the municipal jail was hardly better. He shared his first cell — dirt-floored, windowless — with ten other men, several of them teenagers. Like Aron, they wore the clothes they had been booked in because the jail couldn't afford uniforms. Aron kept to himself in the one corner of the cell that hadn't been claimed, nearest the putrid toilet bucket. The other prisoners were afraid of him at first, partly because he was tall and looked strong but also because they knew he was Mennonite and they wondered whether hurting him would get them into some special kind of trouble. But over time they noticed that the guards extended no more regard toward him than they did toward anyone else, and one afternoon, when the plastic bowls of refried beans and masa mush were passed into the cell for dinner, one prisoner, a wiry, head-shaved American in a green Army jacket, with homemade tattoos of teardrops on his cheek, ripped Aron's bowl from his hands. He poured the contents into his own bowl and put Aron's on top of his head like a helmet. Then he leaned over on his stool, farted deafeningly, and yelled: "Order in the court! Order in the court! The judge is eating beans! His wife's in the bathtub sucking off marines!" and the prisoners who understood a little English howled with laughter.

Aron went three days without food. When the bowls came around on the morning of the fourth day he sprang up and seized the American with the shaved head from behind and yelled in Spanish to the guards that he would break his neck unless he was given his morning bowl and every ounce of food he was owed up to that point. The American didn't resist and began to weep openly, begging for his life. The other prisoners backed up against the walls in unison, as if they had participated in this ceremony before. Five big guards entered the cell, circling Aron and his captive slowly in opposite directions with their batons in their hands, switching directions every so often until one guard was able to get far enough behind Aron to clip him cleanly behind the ear.

For the rest of his time in jail, he was kept in solitary confinement in a small concrete-lined hole topped with a round iron grate, near the guards' headquarters. He stopped speaking Spanish when the guards addressed him, answering only in Low German. After a month in the hole, he asked for a Bible and as a joke one of the guards found him a King James version, which Aron couldn't read, though he tried diligently during the couple of hours each day when there was enough light at the bottom of the hole to see the pages.

He began to pray in German, calling out loudly in the middle of the night:

In Jesu schlaf ich ruhig ein,
Gott, mein Gott will bei mir sein
Gottes Allmacht will mich decken,
Mich soll keine Nacht erschrecken
Gottes Macht kann vor gefahren
Und vor Ungluek mich bewahren.

The guards caught the God and Jesus parts and understood that the man must be saying something religious, so they let him alone for a while, intrigued by the glottal foreign sound echoing through the halls like the chorales in a monastery. But the voice finally began to grate on them and interfere with their naps, so the head guard went out one night and told him to shut up.

"I know you understand me — I know you speak Spanish as well as I do," the guard said in Spanish, bending over and peering down into the darkness of the hole. "Go to sleep or I'm going to come down there and put you to sleep myself." The guard went back to his chair but Aron started up the prayer again, so the guard filled a large plastic bucket with cold water from the hose in the yard and dumped it through the grate. He stared down through the metal gridwork. "Pray in secret — you know? — and your Father will reward you in secret. The Bible says so. Pipe down, *pendejo,* or next time I'm going to get the hose and drown your white ass."

Twice every day a bucket was lowered into the hole with an insufficient amount of pinto bean mush and a plastic container of metallic-tasting water; most mornings, a rope with a hook was lowered to take out his waste bucket. Once, a guard allowed the bucket to tip at the edge of the hole and Aron's own shit and piss rained down on his head. The stench was unbearable for an entire day but he gradually stopped smelling it, and he thought about people he had seen who lived in their own filth and were probably no longer able to smell themselves, either — it was like a consolation prize given by God to the most wretched.

Once a week, an iron pole with rungs welded across it was lowered into the hole so he could climb out and be taken to a secluded yard with no chair or table, nothing except hard dirt and dead grass enclosed by a cinder-block wall, a place where he was allowed to stay by himself for an hour to get sunshine and exercise if he wanted. He had never experienced the sun as such a brutal physical thing, even during the hottest days in the fields in Chihuahua. It wasn't just that the light hurt his eyes after being in the dark for so long; it hurt wherever it shone on his neck or hands and he would try to crowd himself into the shade to escape what they were legally mandated to give him.

What the guards didn't understand was that as cramped and filthy as solitary was, Aron vastly preferred it to being with other men. Being alone was like a thing he had somehow gotten away with, like beating the system, especially because the system thought it was beating him every day it kept him there. The hole, about twenty feet deep, seemed to have been some kind of cistern or storage tank, repurposed into a cell. It was shaped like a bottle with a short neck and a wide bottom and had a bricked-in patch on the floor where a drain had probably been. Because the curved concrete surface had no openings, there were no mice or rats and the roaches and centipedes that got in from the top were easily spotted and killed. Aron began to use the Bible as a pad to sit on, to relieve the throbbing pain the concrete caused his legs and back. He didn't feel right using the Bible this way but he did it anyway, reasoning that if God gave him a Bible he couldn't read He must have intended it to be put to some other use. During one of his lowest moments, gnawed at by hunger, he tried to eat a page of it, but it tasted horrible and the act made him feel physically ill and he prayed for forgiveness.

In the mornings, when a tiny amount of light filtered through the grate, he tried to keep up a regimen of exercise, squatting and running in place to stay healthy. But in the afternoons when the light faded until he could no longer see anything, he lost the will to get up from the floor and fell into waking dreams about the colonia and his campo and the farmland that had been taken from him. He rarely thought about Anna or their other children anymore, but he never stopped thinking about Martha and wondering if he would ever see her again and whether she would still look like a girl or already like a woman. He wondered if they had been able to poison her mind against him. He was sure she was too strong for that, but he told himself that if she wasn't, he would forgive her, and his forgiveness would be enough to win her back to his side.

Oct. 2, 1972

I'm afraid of heights, have been ever since I can remember. I've often thought it must have something to do with growing up in a place as flat as this, where the sweep of the sky is so big that, lying on your back looking into it, you sometimes experience the sensation that you will come loose from the earth and fly up with nothing to prevent your ascent.

One summer night when I was eight or nine Bill Ray tried to cure my fear by carrying me up to the roof. He put a ladder against the storm gutter on the western side of the house and hoisted me astride his back with my legs hanging over his hard forearms and my arms cinched around his neck. He had a fresh cigarette in his mouth and he labored up the rungs with the orange coal on the end flaring and darkening as he breathed. I knew he'd been drinking but it didn't occur to me to be any more afraid than I already was. When we got onto the lip of the roof he turned and let me down and kept a hand on me. The moon was almost full. I'd never been up on the roof of a house before and the expanse of bright white asphalt shingles looked fantastical in the night, lit up like the surface of the moon itself. The roof rose gently to the peak and sank to the left in a shallow valley where the main roof intersected with the smaller gable of the garage. Plumbing vents and attic vents stuck up at random like small dead plants, and the skeletal television antenna lorded over them on a wind-bent aluminum rod.

Bill Ray took my arm and walked me slowly over to where the western face intersected with the southern one. He squatted on his haunches and pulled me down alongside him. I could see out to the far corner of the backyard where we had tomato bushes and black-eyed peas and a stand of overgrown okra already too tall for me and Harlan to pick. The green of the garden looked pale gray in the flat moonlight, like a picture of a forest or a jungle printed on a newspaper page. To the west across the road I could see the evenly parceled posts of the barbed wire fence but the wire itself was invisible in the darkness. On the other side was the pastureland where we hunted Comanche arrowheads that still lay almost unburied where they had fallen wide of a buffalo or some other target maybe not a century before. For twenty miles to the state-line road the pasture ran interrupted only by oilfield tracks and small herds of cattle that wandered looking for tufts of buffalo grass amid caliche and prickly pear. A couple hundred yards out, a pumpjack stood dormant for the night, its big horse head bowed down to the ground. A mile or so beyond flickered the orange of a natural gas flare, a flame that Bill Ray said burned for the sole purpose of reminding him daily of the ocean of wealth lying beneath his property to which he held no mineral rights.

He took another cigarette from the pack in his shirt pocket and lit it. I always liked that first smell — the clean phosphorus of the match and the woodsiness of the just-lit tobacco before it turned stale. It was warm enough but a breeze was blowing and I started to shake a little. Bill Ray didn't say anything for a while. It was cloudless and the stars were so thick they looked like clouds floating just behind the sky. Finally he said, "It's fine up here, above God and people, ain't it? You can see everything, and nobody can see you."

I sat holding my knees, tensing my thigh muscles against the slope. Bill Ray stretched out one leg and pulled a thin metal flask from his front pants pocket and took a drink. He offered it to me, as he always did, and grinned and pushed it back in his pocket. The pearl snaps on his shirt glinted in the moonlight. It was one of his good shirts, and it was pressed, so I knew he was heading somewhere for the night, but he didn't seem to be in any hurry. He seemed willing to stay up there as long as necessary for me to see what it felt like not to be afraid, though I still was. We sat listening to the breeze come and go, carrying the bawl of a dog from a distant backyard.

He stretched out and put his hands behind his head. After a while, he said: "The night your mama and me got married a few boys in town decided to give us a shivaree. We was at the church, and they snuck out and locked all the windows and padlocked the doors on the little house we rented for our honeymoon north of Bronco. We got out there and saw what they'd done. They drove up, every one of 'em drunk as a fiddler's bitch, and announced their intention to kidnap me for the night.

"Rube was wearing a borrowed wedding dress a size too big for her and she had trouble moving around in it at the church. But all of a sudden there she was beside me, out of the pickup without me even hearing her. And when she stood clear I saw she'd reached my Winchester down from the rack behind the seat. She let off a barrel over their heads and one of the boys, the drunkest one, got so scared he fell down like he'd been shot. The others stood there staring at him for a minute to see if he really was shot and then they laughed so hard they nearly pissed. Rube didn't even smile. She let the shotgun come level and said: 'Now let's see which one of you assholes is man enough to come over here and get him.' "

Bill Ray laughed until he fell into a cigarette cough. "They left us there locked out of our own honeymoon bed, so we spent the night on top of an old tarp in the field, staring at the stars, happier than if we was on a goose down mattress."

He looked up at the sky for a while longer, then turned toward me. "You remember much about her?"

"Some," I said. "But it's getting harder to tell what's real and what I've just made up."

"What about Harl?"

"He hasn't said a thing about her for years now."

He put his head back and lay still for a long time.

I told him I needed to take a piss.

"Come on, then."

He got to his feet and pulled me up and walked to the edge on the west side and took a long, leisurely piss onto the strip of sandy Bermuda grass between the fence and the house. I was too scared to go down that far, but I was close to pissing myself, so I pigeon-stepped as far as I dared and unzipped my pants with my shaking hands and saw with gratitude that it made it over the edge into the darkness.

We walked back up the rise to the Y-shaped crest where the three planes of roof intersected. It couldn't have been more than fifteen feet higher than the edge but now it felt like nothing except sky was above us. Bill Ray stood on the peak and looked out over the land for a while. He

> started to laugh again, quietly at first but then so much that he had to take his cigarette out of his mouth. He stood up completely straight like an Indian in a Western movie and swept the cigarette west toward the featureless pasture and south toward the sparse lights of town. "Verily I say unto thee, my son," he said in a booming bass voice. "Someday this will all be yours." I was too young then to understand what was so funny about that, but I laughed along anyway.

Troy and Harlan found a little drop in the lunette formed by the wind along the east side of the lake. Past this ridge the lake seemed to be in rapid retreat — a shocking green rim of salt grass and algae gave way to pale gray sand that grew lighter until it became indistinguishable from the near-white surface of the gyp water, about fifty yards in diameter, rippled whiter with cat's-paws by the evening breeze.

Troy looked up the ridge and saw Harlan with his back to him, silhouetted against the dimming sky, relieving himself at the highest, most conspicuous point possible in the landscape. He stood the way he always did when he pissed, with his hands on his hips and his head bowed, as if presiding over some kind of solemn occasion. Past him a small herd of cattle darkled against the horizon, moving toward a stand of Sudan grass. When Harlan returned the light was almost too low to see him. His arms were wrapped around a tangle of leafless mesquite limbs dangling with long dried bean pods, the kind that underfed horses sometimes ate and died of the colic. Troy, squatting, looked up at him.

"What're you doing?"

"Somebody's been clearing brush. And I found a little outcrop of chert, managed to chip a piece off."

"Chert?"

"Chert. Flint. We don't need matches now."

"I told you no campfire, Harlan, goddamn it. You'll get us spotted."

"You can go to hell. There's nobody to spot anything for thirty miles and I ain't staying out here tonight without a fire. If you want to sleep with the coyotes and rattlers, go out yonder and be my guest."

He squatted down and dumped the wood and arranged the smallest pieces in a tight pile and took a wad of dry buffalo grass from his shirt pocket. He felt the direction of the wind on his face and turned his back to it and hunched down on his knees with the grass almost between them. Digging into his pocket he took out a lock-blade folding knife and opened it and turned it so that the blunt edge of the blade faced out. Then he bent over and began striking the light brown shard of chert against the fattest part of the blade, rhythmically, as if trying to coax music from the steel. At first nothing happened but then thick orange sparks like phosphorescent water droplets began to tumble downward in the dark. He kept hammering the chert against the metal for much longer than seemed necessary and then he picked up the tangle of grass and held it almost against his lips and blew into it gently and then harder, until Troy could smell the grass burning and see smoke begin to curl out. Suddenly, it burst into flame in Harlan's hand and he thrust it rapidly into the woodpile and took a stick and nudged it into the middle and got down on his hands and knees and blew again, into the smoke and flame. He tended it for several minutes, until the larger limbs were burning, then he got up and went to a flat patch of ground five feet away and cleared the weeds out with the heel of his boot and lay down using his bag as a pillow.

Troy stayed where he was, well back from the fire, sitting cross-legged, scanning what was left of the horizon.

The first limbs burned down to coals and Troy thought Harlan had gone to sleep until he grunted and got up and laid on more wood. The din of toads that filled the early night had died down to a stray murmur.

"I'm goddamned thirsty," Troy said after a while. "Lying here next to so much water is making me thirstier. I can smell it."

"You'd rue the day you drank any of that alkaline shit," Harlan said. "It's no good for anything except birds to land on. It's too shallow even to drown in."

Harlan lay down closer to the fire this time.

"I wish I had a Navajo blanket."

"I wish I had a hamburger," Troy said.

"When do the sandhills come here? I can't remember anymore."

"About now. I'm surprised some aren't out there already."

"I didn't realize this was that place. Until we got right up on it. I don't think I ever saw it in good daylight."

"You remember that morning?"

"A little," Troy said. "I remember thinking it was dark enough that we were all going to shoot each other."

Harlan shifted himself on the hard ground so that he was lying on his back. "It was so pitch black I couldn't even tell where the lake was."

Troy was still sitting but he leaned back now and put his elbows on his bag and looked up into the sky. It had been so many years since he had slept outdoors he couldn't believe how many stars there were, how closely strewn, how clear. He scanned the blackness trying to find a constellation but couldn't identify any, even the Little Dipper.

"Jim Bob and Crip had come the winter before," Harlan said. "They knew which way the cranes would come off for food, where we needed to stop. Not too close but close enough so they'd be low when they came over. Those bastards dropped like ten-pound sacks of flour. It sounded like grown men hitting the ground. I'd never seen birds that big before."

Troy badly wanted to sleep but kept his eyes open, looking away from the fire, trying to adjust his vision to the darkness. The morning with the cranes — they were maybe fourteen or fifteen then — started to come back.

"They say they fly through here all the way from Siberia, across thousands of miles of communist airspace, down the whole of America. Then when they stop for a little breather they get shot out of the sky by a bunch of shit-for-brains farm boys with nothing better to do."

"I remember hearing them before I could see them. It didn't sound like wings beating — it almost wasn't a sound at all, but then I knew something was over my head, bodies moving through the air. I started to be able to see them, so many of them, paired up like bombers. It was kind of scary. But pretty, too, I guess. I forgot we'd come out here to kill them 'til Crip pulled the trigger right next to my ear. One fell in front of me. The other of the pair veered and lost altitude, like it was coming down after its mate, but then it straightened out and went on."

Harlan took his hat from his chest and laid it on his forehead, over his eyes. "There wasn't no sport in it. I got five or six before I stopped. I bet Crip and Jim Bob and that other boy killed forty. The ground looked like a goddamned massacre."

"Did we even pick any up? You couldn't eat the damned things."

"I'd sure try now," Harlan said. "Wouldn't you?"

Troy let his eyes close.

"Ask me again in the morning."

Oct. 15, 1972

West Lubbock, sometime in the mid-sixties, the last house I ever robbed. It was a nice ranch-style brick on a residential corner near a shopping strip. The parking lot at the strip stayed busy, giving me cover to case the house in my car in the afternoons and evenings, following the comings and goings. The owner was an older woman, almost certainly a widow — no dog, few visitors, dependable routine; somebody came to take her to buy groceries on Monday mornings, to a ladies' club on Thursday afternoons, to church Wednesday nights and Sunday mornings.

Two weeks in on a Wednesday evening I saw her Pontiac Star Chief gone from the driveway where she kept it. I came back an hour after sunset and parked at the shopping center and crossed to the alley and opened the backyard gate and entered the living room through an unlocked sliding door. I slipped off my shoes, as I always did, and put them in my back pockets, heels out.

I was inside working for twenty minutes, bent down over the jewelry boxes in the bedroom, before I suddenly became aware that I wasn't alone. She moved as soundlessly as a cat — before I saw her, before

I even heard her, the woman was standing directly over me. I made an audible sound and fell backward, scattering necklaces and earrings all over the carpet. I thought my heart was going to burst in my chest. I tried to crawl away on my elbows between the bed and the wall.

She walked after me holding out both hands — hands I expected to see clutching a kitchen knife or a pistol but they were empty, reaching toward me.

"Oh, hon!" she said. "I'm so sorry. I didn't mean to spook you."

She knelt down in front of me and shook her head scornfully. Up close, she looked far older than she had from a distance.

"My lord, Jimmy! Do you know what time it is? It's too late to be up playing now. You put these toys away and you get back to bed."

She bent down and began scooping up jewelry and putting it back in the boxes and I watched her in the weak light coming in from the street. She had me pinned between the bed and the wall and the only way past without knocking her down was over the bed. When she'd cleaned up she stood and drew the quilt coverlet slowly back and waited, looking at me, right at me so hard it seemed she was staring through me at the wall or something on the other side of it.

I stood up, ready to run, but my knees were too weak beneath me.

"What on earth are you still doing up, son?"

I wondered what year it was for her and how old I was supposed to be. I wondered where whoever she thought I was was now.

"I guess I just wasn't tired, mama," I said finally, trying to see what would happen if I played along.

"Well sometimes you're tired and you don't know it. You have to close your eyes and lie real still to find out."

I was dressed in my clothes for night work — dark slacks, dark sweater, black socks. She patted the queen-size bed where the covers were turned down. She didn't move and I finally sat where she indicated. I took my shoes out of my back pockets and put them on the floor. She put a hand on my shoulder and I slumped over and eased my head onto the pillow and pushed my feet clumsily under the sheets looking up at her face over me, wreathed by snow-white hair. She covered me up to the neck and bent down and kissed me clumsily on my cheek very near my mouth. I could feel her cool, odorless breath against my skin.

"Rain's coming," she whispered. "Daddy's taking you and Sis with him tomorrow to help break the new section. You need a good night's sleep, you hear me?"

I don't know how long I lay unmoving in the bed, listening to the quietest quiet I'd ever known. It was like a silence at the bottom of another silence. It didn't matter to me whether I got caught or not; I wanted to spend the rest of the night sleeping in that bed.

Eventually I got up and walked into the hallway and looked into the small adjoining bedroom, which was frilly and must have been Sis's when Sis had lived there. The woman was sleeping in the room, on the twin bed, fully clothed like I was, except that she was lying above the covers, on her back, her arms extended rigidly along her sides.

I couldn't bring myself to take her jewelry, so I stole her small television set instead. Later, it struck me what a terrible decision that had been — she wouldn't have missed the jewelry but the television was probably her best friend.

Martha had no idea how near daylight

might be — the darkness outside was still deepest black. Towing the hunting coat behind her, she climbed quickly over the backseat and found the passenger door handle and pushed it down with great caution, trying to keep it from making any noise. But the handle suddenly gave way under her and she sucked in her breath as the door released and swung open heavily, almost pulling her out of the car before she let go. The door stopped halfway but its opening caused the dome light on the ceiling to burst to life like a powder flare, flooding the car with brightness. Martha sat back up on the seat and turned to stare at the malevolent eye of the dome staring back at her. Before she thought about what she was doing she rolled onto the broad of her back and hoisted both legs in the air and kicked viciously at the light, knocking its plastic cover off with the second kick of her heel and with the third crushing the thumb-size bulb that somehow burned so fiercely.

The darkness covered her again, and she balled up on the floorboard behind the front seat, breathing hard, feeling panic rising in her throat. She clenched her eyes and tried to listen. The wind was completely still now and noises would carry. She waited for voices, feet coming toward her on the hard ground. She raised the top of her head over the seat to look through the back window toward the rise: no human form visible, no movement, yet. She scanned wildly around in the darkness and suddenly realized she could see the horizon, a nearly indiscernible black line running beneath a purplish-yellow blur, still very faint but not for long. She shoved her arms into the sleeves of the canvas hunting coat and dug around in the pockets hoping that Brother Ted had forgotten a pocketknife or a screwdriver, but felt nothing except what seemed to be the ridged casing of a spent shotgun shell.

She could see a little better now but there was almost no moon and the grass-pocked prairieland outside the car door quickly dropped off into void as she tried to make it visible. Where was the dirt road and how long had they been on it? Even if she found it, how many miles would she need to run to get back to pavement and the poor chance of a passing car? If the sun came up and they drove along the road after her where would she hide in this treeless, featureless, colorless godforsaken country?

She started to cry but choked it back, swallowing so hard she couldn't breathe. Rage rose into her chest. She leaned out and slowly pulled the passenger door closed again, not hard enough to shut it completely but enough until she heard it click. Looking out the back window again, she climbed over the front seat to check the glove box for something she could use as a weapon. It was even darker in the car than it was outside. She felt like a sightless creature groping its way through a burrow. Inside the glove box the first thing she felt was plastic and hard and long — an ice scraper, which she shoved into the chest pocket of the coat, in case it might come in handy later, though she couldn't think of how — and then a soft bottle, lotion, maybe car wax, which she dropped on the floor — and a cardboard box that she fumbled to open, spilling out a handful of what she realized were tampons, smooth and medical-feeling. Some sort of folded paper, most likely a state map. A small zipper pouch that she felt around in and recognized the form of a lipstick, a compact, and a bottle of mascara. The compartment was nearly empty but the next time she reached in she felt something that her fingers instantly recognized as crackers. She had to bear down and steady herself to keep from ripping the papery cellophane away and losing them in the dark. She managed to get a fingernail beneath the triangle folded over one end and her hand flew to her mouth. The crackers had probably once been peanut-butter flavored but they were so ancient they tasted like sawdust and she almost gagged as she worked her jaw on the mass and swallowed it and crammed in the next two and the last two, feeling around inside the compartment for more.

At the bottom of the glove box lay the worn plastic bag she knew contained the car papers, the ones that proved the vehicle belonged to you and others apparently so essential you needed to carry them with you always. She was about to leave the bag alone but she swiped her hand beneath it to make sure she wasn't missing anything and heard the jingle of metal, a sound so familiar she thought she must have imagined it. She grabbed one end of the bag and ripped it open and felt around inside; she could hear the metal but couldn't feel it, so she turned the bag over and shook it and crouched down in the mess of the footwell and came up with what she was looking for, two long keys on a small wire loop.

She got back on the ridged bench seat and scooted to the driver's side, keeping her head low. Coming up from the floor, she realized how much brighter it already was outside. She could see the metallic crossbar bisecting the steering wheel and could even read the cursive word incised into the fake silver plaque in the fake wood panel on the driver's door: LUXURY.

It made no sense to her why somebody would keep an extra set of car keys *inside* a car, where they'd be no good to anyone except a person in the situation she was in now. She considered with cold acceptance the great likelihood that the keys were to another car. Her left hand felt out the ignition on the steering column and the other tried clumsily to jam a key into what she hoped was the slot, turning it one way and the other, feeling desperation well up. She brought her face closer to the slot and tried the second key, trembling, holding her breath to steady herself the way hunters did with rifles, but this only made her shake worse. She guided the key slowly toward the center of the chromium circle and wiggled it and suddenly it sank into the curve of the thing like a kitchen knife going into a block.

She nearly screamed, but she understood how meaningless this was; she'd never driven a vehicle in her life other than an ancient tire-less tractor through a Mexican oat field, badly and in fear of being found out. She stared at the rim of the steering wheel looping over the dash, making an arch against the light coming in, a blue that matched the blue tinting at the top of the windshield in such a way that she was unable to tell where the two merged. Any minute now the sun would crest the horizon with no obstacle to prevent it from laying bare all her movements inside the car. The two men would probably be on their way down the hill now anyway, to get a jump on the police. If they weren't it was only because they were a couple of lazy asses on top of being half-ass thieves. Or maybe they'd already killed each other, the way she had read cowboys sometimes do around campfires in the middle of the night.

She sat up on the driver's side and slid beneath the steering wheel and stretched her feet down to probe for the gas and the brake, both of which she could touch, though she had to shift herself so far forward she could barely see over the hood. The dash flared up slightly on the driver's side, mimicking the look of an airplane cockpit. She had heard Johanna make this comparison to women at church, who had seemed envious of such a beautiful new car and suspicious that it was being driven by the pastor's wife. The windshield curved so far around her that it felt wider than the car itself and the crescent of instruments and capitalized English words below looked like photographs she had seen of a jetliner cockpit — VOLUME, SELECTOR, HOT, HI-LO, COOL, ALT, BRAKES, WIPER, OIL, FUEL, LIGHTER, LIGHTS, FLOOR, RELEASE. The letters inside the glass bubble over the steering wheel said PRNDL and she stopped to think about this strange word — PRNDL, it sounded almost German — before remembering what the letters stood for, at least the important ones. She reached down and pumped the gas pedal the way she had seen Aron do. Breathing in and out several times, she felt herself start to cry and she pressed her forehead down against the steering wheel crossbar and closed her eyes and ground her teeth and spat out the word *puta* under her breath. She opened her eyes again and almost reflexively started to recite the Lord's Prayer, the way she always said it in her mind at night, in the language that sounded most convincing to her — "Padre nuestro que estás en el cielo: santificado sea tu nombre, venga tu reino, hágase tu voluntad . . ." — but suddenly the heavy rhythmic phrases seemed unbearably long so she skipped to the end — "el poder, y la gloria, por todos los siglos" — thinking that if God had any plans to help her at this moment, it couldn't matter that much.

When the motor came to life it drowned out all thought and she felt dank air from the air-conditioning vents waft across her face. The starter shrieked metallically for a second until she realized she should let go of the key. She hauled down on the gearshift with the whole weight of her body and the stick wobbled but stayed in place as if it had snagged on something. She pulled it again and shook it violently and this time it fell, propelling the red needle past the D all the way to the right-hand side of the dial, the number 1, and before she could push the stick up again the car lunged into motion. For a split second it heaved forward and threw her back against the seat but then it seemed to come loose from the ground and slip sideways and she realized the tires were spinning out and she eased up on the gas. When she did she was thrown back again and her foot came off the pedal and the big car bounced and came nearly to a stop in a cloud of grayish dirt that rolled past the windows over the hood. She looked over the dashboard down the length of the hood, trying to make out identifiable forms in front of her, anything through the darkness and dirt, but she picked up only the horizon line and the possibility of a pumpjack far in the distance.

Movement was the only thing that counted now. If she was going fast enough maybe it wouldn't matter if she drove the car through a fence. She had a vision of multiple strands of barbed wire snagged across the car's big grille, fence posts being wrenched successively out of the ground, a whole line of fence being dragged and eventually whole fields of it, the station wagon at the apex of a vast inverted V of wire and wood sweeping across the land, scraping everything off its surface. She reached down for the pedal and tried to press it gently but it gave under her and the car lurched violently forward again. This time she tensed her legs and torso and held herself against the steering wheel with both hands to keep from coming off the gas. She felt the car begin to gain momentum and make its way across whatever was in front of it.

Now that she had set things in motion, she felt a sense of calm come over her, as if nothing important could be helped anymore. Her decisions might affect minor details but the overall outcome was no longer within her control. It was a thing that happened sometimes when she was frightened, not so much a religious feeling as a feeling that a mechanism had been triggered whose gears could mesh in only one direction. Instead of being light-headed, as she had heard people say they became when afraid, her head felt fine in these situations, almost too dense. She thought that if she took her hands from the wheel and held them in front of her face, they would have barely shook, though she could still feel her heart thumping wildly behind her eyes, making the visible world pulse in and out.

The station wagon seemed to interpret her actions from a great distance, with a lag, like a lateral nervous system receiving signals from hers through a spinal cord a mile long. She'd never been in a boat before but she thought this was how it must feel to pilot something bulky through deep water.

She hauled herself up on the wheel to get a better bearing of the ground in front of her, but it still looked like nothing, a dark blue slate bisected by a straight black line. On what possible set of facts, she asked herself, had she based the hope that the road lay somewhere ahead and not far to the right or the left? She knew there was a better than even chance that if she didn't hit fence or irrigation line or plowed field she could drive ten miles into open cow prairie without ever coming across a road, or even near one. Then she thought: *Jesus in Heaven, the armageddon of noise I must be letting loose into the quiet of the morning and I still probably haven't gone further than the men could run to catch me, even the big clumsy one.*

She found the gas again with her left foot and stood her weight on it this time, causing the engine to shriek and the steering wheel to yank forward out of her hands as inertia drew her body back. The car bounced hard over tufts of grama and cactus and Martha gave up trying to see what was in front of her but felt herself gain speed and her feet and thighs pressed against the seat registered the freeing sensation of distance starting to spool out between where she was and where she'd been. The car had suddenly decided to switch sides and become her ally.

But just as suddenly it betrayed her again. The dashboard reversed course at great speed and slammed the steering wheel into her chest so hard that she flew back and then bounced forward off the seat and into the wheel again. She felt a vertiginous sensation, as if the back end of the car was coming up above her, into the air. And then she knew that it was. The motor screamed as the back wheels lost contact with the earth and then they came down hard, bouncing the car up and down on the shocks. When it hit the ground the impact caused her to bite her tongue and tears leapt to her eyes. The salt taste of blood flooded her mouth, and she took the name of the Lord in vain in Spanish and Low German. Her chest throbbed where it had struck the top of the steering wheel and her ears filled with an animal roar. Through the noise in her own head, she gradually became aware that something in the world was roaring, too, and she realized it was the engine, though the car itself no longer seemed to be moving forward, only bucking on its frame like a wild animal with its hind legs caught in a trap. A few seconds passed before she understood that she was the cause of the sound — her foot had remained atop the gas pedal, holding it to the floorboard. When she let it up the engine made a long dying wail and the car finally stopped moving.

Latching on to the steering wheel again with both hands, she snaked her foot back to the gas and pressed it several times. But the car only bounced and shuddered more violently and through the rearview mirror she watched red dirt spew up into the morning light.

She let go of the wheel and slumped back

against the seat, knowing what she had done: She had found the road but had found it crossways. The car had barreled through the deep bar ditch perpendicularly, or nearly enough. The front had managed to jump onto the road but the ass end had caught down in the ditch and the middle of the big heavy car had high-centered on the curve of the grade, beached like a whale on one of the only parts of the land un-flat enough to strand it.

Martha came up from the seat onto her knees and shrieked and beat wildly on the steering wheel, causing the station wagon to emit a series of short irregular honks like Morse code.

For a long time she sat behind the wheel not crying, not moving, breathing almost normally again. She raised herself up to look into the rearview mirror, not to see outside this time but to see herself, out of a sudden need to verify her existence — little more than a shadow, a round shape with thin hair clinging to it, a barely legible line for a nose, two small reflections indicating eyes. Past the mirror she saw that the sun had broken the horizon. She reached over and felt out the master lock button on the door and pushed it, listening to all the doors hammer down. She turned the ignition, killing the engine and filling the car with silence again. Then she crawled down into the darkness of the footwell on the passenger side and pulled the hunting coat over her body and lay waiting for them to come.

Oct. 28, 1972

Some of this — maybe all of it — might not be true:

Bettie told me that her given name was Beatriz, though she rarely went by that name after she left home. She said she went by so many names after the age of sixteen that she couldn't remember all of them herself. The couple of times she had been picked up, the police seemed to believe she was from Mexico, but she said she had grown up in a small farming town, now a suburb, west of San Antonio and had never set foot on Mexican soil in her life. Her father was born in Chihuahua and came north under the bracero program, staying on after the war, drifting down into Texas to work cotton. He died before she was two years old in a senseless accident. He and a bunch of hands had lit out on the road between picking jobs, to stay ahead of Immigration. One night the men bedded down near Uvalde between a set of rusted freight rails overgrown with sage and bristlegrass, believing, as many did, that rattlesnakes wouldn't cross a pair of tracks. There were no rattlers that night, but a diesel engine shunting empty feed cars rolled up the spur after midnight because of a broken switch and the engineer, dozing on a double shift, didn't notice. The engine was on top of the men before they woke. It killed three instantly, including Bettie's father. The fourth, his leg badly mangled, got a ride back to Chihuahua hidden under a tarp in the back of a pickup but he bled to death before he got home.

Bettie was raised by her mother, whose family had come to San Antonio from the mining town of Matehuala around the turn of the century. They had done well for themselves in ranch work, but only well enough to understand that they would never be able to afford good land themselves or truly feel like citizens, even once they became citizens. Bettie was a cheerleader. In her junior year of high school she won the sheriff's posse queen by more than a hundred tickets, a stunning achievement in those years for a so-called Spanish girl in a small Texas town. She was just better at speaking to adults — at winning their trust — than the other girls, even those from ranch families with the money to buy the title outright. She showed me a newspaper clipping she kept in the lining of her wallet, from the rodeo where she was crowned. The picture showed her in a tight-fitting denim pantsuit, astride a platinum-maned palomino, small beneath a tall white cowboy hat. She was waving at the camera, flashing a smile whose ferocity people at the time probably didn't notice.

FIVE

Marlan stood with his forehead pressed against the lower half of the glass on the station wagon's driver's-side window. He yelled out again, to no one visible. His voice rolled over the morning, unanswered.

"Nobody in her, Troy! She's empty. Ain't a soul down here!"

The sun had crested, but the raking light hid more than it revealed, throwing deep shadows behind the car and up the ridge.

At the first sound that had jolted them from sleep — the unmistakable sound of a car almost on top of them — Troy's first instinct had been to run and leave everything behind, Harlan included, and in the near-darkness he had tried to pick out a path along the ridge that would conceal him without running him into the silt. But when he had looked to find Harlan he saw that his brother was already in full motion heading the other direction — the wrong direction — clamping his hat to the top of his head as he ran. Before Troy could yell to stop him, he was more than halfway to the bottom of the slope, loping down in a graceless crouch like someone trying to avoid being shot after realizing too late that he was fully exposed.

Based on what had sounded like a lone vehicle, a heavy one, Troy had calculated that it wasn't the law but a wetback hand, maybe a farmer himself, out before daybreak to check irrigation pivots. But even if that were true, even if he could talk them out of the encounter, it wouldn't matter because they'd be seen and word would spread faster than they could outrun.

Troy had drifted into a light sleep just before daybreak and he felt heavy and disoriented as he tried to put his body into motion. He patted his coat jacket for his papers and wallet and stumbled into his boots, hopping toward a stand of arrowhead that hemmed the lake for a hundred feet curving south. He didn't know how to move on foot in the daylight; he'd never been on the run without a car. He thought about Harlan: Harlan running out into the open like that because he had clearly decided in the light of a new day that he was finished with what was happening to him. Whatever lay at the bottom of the hill, sheriff, farmer, hunter, hand — the devil himself — was preferable to present company. And Troy couldn't blame him. But he knew that Harlan wouldn't be able to do otherwise than tell everything.

Troy plunged into the grass through a gale of bugs pelting his face and hands. He could still hear the sound of the vehicle below and in the time it had taken him to find cover the engine had grown so loud and pitched he thought it might actually be headed up the ridge toward him. But as suddenly as the sound mounted, it fell off and died out completely after a series of staccato horn bursts that confused him and made him wonder if something more dangerous wasn't down there after all, parties exchanging signals. To stay in the darkness of the arrowhead he crouched on all fours like an animal and tried to remain absolutely still because he knew his movement could be detected if someone looked to the top of the brush. He listened for a vehicle door opening or closing and for what he thought he might well hear next, a sound he had heard once before, long ago, addressed to him individually — the godlike authority of a voice amplified through a police bullhorn. But he heard only the breeze and the low idiot drone of ten million lake flies. Then he heard Harlan's voice booming out, like a lighted sign visible for miles announcing that somebody was with him, hidden up on the ridge.

Troy looked beneath his armpit, searching for a coyote trail, any kind of clearance to allow him to back away unnoticed through the brush. In front of him he saw only a jungle of green, an alien perspective in this part of the country, and through the verticals of green the coral red of the sun cresting the horizon, an event he never saw like this — outside, through naked eyes — but only through a windshield, down a line of asphalt. He heard his brother's voice again, beckoning him to come down. Though it didn't seem plausible that Harlan could have been coerced to do so, so convincingly, even with a gun on him, Troy remained motionless nevertheless.

At the risk of being heard, he elbow-walked gingerly forward through the arrowhead. Each rustle of the blades felt like an act of violence. He pushed through at the ridge's edge far enough to see almost to the road, but he could make out only a portion of the station wagon and Harlan resting against it to one side, facing away, looking east with sunlight sitting square on his big body. There was no other vehicle in sight — the one they had heard must have been closer to him, Troy thought, obscured by the grass and the slope.

He watched Harlan turn slowly and look almost directly to where he thought he had concealed himself so well in the grass. Harlan rose off the car and scanned the horizon, then climbed onto the station wagon bumper with both feet.

"Car's locked, Troy!" he yelled out. "Somebody must've tried to take her. Come down here with the keys. Let's get the hell out before somebody else shows up."

Troy edged further toward the lip of the ridge, keeping his head so low that he could smell the alkaline funk of wet clay beneath his face. He felt exposed now but the bottom of the rise was still hidden from view. He could see only that the wagon was not where they had left it but T-boned halfway across the road at the end of a scrawl of tire tracks cut deep into the dirt.

Harlan continued staring in his direction. "I can see you moving in the goddamned grass up there, unless that's a javelina ate you in your sleep. Come on down now. We ain't got time for no outlaw shit."

None of what seemed to have happened down the hill made sense to Troy yet. He kept his crouch, watching his brother's body language. He saw Harlan lumber heavily down from the bumper and pace slowly and deliberately in front of the wagon, then bend down and pick up something from the dirt. Suddenly he wheeled and threw it in Troy's direction and Troy knew it was a rock before it sang in the air and snapped at the grass a foot from his head. Harlan looked hard where he had thrown and then spat and bent down and came up throwing again, landing a second shot further afield. But the next one didn't miss — it came right at Troy's camouflaged face and he ducked and felt it skip off the small of his back. He wriggled backward in the grass, looking around for a rock of his own but finding only wet caliche clods that would crumble in his hands. When he was far enough from the incline he raised himself on his haunches and stood bolt upright in a fit of fury, preparing to run but glaring first over the slope at the top half of his brother, who stood as motionless as a prairie dog. Fighting an overwhelming urge to run, Troy advanced three exploratory steps down the hill, to see what he had been unable to see between himself and where the grass expired into colorless dirt at the bottom of the ridge. But there was nothing — no pickup, no cruiser, no man or men. He edged back up the incline out of the grass and looked hard down the dirt road into the cotton fields, then toward the paved road, seeing nothing driving toward him or away, no dust raised by anything having done so recently.

Harlan had hoisted himself onto the hood to sit, turning his sweat-stained back toward his brother. Troy remained in place on the ridge for a long time, racking his mind. Against his better judgment he descended the slope halfway and waited again, listening, keeping an eye on the road. When he finally came all the way onto the flat, inspecting the station wagon warily, Harlan didn't acknowledge him.

"Did you see anybody run?" Troy asked him.

The wagon's back bumper sat almost flush to the ground, half covered in silt above tires that had been sucked into the bar ditch.

"Not a soul. But there was still dust in the air when I got down here. I don't know how in hell somebody got away so fast on foot. We're gonna have to use a couple of fence posts to get her out — she's high-centered."

Harlan climbed off the hood and Troy approached the car slowly, like an animal testing a trap. The sun had reached the ridge where they'd slept and the hard light sat on everything so plainly that Troy suddenly felt the extent of their exposure.

He squatted down to look at the back tires and went around to unlock the driver's-side door, putting in the key and turning it and pushing the latch button. But just as the door came open, a deafening sound, a scream — more like a kettle whistle in the purity of its pitch and violence to the ear — split the morning from inside the car. The shock of the sound propelled Troy backward so forcefully that he fell on his ass and Harlan spun and ran half a dozen bewildered steps into the middle of the dirt road.

The two stared at the station wagon as if a pack of rabid coyotes had materialized on the hardpan in front of them. And as they looked, the big driver's-side door that Troy had tried to open swung out slightly, slowly, and then slammed shut under unseen powers. The clap of steel and rubber at its closing was echoed by the thump of the electric locks battening themselves down again.

Troy scrambled to his feet and ducked. Scanning the ground for cover and realizing that the only place offering any was the car itself, he scuttled up against the faux-wood side of the body, hunching under the window line so that whoever sat inside would be unable to get a bead on him without getting out or shooting through the heavy doors. Harlan remained heedlessly in the middle of the road several dozen feet away, uncertain, crouched on his hams with an outstretched hand, like a football player in a three-point stance.

Nothing manifested itself as they waited. Everything, even the morning breeze, seemed to have stopped moving, anticipating a new revelation.

It was Harlan, through the gleam shooting off the luggage rack, who first saw something rising slowly above the window line: the shape of a head like that of a ghost — a sheath of milky white around a small oval face the same shade. Harlan couldn't make out whether the head was looking back at him. He glanced down at Troy, crouched in the car's shadow, staring up into his brother's face to see what he was seeing.

More quickly than it had appeared, the head sank from view. Harlan advanced a few steps toward the car, careful to keep a margin of road between him and it, wondering if what he had seen was some kind of optical illusion. But then there it was again, ascending gradually, higher this time, staring at him directly and unmistakably, and he realized with more shock than if it had been a ghost that he was looking into the face of a child — a girl, probably no more than ten years old. Her features were partially obscured by the reflection of sky on the windshield but he could see her mouth and eyes clearly. Her face was void of any expression, as if she was indeed only an apparition of a child assuming form inside the car.

He found himself walking almost involuntarily up to the long expanse of hood, keeping his eyes fixed on the girl. As he did, she never moved, never blinked. She seemed more distant than she actually was because of the thick sound barrier of the windshield and the windows surrounding her.

Harlan was close enough to the car now that he lost sight of Troy down beside the flank and he thought his brother had managed to cut and run without being seen. But then a hoarse whisper rose from below. He ignored it and walked slowly from the front to the driver's side of the car, looking more closely in the improving light at the narrow-faced blond-haired girl sitting on her legs, stock still against the steering wheel, staring east across the road. He stopped next to the door and studied the side of her head, the small, oddly too-round ear between parted strands of fine hair. The sun was starting to come straight through the windshield and he squinted around inside the car looking for other occupants, finding none. He refocused his eyes toward the southern horizon and up the road and thought hard before he extended his big right hand and knocked three times on the window.

From below him came the whisper again, sharpened, an adder's rasp.

"What in the fuck, Harlan? What's happening?"

"Stand up and see for yourself."

"Who's in there?"

"I can't say for sure . . . But I don't think she'll shoot you."

The girl didn't turn, didn't move. Harlan leaned forward and brought his face close to the plane of the window and knocked on it again.

"Hello . . . Hello? Little girl? What are you doing in there? Where did you come from?"

Troy scooted out of the shadow toward the back of the car before rising from his crouch, so confounded he had lost a sense of what to do. He looked past Harlan's shoulder through the window and saw what Harlan had seen, the form of a sallow prepubescent girl who gave the impression not only of being miles distant from where she sat but of inhabiting a dimension different from the one Troy thought he inhabited, where the presence of such a girl inside the car was inconceivable.

"Who the hell is that?"

"I can't make sense of it. Maybe she's from some farm 'round here."

"What would a little girl be doing out in a cow pasture before dawn?"

"You tell me. Maybe she's lost. Maybe there's something the matter with her."

Troy looked southeast toward the picked cotton fields to see if he could spot a farmhouse, knowing the closest one was easily a dozen miles away. He walked up beside Harlan and stooped toward the window and studied the girl's strange pellucid hair and her hands folded in her lap as if she was waiting for someone. He could see the key in the ignition and the glove box door hanging open.

He addressed her through the window, more sternly than Harlan had, enunciating his words in a way that felt instantly absurd. "Hey! Can you hear me? What are you doing in there?"

"I think she can hear us all right," Harlan said. "She just don't want to."

Troy repeated his question and walked to the corner of the windshield, looking through it to try to catch the girl's eyes, which admitted not in the least his presence. He realized that the keys were still dangling from the door and he walked back to it and leaned down and spoke loudly this time.

"I'm going to open up the door now so we can talk, all right?"

He reached for the key but before he was able to turn it fully the inanimate girl sprang to life and leapt with astonishing speed toward the door side and hammered down the electric locks. Troy tried again, working the key, grabbing hold with both hands. But the girl parried him at each turn, pumping the switch rhythmically on the other side of the door until Troy yanked the key from the handle with an exaggerated sweep of his arm and smashed a boot into the bottom of the door.

"Hey, you open up the goddamned door right now! *Who are you?* Open that door this second and get out of our car!"

Martha's head was bowed toward the floorboard and they couldn't see her face, so when she finally spoke it seemed to come from nowhere. It was a high, raspy, strangely accented voice that sounded remote through the glass, like a radio broadcast:

"This isn't your car, *ladrón*! This car belongs to my aunt Johanna and you robbed it from her in broad daylight. *Ladrones sucios!* You left her to walk. And you didn't just take her car, you stupid dirty *pendejo* robbers — you took me! So now you're gonna pay. Because I know your *pendejo* names and I know all about the both of you. *Pendejos!* I know where you live and what you do and I know the police are already looking out for you. So you better run right now before they get here to lock you up for the rest of your lives."

Troy and Harlan stood dumbfounded. Harlan failed to grasp the significance of what the girl had just said but Troy understood immediately. He stood back and looked at her as if seeing her for the first time.

"I'll be goddamned." He turned toward Harlan. "She was in the back of the car. The *whole* goddamned time."

Harlan continued to stare at the girl, playing her speech over in his head. "What time?"

"All the time. All night. We never looked."

"When did she get in?"

"She never *got in,* Harlan. She *was* in. She belonged to that woman in Tahoka. She was lying in the back there when we drove off and we've had her with us since yesterday and we never thought to look. She didn't make a sound."

Harlan looked at Troy. "There wasn't nobody else in that car with us yesterday. We drove forty miles."

"Did you ever think to check behind the backseat? Of course you didn't. Neither did I because you don't think about a thing like that, looking behind the seat of a car for a child asleep when you're stealing the car. She probably woke up and thought we were going to kill her. She's Mennonite I bet. Just like those two boys who got out. The woman, too, probably."

The crown of Martha's head was the only part of her visible above the window line. Troy ran his hand over the damp of his face and looked down at the colorless dirt caked on the knees of his suit pants and the toes of his boots, the ones that belonged to the livestock judge in Fort Sumner.

"She's been gone more than twelve hours. By now half the state of Texas is out looking for her — we're a couple of dead men, Harlan. They're looking for kidnappers."

Harlan made a guttural sound protesting the lunacy of such an idea. He started to say something to Troy but nothing came out. He fixed again on the girl, whose wan half-oval of a forehead had sunk lower behind the glass, as if she was in prayer or becoming sick. A look of disgust spread over Harlan's face, then one of stupefied denial — not at the facts, which were too plain to dispute, but at how rapidly everything he had once thought about his life was becoming untrue.

From somewhere a diesel pump on a timer rattled to life, marking the divide between daybreak and day. Trying to think through the situation as it stood now, Troy turned and sprinted up the rise to get the bags, taking a long look from the crest over the road. On the hood of the car, he opened his suitcase and spread out the contents and held up a shiny leather wallet and counted the bills inside. He repacked everything except the wallet and went to where Harlan had taken up a position a few yards down the road, looking back at the car and its occupant.

"We can't leave her out here."

"That's what we're going to do," Troy said. He put some of the money into his coat pocket and bent to tuck the rest into the shaft of his right boot. "She can ID us, Harlan. She can give them a rendering — she's been looking right at us. The only shot we have is to get down the road while it's still early, make it south maybe an hour, get another car before she gets to the road and somebody picks her up. Even then it's a shot in hell — that station wagon is one thousand percent radioactive."

Troy looked at the car without turning his head and saw the girl facing them now, her hair reflecting the sunlight and her large eyes skimming the door top like an exotic mammal peering from a terrarium in a zoo. It was almost too much to take in — stranded at daybreak on a dirt road in the middle of nowhere, looking at a strange child locked inside a car, locking you *out* of a car you needed worse than any you'd ever needed before. Troy wondered how long it would take her to make it back to the main road and how long before a pickup came down this one.

"If we drive straight through and we're lucky, we can make Presidio before dark and get over into Ojinaga."

Harlan squinted into the sun and pulled his hat down on his brow. "Ojinaga? In Old Mexico? For how long?"

"I don't know. We might have to stay for a while. Or we might need to keep on the move. It depends on what kind of case they make after she turns up."

Harlan looked past Troy into the nothingness of pastureland. "I can't believe this. I truly can't."

"You better get started."

"I don't want to go down into Mexico."

"Then you can stay here by yourself and see what happens."

"I've spent my whole life here, Troy. Inside of a ten-mile radius. I don't know how to live no place else."

"And look at what it's gotten you."

Harlan walked to the far lip of the road and spat into the bar ditch and turned back and yelled: "As compared to what the life you're leading has gotten you? Look at the truckload of shit you've brought down on both our heads *in under a day's time*! It has to be some kinda record . . . all in the name of coming here to *help me*!"

Troy walked back to the car, keeping a deferential distance. The girl's face remained at the side window in his direction but she wouldn't meet his eyes.

He enunciated clearly, like a grade school teacher: "Hello. If you know my name, why don't you tell me yours? That would be nice, wouldn't it? Why don't you turn the key and roll down the window a little so we can have a talk. Word of honor I won't get any closer."

Harlan watched from the road. Troy might as well have been addressing the automobile.

"It's not going to do anybody any good

sitting out here in a cow pasture. If you let us get back in the car, we'll drive you to the city limits in Seagraves and drop you off and your mama can come get you. I promise you, we're not going to hurt you."

The girl turned — only slightly, to look in Harlan's direction, though any movement seemed consequential. She turned again to Troy, showing no signs of willingness to crack the window, much less open any doors. He took a couple of exploratory steps toward the wagon and she pulled back and he stopped.

She looked in his direction for a long time, as if she had lapsed into a trance, but then he heard her voice again, barely audible.

"I want you to take me to El Paso."

Her speaking was so unexpected he wasn't sure he had heard her correctly. "You want what?"

"To go to El Paso."

Troy shot a glance at Harlan and then at the girl.

"El Paso?"

"Yes."

Troy turned back to Harlan, who was watching from his removed position as if the exchange no longer involved him.

"Now" — Troy tried to smile at the girl — "El Paso's not where we're headed. We can't take you anywhere. You don't belong to us. We never knew we had you in the first place or things wouldn't have turned out like this. We're going to take you to a pay phone so you can call your mama and she can come get you."

The girl didn't move or change expression. "That's not my mama. That's my aunt Johanna. I'm not going to go back to her. I want you to take me to El Paso to my papa." Her voice was growing louder now, clearer, with the curious loping Germanic accent Troy knew to be Mennonite.

"Listen, why don't you roll down that window a tad, so we can have a real conversation?"

The girl looked at him for a while, seeming to review the pros and cons of cooperating, then moved carefully to her right, keeping her eyes on Troy as she reached toward the steering column with her right hand. Suddenly the wipers jumped and banged noisily back and forth across the dusty windshield and the girl turned and fumbled with the levers branching off the column, trying to find the one to stop them. Her head sank from view again, while a worrisome hissing sound issued from beneath the car. In a few seconds the driver's window descended several inches before quickly reversing course and heading back up, stopping to leave only a tiny breach, no more than two inches. The girl lifted herself up to this fissure and stuck the fingers of one hand through and tilted her head to bring her mouth closer to the opening. When she spoke this time, it was with new assurance in her voice.

"I want you to take me to El Paso right now."

Troy maintained his position near the car as if it was a thing that had been established in negotiation. Harlan advanced a few steps, turning his head to listen.

"Like I said, now, we're not headed to El Paso, so we can't take you there. Maybe your papa can come here and pick you up."

"My papa can't come pick me up."

"Why not?"

She looked at him for a second. "Because he can't go anywhere. They have locked him up in El Paso. Over on the other side. In Juárez."

Troy received this information without being able to fit it anywhere into his conception of the girl in front of him.

"Will you tell me your name now, so we can talk?"

She paused, seeming to gather her thoughts. "I don't have anything to talk to you about," she said. Her voice was growing shriller now. "I know *your* name and that's enough. You take me to El Paso and I'll never tell your name to a soul, nor his over there, I swear it on a Bible. But if you leave me here, I'm going to tell the police everything. I'm going to tell them that you hurt me, that you touched me in the nighttime where you're not supposed to touch a girl. And they're going to track both of you rotten *pendejos* down and lock you up for the rest of your born days. So you better start driving. Or else you better kill me and get it over with."

"Jesus Christ," said Harlan, who had been lured almost back to the car.

Troy put his open hands out in front of him. "Hey now, nobody's gonna kill anybody here."

He could hear the playacting in the girl's voice, the way she managed to say everything she said because it wasn't really her saying it — it was some tough girl she'd seen on television. But it didn't make much difference because she meant what she said and she wasn't getting out of the car.

Troy approached gradually, bending in humility, addressing her through the glass. "We need to get you back to your family, to your aunt. She can take you to your papa.

We can't be traipsing around the countryside with a little girl that doesn't belong to us."

"I'm not going back to Tahoka."

Troy ventured a couple more exploratory steps.

"Well, then, we need to figure out a way to make a deal here because we're not going to El Paso. We can't take you *anywhere.* If you'd just open the door and maybe let —"

Whatever words came next were smothered under a blanket of sound so immense it seemed to come from nowhere and everywhere at once, except that Troy had seen the girl's hands move. The station wagon's horn bawled from beneath the hood, at first with a sour, bovine uncertainty but then with gale force that split the morning. Hearing it, Harlan turned and began walking down the road, as if the sound signaled the end, definitively, of everything that had happened to him in the last twenty-four hours. Troy backed away with his hands above his head in surrender.

The blast lasted several seconds before dying out in a train of echoes. The girl faced the wheel, slumped into it, staring at the center with both hands joined there at chest level. Then she bent in again and the sound reexploded, flushing a covey of bobwhite quail from a mesquite patch on the far side of the road, the drone masking the flutter of their wings.

The sound was so deafening Troy felt it as a physical assault. He ran up to the driver's-side door and pounded on it frantically. "Okay, okay, okay! Goddamn it! *Let up! Ease up!*"

Through the window he saw the girl's hands rise but remain poised together, one atop the other. It took him a second to realize that the sound had stopped and he could be heard.

"*That's enough!* There's no need for any more of that! *You want to go to El Paso?* We'll take you wherever the hell you say. We'll take you clear to Hong Kong if that's where you want to go."

The girl didn't look at him but withdrew her hands and used one to clear her stringy hair from her face before letting both sink slowly into her lap. She looked strangely formal, like someone posing for a picture. Troy's face was pressed nearly up against the glass now and his breath made coins of fog that evaporated and replaced each other rapidly in the dryness.

He stared in, not knowing what would happen next. And then, with his eyes locked on hers, without thinking about what he was doing, he punched the key still in his hand into the keyhole and reached for the handle and yanked the driver's door open as hard as he could, pulling the girl, who had grabbed for her own side too late, half out of the car with it. He reached down where she dangled from the handle over the road and grasped her bony upper arm and wrenched her from the car onto her feet, standing her straight upright on the hard dirt. And then with the momentum generated by this action he swung neatly around into her place and plunked himself into the driver's seat and slammed the door shut behind him and locked it with the other hand.

After everything that had come before, this rapid exchange of positions ended up appearing oddly nonviolent, practically prearranged, a do-si-do during which the stunned girl made no sound and ended up standing awkwardly beside the car facing Harlan, seeming utterly at a loss about what to do next — except that she made no move to run.

When she heard the engine jump to life behind her she startled and scooted several steps from the car and turned to look at Troy, who had put the wagon quickly down into drive to try to free its back wheels from the bar ditch. The engine heaved and the tires seemed to grip and the car's enormous back end rose a foot and a half off the road. But it was only a bluff; the dirt under the wheels crumbled and the tires sank back into the breach and spun free, kicking up a plume of red dust like a rooster tail. Troy gunned it and dropped the motor into a lower gear, but the engine only screamed and the tires spun faster, shimmying, going nowhere.

The dust cloud drifted toward the lake, casting a shadow beneath it. Troy rolled down the window a few more inches and yelled at Harlan, thirty feet up the road behind the girl, the two of them staring dumbly together toward him:

"*Go find something to help me!* Grab a goddamned piece of wood, a fence post. See if you can lever us out."

But Harlan didn't take a step from where he stood. Troy gunned the wagon again and finally let off and the engine idled down.

Shaking his head exaggeratedly to make the gesture visible, Harlan yelled back, cupping his hands to his mouth:

"I ain't gonna. I ain't leaving a little girl out here in a field like this, Troy. Let her back in the car. Or I ain't coming back, either."

Planted where she was next to the car, the girl almost blocked Troy's view of Harlan and Troy felt as if he was talking to her.

"We can't have her in here, Harlan," Troy yelled. "It's bad enough as it is."

"Well we're gonna take her somewhere. We ain't leaving her. Least I'm not."

Troy's heart pounded now. He was so furious he felt as if he couldn't see, and a vision suddenly came to him of everything that was happening, except observed from high above, from a helicopter, soundless but distinct: two grown men and a ghost-pale girl against an eternity of scrubland by a gyp water lake, going through the movements of an obscure ritual or fit of madness whose object seemed to be an immense immobilized vehicle. And from further out, on every road within a two-hundred-mile radius, other vehicles, too numerous to count, hurtling toward them, converging on the spot where they stood. The absurdity of it rained down around him. He thought about getting out of the car and just walking away, but he knew he no longer had the ability to disappear like that, the way he once had. He thought about climbing on top of the station wagon and stretching out spread-eagle in the sun, closing his eyes and sleeping for a whole month, not letting anybody wake him, not even the police, because he knew it was all over now. It had been over since he decided to come back home, but he never imagined it ending like this, in complete idiocy. He felt bad that Harlan was going to get caught up in it, especially with a child involved, but that's just the way things happened — Harlan had no record; he probably wouldn't end up doing much jail time.

Troy looked at the girl, who hadn't moved but seemed to be crying silently now, her impassive face glinting in the sun. Harlan stood where he was, holding his ground. The sun behind him made him into a silhouette and obscured his face beneath his hat. Troy killed the engine and sat for a long time looking out toward the two of them through the dusty glass. The sound of a passing semi rose and swelled and died away and he thought about the nearness of the paved road.

He unlocked all the locks and opened his door, the bottom of which scraped against the caliche. He walked back to the bumper to see how hopelessly mired the wheels were in the ditch and then he stared at the girl. Though it was difficult to tell, she didn't appear frightened or angry, just wholly forsaken, as if she had nowhere else to go.

"What's your name, girl?"

There was no answer.

"We're not taking you to El Paso."

She looked somewhere over his shoulder.

"We'll drop you close to the nearest bus depot and give you fare and you can go wherever you want to go from there. It's the best deal you're going to get. And if you want it, you better make up your mind because our problems just became yours. If we sit out here yanking each other's chains, you're going to end up in somebody's custody like we are. No El Paso, no nowhere."

The girl didn't acknowledge she had heard what he said but she walked rapidly back to the station wagon and opened the passenger door and got in and pulled it shut hard behind her and reached and pushed down the locks on both back doors. She leaned over the front seat between the headrests and retrieved the large canvas coat lying in the footwell and with it in tow she pushed herself over the backseat, returning to the place where she had somehow made herself incorporeal for so long, listening to every word they had said. She didn't lie down this time but took up a seated position facing forward, legs crossed Indian-style, and took the coat and pulled it over her shoulders and didn't move again.

Troy waited a minute, watching her, then went to the driver's-side door and opened it slowly and sat sideways on the seat and restarted the engine, listening more closely this time to discern whether it was functional. The girl stared through him toward the windshield. She addressed him calmly, flatly: "Leave both of the back doors locked. You can throw your stuff in over the front seat. If you unlock either of the back doors I'll scream. If you try to touch me I'll scream and I will bite you."

Troy stood up and put his fingers to his lips and whistled over the sound of the motor. Harlan looked at him without moving, but Troy knew he would come back to the car.

With a piece of cedar post wedged under the back tires it took ten minutes to get the wagon up from its rut, mostly because of the extra weight of the girl, who sat firmly in her place in the back, watching them. After Troy and Harlan had both settled themselves inside, she leapt suddenly over the backseat toward them and wrestled the left passenger door open. For a second it seemed as if she had changed her mind and decided to bolt, but she sprawled over the backseat with her body stretched out and choked and vomited onto the road, somehow managing to get none of it on the car. When she finished, she closed the door and pulled herself back over the seat and wiped her mouth with the sleeve of the coat and resumed her previous position.

Under way again down the dirt road, the car made a ragged, disturbing sound behind the dashboard, like the clattering of an old film projector out of sync. To their right the sun was already well clear of the horizon. Troy looked down at his wrist and realized he had lost his watch during everything. He glanced in the rearview mirror at the hard set of the girl's face.

"Once we get to the main road, you get yourself down, out of sight, like you were when you got us into this. Understand?"

Harlan turned around to get a good look at the girl for the first time, but she had already sunk behind the seat. He thought about whether Troy was thinking of pulling over and throwing her out before they reached the paved road, and what he would do if he did. But Troy just laid on the gas and the dust whorled behind them in two vortexes and when they reached the Y of the farm-to-market road the wheels hauled left, heaving the car sideways onto the blacktop, due west. The girl's head rose up slightly to see the two lanes of pavement, empty in both directions.

SIX

The longer Aron stayed in the hole the further back into the past his memory ranged. He started to retrieve powerfully vivid images of riding in a dark train car, in the middle of the night, swaying and rocking, trying desperately to stay awake because he didn't want to miss any of what was happening to him. It was the first time he had ridden in a train; it was the first time he had ever even seen one, inside or out, and his mind couldn't encompass it. He was ten, maybe eleven. His father, also named Aron, his two younger brothers, and his two sisters, one older, one younger, were in the car with him, crowded up against each other on the seats and the floor. The baby, Naomi, not yet two, dozed on their mother's lap. She had been holding a rattle made from a tobacco can with peanut shells sealed inside but she had let it drop to the floor and it rolled around among tangled arms and legs as the train rocked back and forth. The porter in St. Paul had allowed them to crowd into the tiny roomette sleeper as a family because he knew by sight who they were and what they were doing — heading back to Manitoba, like many Mennonites from Mexico he had seen in those years. The train was half empty anyway so it wouldn't matter. The family looked like the rest had — like mourners, dressed head to toe in black except for the little girls, whose head kerchiefs were embroidered with small blue and yellow flowers.

Aron was against the fold-down bed, near the window, and he could see by the moonlight that the land was becoming flat again, like West Texas and the Chihuahua grassland. On the train platforms he made out in English some of the funny names of the towns they passed through — Carlos, Winger, Plummer, Thief River Falls. They had not been able to take much when they left the campo; everything Aron thought of as his own occupied a third of a cardboard suitcase with his brothers' things.

Before the sun rose they came to Noyes, the last American city before Emerson on the Manitoba side, and Aron's father told them to wait in the train while he took care of the papers. But after he left, the porter told them they couldn't stay in the train and so his mother, crying softly now, dragged the suitcases and trunk with the help of the boys into the station, a small wood-paneled waiting room with benches built in along the walls. Aron's father stood with his hat held respectfully over his chest, talking to the ticket taker. The man had come out of the little booth into the open doorway, looking around as if he needed help. When the man saw Aron's mother and the rest of the family pulling their possessions into the station he looked down at the floor and shook his head and started talking to Aron's father again, more slowly. But he spoke English and couldn't understand much said to him in Spanish, nothing in Low German. After a while the man went back inside the office and Aron's father came and stood next to his mother and told her that it was going to take time; this is what happened at borders and it was too early in the morning. But when the sun came up two other men arrived, wearing uniforms a different color from that of the ticket man, who emerged from his office again and stood alongside the others, looking gravely at Aron's father; one of the new men spoke Spanish and Aron overheard him telling his father that as far as he could determine he and Aron's mother were not Canadian citizens; they were Mexicans. And the children were certainly Mexican, having been born there.

"But I was born here, in this land!" Aron's father said in Spanish, trying to keep his voice under control. "Mrs. Zacharias was born here. We are citizens of the Dominion. We are Manitobans."

"You're not in Manitoba, sir," one of the new men said. "You're on this side of the line, and we can't let everyone come back just because they say they belong and want to. We have laws to follow. We can't do anything about the laws."

The men took a shoebox full of the family's papers and told Aron's father to come with them. After a few hours, three women from a local church arrived with a pot of chili and hard rolls for the family. But right behind them came two men who looked like police officers, indicating with their hands to Aron's mother that they needed to take the luggage. They carried the suitcases and the trunk out to the platform and opened them and spread everything — clothes, blankets, tools, kitchen utensils, keepsakes, undergarments — out on the paving stones. They tied white cloths like doctor's masks around their faces and using a silver canister with a brown rubber hose they sprayed all the family's possessions against hoof-and-mouth disease as Aron and the other children watched transfixed through the station window, their mouths full of bread.

"Schau! Regenbogen!" Aron said to his brothers and sisters, and a rainbow did hover momentarily over the white mist that emerged from the hose and spread over the platform. It looked like a beautiful earthbound cloud but it stank like kerosene. The women from the church seemed embarrassed and said nothing to Aron's mother, who sat rocking the baby, staring dead-eyed at the windowless wall on the other side of the station.

By nightfall, the family was aboard another train, their tickets paid back through St. Paul, their luggage separated from them in a freight car, fumigated for no reason. Aron had no recollection of passing through Minnesota again or how they got from there the rest of the way back to Chihuahua, and years later the whole journey came back to him less like a memory than like a dream, punctuated with flashes of strange passing landscape, sudden waking, fear, and hunger.

Once they got back to the campo nothing seemed to change; he didn't remember anyone even welcoming them back, only people acting as if they had never tried to leave. That summer was as dry and hot as the one before and they all worked just as hard on the land and the only difference was that the new house where they lived was smaller and more flies got in through the window screens.

Above him, Aron heard the familiar metallic keening and he looked up to see the circle of grayish light, now unobstructed by the grate. As the ladder was lowered down he stood up against the side of the hole to keep from being struck. A voice told him to climb out and to carry the Bible up with him this time.

"Why?"

"Because I said so. What other reason is there?"

He put his feet on the rungs but he felt this time, for the first time, that he was not going to make it all the way to the top. He put the Bible under his arm and began to climb but managed only four rungs before he had to rest. The light in the hole went away — the guard's head was blotting it out as he stared down inside to see what the problem was. "Ándale!" he said and shook the ladder and Aron fell off, landing painfully on the heels of his bare feet. He picked up the Bible and made it high enough the second time that the guard was able to reach down and latch on to his collar and haul him up the rest of the way.

"Please don't take it," he said, remaining on his knees clutching the Bible, squinting painfully into the morning light, speaking Spanish for the first time in months.

"I'm not going to take it, *cabrón,*" he said, laughing. "You're going to take it. As a souvenir of your stay here at our tropical resort." The guard picked up the black faux-leather-bound Bible, which was bursting at the seams, its browned pages bulging out like dead leaves.

The guard turned his head away. "It stinks like *shit.* It stinks even worse than you do, alemán."

He took Aron to a regular, empty cell and told him to remove the decaying clothes he had arrived in. Two other guards hosed him down with cold water and gave him a towel. They handed him a pair of white cotton pants and a shirt of the same material, thin like children's pajamas, and a pair of stiff huaraches that were too small, fitting only the front part of his feet. He knew that by law he was supposed to be given back the bills and coins he had had in his pocket when he was arrested, but they gave him only a release paper and escorted him through a series of offices he had never seen before and out a garage door into an empty parking lot. He covered his eyes with one hand and stood for several minutes outside the closed door, stooping as if the sunlight and wide-open space were pushing him to the ground. Finally, he bent and put the Bible on the asphalt next to the jail wall and sat on it to wait until someone came to tell him what to do next.

Troy stayed on the farm and ranch roads but not the dirt roads, heading southwest at right angles toward Kermit, near the western elbow of the Panhandle. He chanced going that far in the station wagon only because every mile they put between themselves and Tahoka, keeping away from the larger towns and moving into the truly unpopulated stretches of the state, the better the chances of getting another car unnoticed. They couldn't make a switch in a town now, even at the edge of one. This left primarily farmhouses, which presented no small risks of their own, risks that belied their isolation: dogs — vicious, scabby, near-feral ones, sometimes in number, unfenced and unpredictably located; entry by dirt road, which meant the impossibility of approach without raising a cloud of dust, signaling anybody a mile out; houses loaded with guns, more at the ready than they would be in town; available cars sitting outside with no cover, in the sun, like bait in a trap.

On a one-lane ranch road between Kermit and Monahans they passed a house unusually hard against the pavement, a tiny place. Someone had begun to stucco it but had run out of money or will, leaving only black tar paper halfway up to the eaves. Chickens, a few of which could be seen crowding into the small shadows, had rendered the yard grassless. There was no good way to tell if anyone was home. The door was closed behind the screen door and the two front windows, facing south, were covered with foil to keep out the sun.

Troy passed, slowing slightly, but once they had gone several hundred yards beyond the house he yanked the car off the narrow road, bounced it into the bar ditch, back up onto the road and down into the opposite ditch before pulling onto the pavement again, headed the way they had come. He went by the house at full speed and traveled a hundred yards more before he took the car gently into the ditch and onto a harvested milo field alongside a windbreak ridge thick with tumbleweeds snagged in mesquite and shinnery oak.

He cut the motor. After being in the car so long with the roar of the engine and the road, the silence was stupefying. Being in a car on the run made it seem even more so. To Troy it sounded like death. He looked back and saw no evidence of the girl. Harlan might as well not have been in the car, either — he had said nothing for more than an hour, staring ahead with his right elbow hanging out the open passenger window; he looked as if he no longer cared what happened to him or where he was being taken.

"I'm leaving the keys in the ignition," Troy said. "If you see anybody coming around this windbreak except me, scoot like hell behind the wheel and take off and lay on the horn. Roll up your window and lock the doors as soon as I get out."

Troy left with no hope that Harlan would do any of these things but it turned out not to matter. He was back in less than five minutes, moving at a trot. He knocked on the station wagon's rear window and motioned to Harlan and the girl, who rose tentatively into sight. Harlan looked in the side-view mirror and caught sight of the rounded nose of some highly burnished black thing parked on the road behind them, most of it obscured by the brush. It looked like the front end of a hearse.

Troy reached in to unlock the back door and grabbed the bags and told the girl to climb over and get out in a hurry. Harlan walked around a stand of mesquite and saw the entirety of what Troy had found, a black 1950 Ford Business Coupe so pristine it could have just come off the factory floor. The whitewalls were as bright as new-fallen snow and the grille, decorated with a finned chromium bullet between the headlights, reflected the sun so that you could not look at it directly. Harlan laid his hand on the curve of the rear fender.

"Well, I guess as long as we're all being thieves here, I'd say this is something else."

Troy opened the driver's-side door and threw in the bags and held it open.

"It's a shame, is what it is," he said. "This isn't just a car. It's like stealing somebody's child. On top of which, it's going to be like driving a bullhorn down the road blaring out to everybody we pass: 'Take a real good look at the people in the old antique! What a car! Tell your friends and neighbors!' We're going to get rid of it as soon as we have the chance and we're going to make sure it gets left in the condition we found it."

Troy looked at the girl, who had followed them to the paved road trailing the immense beige hunting jacket that seemed to be her only possession in the world. She stared blankly at the side of the coupe, seeming to make an effort to strike a pose of tractability, of waiting for instructions. Troy pushed the seat up and she got into the back of the car, which seemed somehow far larger than it did from the outside; it looked as if she was sitting on a sofa in a tea parlor. She put her arms into the hunting coat and situated herself in the middle of the wide leather bench and withdrew her head into the corduroy collar and her hands up the sleeves, turtlelike, disappearing except for her legs and the opalescent top of her head.

The interior of the coupe smelled of Pine-Sol and lanolin. It was plain no one had ever been allowed to smoke inside it and the odometer showed just under three thousand miles. It was only a two-door, but it felt much roomier than the station wagon — as if its contours possessed the ability to contract and expand at will. Troy forbade the touching of anything, even the window handles, though the car remained cool inside with the windows up; it had been sitting in a darkened garage probably for years, dusted weekly. Polished walnut grain covered the dash and door panels and the seats were brown leather, pleated every three inches for air flow, firm and high to provide the best view out the windows, tinted faintly green like the glass of a Coca-Cola bottle.

For the first few minutes after they started down the road again Troy felt exhilarated to be in such a vehicle, atop such splendid shock absorbers; it was more like being inside a car museum than a car. But after a few miles the immaculateness began to feel strange, as if the owner perversely wanted the car to seem to have no owner at all, never to have been driven. It reminded him of a Chevy 210 he was once supposed to deposit in Fort Worth. The interior had smelled powerfully of some orange-scented disinfectant, pleasant in itself, but it made Troy begin to wonder if the odor was intended to cover up another. Had there been an accident? Had someone *died* in the car? The smell worked on his imagination until it gave him the willies, and he ditched the car before he got to Abilene.

As they moved south on roads around the town of Monahans, the prairie became paler and sandier, no longer covered by emptied furrows but by shinnery oak, the only thing that kept the dry soil, formed by millions of years of erosion and wind, from eroding entirely and blowing away. Viewed toward the horizon the whole prairie still appeared to be tableland but low dunes swelled up now, obscured by their uniformity, an optical illusion broken only when the black rocker of a pumpjack appeared and disappeared among them, tugging rhythmically at its rod. Fifteen minutes outside town they crossed the Pecos River, whose historical importance to the Old West was marked at that point by nothing but a short stretch of raised road bracketed by a pair of rusted guardrails. In the distance to the southwest the Davis Mountains spread a bar between land and sky, marking the end of the flatland until it picked up again in the desert on the Mexican side.

They took the farm roads south of Pecos toward the small town of Balmorhea, passing only a few people, mostly farm pickups. The men behind the windshields waved reflexively, raising two fingers from the tops of their steering wheels before registering the sight approaching them and turning their heads to watch the coupe shoot past.

Harlan had stopped thinking about how many people must be trying to find them by now — they had blurred into an abstraction too big to encompass. The girl was not visible in the mirror from his vantage point on the passenger side so he pushed himself sideways on the seat, turning his head slowly to see that she had fallen asleep. She was slumped over on the seat as if she had suddenly lost consciousness, her head pushed awkwardly against Troy's bag and her thin body crooked across the seat. Harlan could see that she had bad teeth, too small and too widely spaced against her pink gums, like pickets in a fence. The hunting jacket had come off her shoulders and lay bunched around her legs. The bare tops of her arms, below the short sleeves of her blouse, were smooth and unmarked, without the moonlike smallpox scar that the arm of an American child her age would have had. But she didn't look so different from an American child, not as different close up as he had expected, except for the paleness of her complexion and her hair. She wore faded blue jeans cut for a boy and a rose-print button-up shirt that looked handed down but not homemade. Harlan wondered if Germans in Germany, or wherever Mennonites came from originally, were this pale or whether living in Mexico had somehow had the effect of bleaching their skin and hair even lighter, marking them even more deeply as the outsiders they were. A Mennonite farmhand once told him they called themselves "the quiet in the land" and he had remembered this because it had such a nice ring but also because it seemed to describe them perfectly, or his experience of the ones he knew, a people who were always around but never fully present.

After half an hour of silence, Harlan turned on the radio, which was tuned to a Spanish station and filled the car with jaunty music played with tubas and trumpets, clean and clear, as if the radio station was somewhere just outside the car.

Troy reached down and turned it off. He had put his sunglasses on and sat up close to the wheel, holding it anxiously at ten and two like a young driving student, eyeing the speedometer to see how far he could push the engine.

"What're we going to do with her?" Harlan said. "She can't be more than ten years old."

Troy tensed his thighs to raise himself and look at the girl in the rearview mirror.

"We just keep driving for now. Maybe we figure out a way to drop her in Fort Davis if we make it that far — wait until the sun goes down. They'll pick her up trying to take a bus and have her back in Tahoka by tomorrow. She'll be fine."

"Where do we go then?"

"Presidio's the straight shot, straight south. Once we get below the highway there's nothing between here and Mexico but empty road. I might know somebody there who can help us get across."

"You always seem to know somebody but I haven't seen a soul yet with my own eyes. I bet you know as many people in Presidio as I do. How much Spanish have you got?"

"Enough to get along. You must know some yourself by now."

"A few words, from Inés, that I remember. She liked to teach me. Bettie never would. She told me she wanted to leave her old language behind for good. She picked up English real fast."

The girl began to stir behind them, making a muffled sound like crying, but then she seemed to wake and catch herself and fell silent again. She sat up and pulled the coat around her, leaving her long hair straggled across her face like a threadbare curtain, a defective sight barrier between her and the two men in front of her.

Troy and Harlan left off speaking, staring through the windshield at the approaching mountains. After ten minutes the girl's voice broke the silence:

"I'm very hungry, Troy, can we please pull over somewhere to eat? I need to go to the bathroom, too."

No one besides Harlan had called Troy by his real name for more than two years. Martha used it only because she had been brought up to address adults properly and she didn't know his family name.

"Don't call me that — that's not my real name," Troy said. "If you want something just ask for it."

Martha looked at the back of Troy's neck, which was pale, not reddish brown from the sun like those of all the grown men she had known in her life.

"That's what your brother calls you."

"What makes you think he's my brother?"

Martha stopped to think about how she should answer.

"I have ears," she said.

"You don't know a true thing about either one of us, even if you think you do. None of us is going to get to know each other long enough for names. As soon as nightfall comes we're going to get you to a bus depot and you're on your own."

"I heard what you said before, that they'll take me back to Tahoka if I try to get on a bus."

Troy looked into the mirror at her again and she met his eyes. "You're a hell of a listener, aren't you? You're a little young to be on a Greyhound by yourself. But who knows? You might get lucky."

"Maybe I'll tell them things about you,"

she said.

Troy put his eyes back on the road.

"You knock yourself out, little lady. As deep as we are in this, nothing you say is going to make it any worse."

She waited before she said what occurred to her to say next. "It's not that I don't want to go back to Tahoka," she said. "It's just . . . I can't go back there."

Troy looked at her.

"Why is that?"

She didn't say anything and Troy had to ask her again what she meant.

"Because they hurt me," she said.

Harlan turned his head toward Troy, who was holding Martha's eyes in the mirror.

"Who hurts you?"

She waited.

"Your uncle? Your aunt? What do you mean they hurt you?"

She decided to leave it there, to fall silent now, to see what effect her words would have. She had never told a lie so outrageously wicked before and she was frightened at how convincingly she had been able to do it, with so few words, looking directly into a man's eyes.

Neither Troy nor Harlan spoke again and they drove in silence for a long time afterward.

She watched the one called Harlan, who had turned slightly in her direction, as if he wanted to talk. If she hadn't already listened to his voice and gained a sense of what he was like, she would have been more afraid of him than the other one because he had a harder face, the look of someone she probably wouldn't talk to if she had a choice. His cheeks bristled with gray-brown whiskers that looked as stiff as wire, and he wore a sweat-stained cowboy hat inside the car, set back so that all of his high forehead showed — tanned, leathery, laced across with hundreds of threadlike wrinkles.

He faced her fully now.

"My name is Harlan," he said. "What is your name, girl?"

She could tell by the way he looked at her that he really wanted to know.

"Martha."

"What's your family name?"

"My full name is Martha Mary Zacharias."

As soon as she said it she wondered whether she should have let it be known, fearing that it might give them back some of the power her knowledge of their names had given her. The larger brother made no response but looked at her with his big face, as if trying to reconcile her name to her appearance or some experience he had had with a name like it before. She didn't meet his eyes, but feeling them on her she became self-conscious and turned to stare out at the passing land, which was beginning to look wilder, less like Texas, more like Chihuahua. She knew enough of the Texas map — especially the parts in the Southwest with so few towns — to have a sense of where they were now.

"I need to eat," she repeated. "I haven't had any food in a whole day."

Troy wished desperately that he still had a watch. He looked out the peak of the windshield to find the sun, which appeared well past the meridian, though it was hard to tell. Even this far into fall the Texas sun was still as powerful as it was in summer, but it was coming from the wrong angle, the angle of descent, straight into your eyes. On the left side of the car hard shadows angled off the telephone poles, though the wires connecting the poles cast no visible shadows, as if the sun obliterated them.

Troy had no intention of pulling over somewhere before they reached Presidio. Even a drive-through would pose an unacceptable level of risk. But five miles before the highway, a state trooper passed them headed the other way. The girl saw it, too.

The cruiser's lights were not flashing but it was headed somewhere in a hurry, bounding on its shocks, growing rapidly smaller before receding into nothingness in less than fifteen seconds.

When they crossed beneath the interstate and slowed to a halt on the other side, Troy remained at the stop signs for an unusually long time with no cars coming. The roar of trucks on the highway built and died away from both sides in a sprung rhythm. Instead of going through the intersection to continue south on the farm road Troy turned right on the federally maintained highway frontage and eventually took a small paved road that angled under the highway, continuing past an alarming number of structures and vehicles until they entered the outskirts of the town of Balmorhea. Without being told to, Martha got down and hid herself. Troy seemed to know where he was going once they got onto the gridded streets. He took several right turns past trailer houses and tiny stuccoed houses before driving twice around a shabby low-slung motel. The motel was constructed from painted cinder block and attached to a chain-link-fenced courtyard with a swimming pool that seemed against all odds to be full of water.

He stopped at the corner before pulling into the motel's parking lot. He turned partway toward the girl hidden below the backseat.

"We're going to get you something to eat now. But I want you to stay down there and cover yourself up all the way with that coat and be quiet until we come get you. Can you do that?"

Nov. 5, 1972

I didn't feel Bill Ray's death for months. I hadn't seen him in such a long time that it didn't change anything in the short term, even though it changed everything forever. After it hit me I started to picture grief as a snake endlessly circling a rock, trying to find a way to get inside. It would slither around and around it and suddenly it would spring and bite at the rock and the pain would be unbearable. At first the snake would try furiously to get in, over and over. As time went by it would try less often, but when it did the pain would be the same, maybe worse because the memory of how horrible it was had faded in the intervals. In this setup, it might seem as if it was the snake that felt the pain. But I always thought of it as the rock, which couldn't be broken or moved. The snake was just life. The rock was me and unchangeable fact.

I remember the last time I talked to Bill Ray on the phone, though the passage of time has worn down the memory, distorting it more with each month. Now it seems to me as if I had been aware during the call that the heart attack was imminent and I had somehow been able to reach him in the final days of his life by dialing a nonexistent number to a black telephone at the bottom of a cave a thousand miles below the surface of the earth, where he had fled to elude the angel of death.

This makes it all the more strange to recall the content of the conversation, which was as brief as most. It revolved around the weather, a little inconsequential town news, his recent engine troubles — the actual subject, unspoken, as always, being the careful avoidance by both father and son of the question of what I was up to (stealing cars), how I was supporting myself (same), and when I planned to pay a visit home (no time soon, for reasons having to do with the former). The memory of that conversation has a parallel in a recurrent dream I'm having now, a dream in which I accidentally discover a means of speaking to my already dead father by phone. It's always a particular telephone in a diner booth at a truck stop on Interstate 10 near Fort Stockton, a real place where I sometimes eat and use the pay showers.

In the dream, I sit in the booth and order a cup of coffee and wait, sometimes only minutes, but sometimes hours into the night, staring at the maroon handset attached to the wall above the tabletop, next to a miniature jukebox. In reality, this is the kind of phone that can't receive incoming calls and is used only to place orders. But eventually, the phone rings and his voice is on the other end. He sounds happy and relaxed, maybe a little sleepy. He speaks in hushed tones, as if he's being careful not to be overheard. I take it from this that he's not allowed to say anything about where he is or what it's like, so the calls have to be circumscribed, filled with everyday chitchat, him changing the subject anytime the conversation wanders too close to anything. But it wouldn't have mattered to me if we were talking about lawncare. In the dream, I lived for these calls, something I knew no other human being in history had been able to receive.

■ ■ ■ ■

Troy knocked as much of the dried dirt as he could off his suit and checked into the room while Harlan stood near him in the tiny motel vestibule, furnished with a folding chair, a dusty aloe vera plant, and a small television set on top of a wire shelf. Troy had prepared a story for the proprietor, a short, shiny-faced Hispanic man, but the man showed no interest in where they had come from or where they were going. He had obviously looked outside and seen the gleaming old Ford sitting in the parking lot but he didn't remark on it. Though Troy didn't intend to stay all of one night, he paid sixteen dollars for two and took the room key, connected to an absurdly large plastic fob. Inside the room he extracted a flimsy piece of metal from the lining of his wallet and, inserting it into the knob of the door to the adjoining room, popped the lock and then went in and put the chain on the front door and closed the curtains all the way.

"Go back to the office and ask him something," Troy said. "Keep yourself between him and the window for a minute."

"What do you want me to ask him?"

"Ask him how long the rooms have smelled like this."

Troy cracked the door and looked out at the car and the road.

"I'm kidding. Don't get on his bad side. And don't try to make small talk. Just ask for extra towels. That'll take him long enough."

Harlan walked to the office and as soon as he was inside, Troy went to the coupe and opened the passenger door and took out his bag and pulled the coat off the girl and told her to get out in a hurry and say nothing. He kept the bag in his left hand and his body between the girl and the end of the motel where the office sat, guiding her toward the open room door. She was unsteady on her feet and looked scared now and tried to resist going in with him but he pulled her inside and kept pulling until he had her in the adjoining room.

"This is your own room, by yourself. If you can be quiet in here, I'm going to get you something to eat."

She stood just past the threshold of the darkened room, not committing to being inside it.

"I don't want to stay here," she said. "I want you to keep driving."

"That makes two of us. We won't be

spending the night. I just need some time to take care of something."

"I don't want a room. I want to sleep in the car."

"You can't stay in the car. We're going to have a different car now. Go sit down on the bed and be quiet and I'll get you some food. Don't turn on the TV. If anybody knocks on the outside door, don't say a word, and don't move. You understand me? If you help us everything's going to be fine. We're going to get you as close to El Paso as we can."

He pulled the door shut between them and looked for the first time at the room, which was even worse than he had expected — two low-slung pine singles, thin sagging mattresses without box springs; television bolted to the wall; sink, disconcertingly flesh colored, inside the room itself, alongside a dresser-desk combo; paint peeling off the bottommost cinder blocks because of some descending damp that lent the whole room a digestive odor; cheap framed print on the wall depicting a cowboy on a bucking horse, from whose ass a previous guest had scrawled a cartoon cloud of flatulence shooting out.

Troy waited for Harlan to return and then went out and found the breezeway with the ice and vending machines. The change machine worked and he fed several bills into it and put the change into the Coke machine and the snack machine, punching buttons at random until he had an armful of chocolate bars and brightly colored bags. He carried these the long way around, to get a look at the few cars parked along the motel's perimeter. He passed the pool and could hear voices inside but couldn't see who was swimming because of the green and white fiberglass slats woven into the chain link.

When he got back to the room, he threw some of the food down on the desk for him and Harlan and knocked on the door to give the girl the rest and the Coke. She parted the door a crack and looked at the cellophane-wrapped offerings in Troy's hands and took them wordlessly one by one and closed the door again.

"You stay with her — I'm going to scout around," Troy said.

"The old man in the front knows something. He was giving me a shit-eating grin while I stood there."

"He must have seen the girl, that's all. Let him think we've got ourselves a girl. It won't be the first time he's seen it."

"What if she starts making noise?"

"She won't — she wants to get as far away

as she can, too. But don't leave the room. The less people see of us the better."

Troy left his jacket in the room. He went to the Coke machine and got a bottle of Sprite and walked over to the swimming pool and opened the gate and went in. At the deep end of the pool were three blond-headed boys who looked almost identical and seemed very close in age, all maybe under the age of ten or eleven, and a man with a blond crew cut who was indisputably their father, standing in the shallow end clutching a volleyball tightly in both hands, watching the boys perform what seemed like carefully rehearsed acrobatics off the diving board.

The man glanced quickly in Troy's direction as he came through the gate but didn't acknowledge him. He was focused intently on the boys' successive flips and dives, directing their order and complexity by shifting the volleyball up and down and to the sides in some kind of private semaphore.

"All right, let's do the full gainer again. I want those tucks tight this time. I'm talking to you, Mark."

One of the boys, Troy couldn't tell which, said "Yes, sir" and the three lined up by height, the tallest first, at the step of the low diving board and went down it one after another in quick succession, springing out high over the water and hurling themselves in a knot of elbows and knees and torso muscle back toward the diving board, coming over the top of the flip and straightening out their bodies so that they entered the water noiselessly, somehow almost slowly. They did it with so little effort they seemed like dolphins.

The man stood watching after they finished and didn't say anything, holding the volleyball in front of him with his arms straightened.

Then he yelled: *"Mark!"*

The middle-size blond boy, a little chunkier than the other two, climbed silently out of the pool by himself and walked over to the step of the springboard and stopped and stared at the concrete and seemed to hold his breath. He didn't look out to meet the eyes watching him stand there. Then he quickly mounted the board and went down it and performed the gainer again. To Troy's eyes there was no difference between it and the one he had done before, but this time he was allowed to join his brothers treading water at the midpoint of the pool and the man watched them all for a minute before yelling, "Okay, fiver." The three boys climbed languorously out of the water and went to the metal patio table where their towels were and sat down, their bodies raked by the golden afternoon sunlight in a way that made them look slightly unreal, like Roman statues. They didn't speak a word to each other, staring out at the road.

The man, whose hair and upper body were completely dry, remained in the pool in the shallow end, in water up to his middle thighs. He was tan and at first glance appeared as fit as his boys. He had meaty forearms and pectorals that made wing shapes from his sternum to his armpits, but below this was a body belonging to another man; a gut like a gourd cantilevered over the waistband of his tight blue trunks and pale haunches hanging from the sides of his backbone. He seemed to register Troy's presence now. He looked in his direction and began popping the volleyball off the inside crook of his elbow, snapping his arm straight so quickly that the ball flew a remarkable distance into the air directly above him and came down into his other hand without his having to look to catch it, like a circus trick. After a couple minutes of not missing a pop or a catch, he waded to the side of the pool and picked up a pack of cigarettes lying on the brick rim and lit one and rested his arm on top of the volleyball.

"Smoke?" he said, holding out the pack toward Troy.

"No, thank you, I'm trying to quit," Troy said. He leaned forward with his elbows on his knees in a gesture of friendliness toward the man and the boys.

"I hear that," the man said.

"Don't mind us if you want to take a dip. I'll keep these boys out of your way."

Troy shook his head, finishing a sip of the Sprite. "I'm just passing through on business. I didn't even bring a pair of trunks with me."

"That's a shame, nice day like this. They say a cold snap's coming."

Troy looked out past him to the sunset.

"You and your boys out here on vacation?"

The man kept the cigarette in his mouth and waded back to the middle of the pool. "Just a little R&R."

"They sure can swim. You must have started them early."

"Well, I'm a coach. JV football and track. They're a lot better on land than they are in the water. You should see these boys with a pigskin in their hands. Say hello to this man — Matt, Mark, Luke."

Troy looked in the direction of the boys, who looked collectively back at him without saying hello.

"Where's John?"

The man looked at Troy for a second before laughing.

"That's a good one. I never thought of that. That'd sure round it out, wouldn't it? But I don't think we'll get to that fourth one."

Troy wondered what had brought them to a motel like this on a Sunday evening during the school year. He didn't have to ask whether there was a wife, a mother, who was back in the room because he knew there wasn't.

After sitting for a while watching the man smoke, Troy asked: "Did you see that polished-up Ford jalopy in the parking lot? I wonder who's driving that baby. She looks damned near new."

"I saw that pull in," the man said. "I'm glad she ain't mine. I wouldn't have the heart to put the key in the ignition. I'd have to moon over her in the garage and weep."

Taking another drink of his Sprite and looking out across the water Troy asked, "What are y'all driving?" — knowing it would sound like a strange question but hoping it came off casually.

"Us? Nothing to weep over, except when it breaks down. That big yellow Biscayne out front, the one that needs a paint job. But it gets us where we're going. And it's roomy enough the boys can pound on each other in the back without getting any blood on me. Ain't that right?"

One of the boys, the smallest one, either Matthew or Luke — Troy wasn't sure of the Gospel order — seemed to take this as authorization and doubled up his fist and punched the middle one, Mark, the pudgier one, the weak diver, viciously in the stomach. Mark was caught by surprise and doubled over at the blow. Before another fist landed, the biggest brother grabbed the one who had thrown the punch and squeezed his head beneath his armpit until he seemed unable to breathe and started making screeching noises, flailing helplessly at his attacker's ribs.

Wading in the boys' direction with the cigarette dangling from his mouth, the man yelled, "*Luke,* if I have to come over there, you and me both are gonna end up in the hospital — you to get a boot out of your ass and me to get my boot back!"

Luke said "Haw!" and snorted but didn't seem to want to cross his father so he let his brother go after giving him a parting punch to the top of the head. Mark, still hunched over from the fist to the stomach, glared murderously at both of them and relocated to a metal patio chair further away.

Troy acted as if none of this had happened, which was how he assumed most strangers interacted with this family.

He asked: "Can you tell me anything about the café hitched to this place?"

"There's better joints around but why bother when you can walk, right? Besides, being Meskins, they do a good number with enchiladas."

"Do they?"

"Yessir. Good and greasy. But good. That's where we'll be tonight."

Troy finished his bottle and stood up and smoothed the front of his pants.

"You leaving so quick? Why don't you stay for a little while and let me put these boys through some paces for you before we lose the daylight." The man looked Troy in the eye now, as if they had established some kind of simpatico. He took up his post in the middle of the pool again with the volleyball in both hands.

"I'd love to see that, I really would," said Troy, "but I have a little business to attend to."

"Suit yourself. Man's got to work," the man said, and put two fingers to his mouth and whistled to get the attention of his sons, who had fallen silent and motionless again. "You're going to miss a good show."

"I bet I am," Troy said. He looked over at the boys, who had stood up and, without being told to, arranged themselves instinctively in height order again. As they made their way back to the diving board under their father's gaze, Troy walked to the gate and looked down at the gold number painted on the big key fob sitting atop their towels.

Raising his voice to address the boys for the first time, Troy said: "You boys keep up the good work! And pay attention to your daddy here. He knows what he's doing."

He walked directly to room number 14, located providentially in the back of the motel, where there was no space for a parking lot but only a covered sidewalk and a gravel strip between the doors and a pine-board fence. He popped the lock and let himself in and found the key to the Biscayne in the man's right front pants pocket and rolled it off the ring. He still had the key to the Nova they had left behind. He took it off the key ring he had in his own pocket and put it on the man's ring and put that ring back in the pants and laid them carefully across the bed the way he had found them.

Except for the station wagon in Tahoka, where he'd had no choice, he had never stolen a car from a family. But he needed this one and he couldn't bring himself to feel bad about it. The only thing that nagged him was the make of the car, a Biscayne, a standard-issue police vehicle. The shape of the body alone — formed around a line starting at the trunk and mounting steadily until it crested the fender, giving the car a feral aspect, the look of something springing at you — put an itch in him to look around. But the motel was three-quarters empty and he knew it was the best he would get.

He walked to the café and ordered three hamburgers, three bags of French fries, and three bottles of Coca-Cola from the counter and took them back to the room. The television was on inside and when he knocked Harlan turned down the volume and peered through a half-inch gap in the curtain before letting him in. He was watching some sort of nature program and Troy stood with the burgers in his hand, watching for a minute himself, trying to figure out what was happening on the tiny, grainy black-and-white screen, which seemed to show large, dark lumps of something scattered up and down an expanse of beach at sundown. It took him a while to figure out that the lumps were turtles, emerging from the sea to lay their eggs, using their awkward flippers in a mostly futile attempt to cover their eggs before vultures descended to eat them, as the announcer on the television explained.

Harlan leaned forward and raised the volume and kept watching. Troy knocked on the adjoining door and when the girl parted it narrowly, he held out the bag of fries and the burger wrapped in wax paper. She took the Coca-Cola from his hand.

"I don't like hamburgers," she said.

He could barely make out her face in the curtained darkness of the room. He bent over and put the bag down at the threshold of the door and settled the wrapped burger on top of it.

"Eat it or not," he said. "It doesn't matter to me. But I'd get some sleep if I were you. We're leaving here in the night, as soon as everything's quiet." Troy took the tip of his boot and scooted the bag past the door-frame into her room and closed the door.

He went into the bathroom and took a shower. The water from the pipes smelled ancient, as if the taps hadn't been turned on in years. He made the water as hot as he could stand and let it run over his head until it covered his ears in a waterfall roar, drowning out thought. When he came out he got completely dressed and filled two motel glasses with Coke and gave Harlan one and they ate their hamburgers and fries together on their respective beds. They sat unspeaking for a while and then Harlan got up and turned the television back on, to some kind of detective movie already in progress. From the way everyone in the scene was dressed, it seemed like a relatively recent show, though it was hard to tell because the picture was so bad. On the screen a man could be seen in a room, gagged and tied to a chair. Three tough-looking, paunchy men in Western-cut suits and cowboy hats stood around him. The one who seemed to be the chief cowboy addressed the man tied to the chair: *"Now look, son, I don't know you from a hole in the ground. I don't know what you did do or didn't do. Hell, in my book, this ain't even about you. But I work for some serious people and when they ask me to do a job, there's usually a good reason or they wouldn't come to me to make sure it got done."*

The man paused and sighed almost sympathetically on the screen. *"I guess what I'm tryin' to say is: This just ain't your lucky day, hoss."* Then he turned casually to one of the other men in the room: *"Benny, go over and make sure the door's locked."*

Troy got up and turned the channel knob. Harlan protested bitterly.

"Hell, you didn't give us a chance to figure out what it was about. Turn it back."

Troy ignored him. "I can't watch something like that right now, Harlan. I need cartoons or something." He kept turning the knob until he landed on a local news show with a white-haired weatherman standing in front of an oversize map of Texas covered with plastic numbers and plastic representations of suns and clouds. The weatherman talked for a long time about an unseasonable cold front moving into the Big Bend, and then the picture cut to an attractive young newswoman inside what seemed to be a supermarket. The woman was talking about Thanksgiving to a group of children standing around a card table, upon which sat an aluminum roasting pan and a trussed turkey the size of a suitcase.

Troy took off his suit jacket and boots and put them on the floor close to the side of the bed, but before stretching out on top of the covers he went to the bathroom and filled his glass a half dozen times from the tap and drank as much water as he could hold — a trick known as the Indian alarm clock, to keep him from oversleeping in his exhaustion.

Harlan took off his pants and shirt and in the light coming from the bathroom Troy looked at his brother's body for the first time in years, his white legs so hairless they looked depilated, solid but somehow not big enough to keep his white briefs from hanging loose around the leg holes like curtains. His shoulders were still broad but his chest was soft, like Bill Ray's had begun to look after he did less work with his hands. The tan on Harlan's neck and forearms was the only color on his pale body. Troy watched as he placed his hat on the little nightstand and pulled the covers all the way down to inspect the sheets before getting in, settling himself on his back, drawing up the blanket, folding his hands across his chest, and falling to sleep before he had taken a dozen breaths.

After Troy pushed the food into her room, Martha waited until the door was closed and picked up the two oil-soaked bundles of paper and carried them to the tile counter next to the sink outside the bathroom. She had smelled the dull, meaty, mustardy smell rising from the food and had come close to throwing it into the trash can below. But her stomach had grabbed at her painfully and she tore the burger wrapper away and ripped the bun and meat into pieces with her hands and ate it and stuffed the fries into her mouth and leaned down to drink straight from the faucet.

She didn't want to sit on the bed for fear of falling asleep, so she sat in the one chair the room provided, hard, with a green Naugahyde cover, and drank her Coke. Trying to keep her breathing shallow, she listened to the two men talking and then to the sound of the television, and finally, after what seemed like two hours, the television stopped and she could no longer hear anything, even when she pressed her ear to the wall.

She waited to make sure of the silence and bent down and slipped off her shoes and walked in her socks to the bathroom and got a towel and folded it longways and pushed it carefully up against the crack beneath the adjoining door. She put the hunting coat around her and rolled the long sleeves off her hands and went to the front door. By the light coming from the bathroom, she slipped the chain off the door, moving as slowly as her hands would let her. She turned the doorknob to see if it made any noise and when she was sure it didn't she turned it further, pressing her shoulder against the door to keep it from clicking when the catch came out. When she finally pulled the door, keeping the knob tightly turned, she was amazed at how silently it opened to let the night air wash across her face and flood into the room. It was much colder out than she had expected and she caught her breath and quickly stepped to the other side and allowed the knob to turn back and pushed the door closed without shutting it all the way. She hadn't thought to inspect the porchway first to see if anyone was there, watching a young girl sneak from a motel room in the dead of night. But when she looked right and left and into the parking lot, she saw no one, heard no sounds, not even distant traffic — maybe people here went to bed as early as people did in Chihuahua, not because they needed to be up before dawn to farm but because they had no reason to stay awake any longer than necessary.

The vacancy sign in the distance glowed pale blue but no other light shone from the office windows. Martha guessed which way to go and turned right and found the small breezeway between the motel's two sides, the site of an ice machine, a cigarette machine, a candy machine, a Coke machine, a change machine, and, next to a plastic-windowed laundry room door, a pay phone fixed to the wall. She looked around again and listened hard and lifted the receiver off the cradle. For several seconds there was only silence and she felt a plunge in her stomach but then she heard a click and the dial tone droned loudly into her ear and she reached up and dialed zero and gave the operator her name and a Juárez, Mexico, number that she had never called before but had not forgotten. It took a while for the international exchange and the line rang nine times before a woman's voice answered sleepily in English and fell silent and then accepted the charges.

Shivering, Martha cupped a hand over the phone and whispered in Spanish. The woman, after a silence that went on for a long time, asked her, in Plautdietsch, where she was calling from. Martha wondered if she had heard what had happened in Tahoka. If so, she didn't think to ask whether Martha was okay.

"No puedo hablar," she whispered. "Me van a escuchar."

She looked up and down the breezeway, feeling as if everyone in the motel could hear her now. "Puedes decirme dónde llamarlo?" She waited. "Por favor. *Por favor.*"

The woman on the other end was quiet

again, for so long that Martha thought the connection had been lost. But then, still speaking in German, she gave Martha another Juárez phone number. Martha closed her eyes and repeated the number slowly and the woman said yes and when the woman started to say something else Martha reached up and pushed down the metal hook switch.

Her hands were shaking now. She dialed zero and asked for a collect call and said her name and repeated the number to the operator.

It rang just once before it was picked up and Aron's voice, a voice she almost didn't recognize, a voice that sounded far older than she remembered, said: "Bueno?"

SEVEN

Nov. 10, 1972

As I walked by the open motel door I saw the man — more of a boy, really — with a guitar on his lap, sitting on the bed shirtless, facing the parking lot. If I could keep from it I never talked to fellow lodgers in the motels where I stayed. But the place was dead silent and I was on my way to my room and I heard a song being played so I stopped. The guitar was beautiful, a Fender Stratocaster with a sunburst finish and chrome hardware, polished up, maybe brand new. He didn't have it plugged in or even seem to have an amplifier anywhere.

He was playing an old country song whose name I couldn't bring to mind, and he either didn't know the words or wasn't the kind who liked to sing. He was concentrating hard as he played and when he saw me he just nodded and kept on. He was strumming with a playing card torn in two and doubled over. It was this detail and the lack of an amplifier that made me fairly sure the guitar wasn't his, that he had probably stolen it from someone recently. I glanced behind him into the room and saw only the guitar case and some clothes scattered around. A bottle of whiskey a third full sat on the floor near his boots.

After a minute he stopped playing and lit a cigarette and took a swig from the bottle and offered it to me and I stepped forward and took a drink.

"That's sure a guitar," I said.

"You wanna buy it?" he said. "I don't need it. I'm no damned good at it."

"I couldn't afford it."

"I'll make you a deal."

"I don't play."

"Hell, you could turn around and sell it to somebody for three times the price I'd give you. I just need a little to get me out of town. Here, listen to this."

He strummed again and the unelectrified strings made a soft, faraway sound, like a guitar being played in another motel, another city. He sang this time, under his breath:

I can't believe it's really me
Hurting like I do
Just because you left me
All alone
I've seen it happen many times
To other guys you knew
Surely I must be somebody else
you've known.

I tried to figure out how old he was — maybe twenty, no more than twenty-five. He was thin and frail-looking, his naked torso pale and almost hairless. He seemed to have some kind of birth defect, a deep hollow right in the middle of the bones of his chest, sunk far in, as if someone had hit him there with a gigantic hammer.

He finished the song and offered me another drink. He said he was from Columbus, Ohio, and this was his first time through Texas. He couldn't believe how big it was.

"You heard the one about the guy from the city who moved out to the frontier?"

"Probably not," I said.

"The guy's so damned lonely out in the country he's about to pack it in. All of a sudden there's a knock at the door. 'Howdy, neighbor,' says a fellow standing there. 'I just come over to introduce myself, welcome you to the territory. There's a party at my place tonight, and you're invited. It's gonna be a humdinger — dancin' and drinkin' and fightin' and fuckin'! Come on over!'

"The city man thinks, 'Hell, maybe I misjudged this place!' He says to the neighbor, 'I'll be there!' Then he calls out after him: 'Listen, how fancy's this party gonna be? Should I wear my good suit?'

"The neighbor turns around and says, 'Oh, it don't matter none. It's just gonna be me and you.' "

The boy slapped the side of the guitar and hooted. Then he stretched out on the bed with the guitar beside him as if it was a person.

"You have any money at all?" he said, looking at me and grinning a boyish grin. "You could stay the night."

I looked at him. "I've got a little money. But I've got my own room." I reached into my coat pocket and took out some bills and stepped into his room and put a fifty on the nightstand and stepped back out onto the porchway.

"You know, you really ought to keep that guitar. It might be the prettiest thing you'll ever own."

■ ■ ■ ■

Martha woke to a knock on the inside door, soft, like someone knocking with the palm of a hand. She had left the bathroom light on but had fallen asleep anyway, sitting up in the chair. She looked at the clock on the nightstand next to the bed and it said eight-fifteen but she followed the path of its frayed cord and saw that it ended with no plug, dangling above the carpet. The door to the adjoining room opened and the larger brother put his head in without looking at her, making a point of staring up at the ceiling.

"We're fixin' to go," he whispered. "Can you get yourself ready?"

Martha stood up from the chair and slipped into the hunting jacket.

"I'm ready."

The adjoining room smelled like men even though the two brothers had been in it only half a night. It was almost completely dark, except for a light near the sink, by which Martha saw Troy, in his suit and jacket, at the mirror, washing his face. He looked like he hadn't slept, hadn't even sat down, since she saw him last. He combed his hair and told Harlan to wait until he heard the engine. Then he opened the front door slowly and walked out into the night in his sock feet. A couple of minutes later the sound of a car rumbled low outside the window and Harlan put Troy's suitcase under his arm and picked up his own with the same hand while grabbing Troy's boots with the other. He told Martha to wait. He opened the door and stepped out, then motioned back and she covered the half dozen steps from the room to the open back door of the car as quickly as she could, feeling cold drops of rain on her face in the dark. Troy told her and Harlan to hold on to their doors but not to shut them. He idled slowly out of the parking lot and onto the darkened road, which seemed to lie beyond the boundary of the city's utilities. When they came to an intersection Troy closed his door and Harlan jumped out and closed Martha's and got in and closed his and they drove on.

It was colder in the car than it was outside, a metallic cold, but Martha could feel the heater starting to work. The windshield wipers pushed against the rain and the water coming down the windows obscured the town, leaving only smears of streetlights and store signs as they passed through and out. Martha wrapped herself in her coat and lay down across the backseat and drew her legs up against her and in a minute the inside of the car was so dark again she couldn't see anything.

There was some talk of how to go and Troy said they had no choice but to take 17, the main road, because no farm roads ran through the Davis Mountains, as low as they were, mountains only in a Texas sense. But it was safe enough this time of morning because there was essentially no habitation along the road between Toyahvale and Fort Davis.

Harlan seemed to have some knowledge about where they were, and as Martha drifted in and out of sleep she heard him tell his brother a long, meandering story about a band of Apaches who had robbed a mail coach on its way from San Antonio to El Paso, bound from there for California, heading through a notch in these mountains with the musical name of Wild Rose Pass. The Apaches had slaughtered the driver and guard. Then they took the sacks of mail and opened them and, while marveling at the pictures in the illustrated magazines they had found, they became so spellbound they allowed themselves to be ambushed. The ones who escaped with their lives spread the word that pictures were bad luck, a bad idea, to be avoided at all costs. Troy didn't respond to the story or even acknowledge that one had been told, and Martha thought maybe she had dreamed it, though she had never dreamed about Apaches or stage-coaches before.

When she opened her eyes again the rain had stopped and weak daylight filtered into the car. She raised herself on her elbow and saw that they were in flat land once again, though not as flat as that of the Panhandle. Fenced yellow-brown pastureland stretched out on either side of the road as far as the eye could see and in the distance low mountains crossed the horizon, different mountains than before. Small houses and low metal barns passed and she waited to see if they were approaching a town or leaving one. When the frequency of the buildings increased she kept her eye out for a city limits.

"Keep down," Troy said to her. "People are up by now."

Martha lowered herself but she saw the sun-bleached green state sign when they passed it — ALPINE, POP. 5971. They took a left before they were all the way into town and from her vantage point on the seat looking up out the window she could see the tops of trees, almost leafless, and the tops of municipal light poles and after a few minutes what she took to be the uppermost seats of the bleachers of a high school football field or a rodeo arena. Then the treetops came less often until there were no more and they seemed to be out of town again, back on the open road. The sun was up on the left side of the car and began to illuminate the condition of its interior, which she had sensed in the dark — filth: empty RC Cola cans, food wrappers, pulverized corn chips, and gobs of dried food spread on top of a dungheap of dirt-gray socks and other items of clothing filling the footwells; the back of the driver's seat had been gashed in several places as if someone had attacked it with a knife, and the yellow foam stuffing bulged out. A vinyl Dallas Cowboys sticker in the shape of a pennant had been pasted across the gouges, to stanch the hemorrhaging or maybe just for comic effect. The seat beneath Martha's head smelled like her brothers had up against her in bed after a day of moving pigs in August. She reached and pulled hard on the window handle and cracked the window and no one in front objected. She tried not to breathe through her nose and looked out at the sky, covered with streaky white clouds like smears across the purity of the blue.

After the car picked up speed again she said: “I want to sit up now.” Harlan looked back and told her she could and she pulled herself upright and took in the new landscape for the first time. It was starting to look like Mexico now — terrain that rolled instead of lying flat for plowing and grazing, wilder scrubland covered with miles of yellow grama grass and cholla cactus that made her heart leap because this was *Mexican* cactus that you never saw further north in Texas. She remembered that the drive from Cuauhtémoc to Juárez in a broken-down pickup had taken a little more than six hours and so she estimated that the distance to Cuauhtémoc from where they were now in Texas, so far south, probably wasn’t much longer. Her mind went ahead of them, further south, to the Rio Grande and she started to think about the river — which she had never considered as a river but as a divine demarcation inscribed on the earth by God himself to separate two profoundly separate places. Now she thought that it was just a river after all, in places not even a very good one, a dirty, shallow course through a countryside more or less exactly the same on one side as the other for miles north and south. The river wasn’t important, really, even as a barrier.

It wasn't anything. Some of the year, in some places, you could wade across it the way you would a muddy irrigation ditch, without even getting your shirt wet. She remembered something an old woman in the campo had told her about how German women performed auguries in rivers in ancient times, reading omens in the currents, but they wouldn't be able to predict much in those parts. The Mexicans called it the Río Bravo, the wild river, which had some truth to it in the winding of its course. But Grande seemed wrong to Martha, an American exaggeration only because it drew a portion of the form of their country.

She was making herself sleepy again. She looked out at the road, a narrow crumbling two-lane asphalt strait with no shoulder except for a margin of dirt that the traffic kept clear of brush on either side. She could see five miles ahead and spotted no vehicles coming toward them or headed the same way. In the front, the larger brother reached down into the rucksack at his feet and produced a plastic ice bucket that he had apparently taken from the motel room. He also took out something else wadded inside, a beige polyester foam blanket that Martha recognized as the kind she had seen on the motel beds. He turned and handed the blanket over the seat to her. Then he situated the bucket between his legs and took a large wad of tobacco from a paper pouch and shoved it behind his lower lip and spat every few minutes, ruminatively, like the old men Martha had known in the campo.

"It smells very bad in here," Martha said.

Harlan spat into his bucket. "This car is a hovel, Troy," he said. "Couldn't you have rustled us something better?"

Martha leaned over and rolled her window lower.

"Roll up the goddamned window. You're going to freeze us out."

But she left it open to the cold wind singing in. Harlan held on to his bucket with one hand and rolled his window down, too. The roar in the car grew deafening and began to oscillate in their ears.

"The girl's right — we need to air this pigsty out," Harlan yelled and he began to laugh, the first time Martha had seen either of the men express any kind of strong emotion other than anger. Harlan clamped his hat on top of his head with the flat of his hand. "Smell that Texas air! Don't it feel nice? Breathe it in while you've still got the chance."

Troy let off the gas and allowed the Biscayne to slow until the sound from the windows was replaced again by the rumble of the car's big V8 engine. He rolled his window down, too, and flipped up the collar on his suit jacket and pulled it around his neck and let the car wander to the side of the blacktop as the speedometer needle fell below thirty.

Harlan began to whistle and then to sing, his voice drifting aimlessly:

> My horses ain't hungry, they won't eat your hay
> So fare thee well, darlin', I'm goin' away
> Your parents don't like me, they say I'm too poor
> They say I'm not worthy to enter your door.

Troy reached down and turned on the radio. It was tuned to a border X station playing a song with a pretty melody, an old-timey country ballad, maybe a church hymn:

> In a little rosewood casket
> That is resting on a stand
> Is a package of old letters
> Written by a lover's hand.

But the lyrics of the song bothered him and he turned the radio off again.

"We've got two hours, maybe not even,

Harlan. Can you hold it together that long?"

"I'm holding everything together. I'm holding it together *just fine.*" Harlan leaned and spat out the window instead of into the ice bucket and began to whistle again. "You know why? Because I've decided not to worry anymore. I woke up this morning and I decided — what's the use in worrying? This train's headed in one direction and it ain't ever coming back. I've decided I'm all ready for my new life in Old Mexico."

The clouds had thickened and the sky had turned a dark gray, like a lead helmet over everything, but it didn't rain. Troy picked up speed and eased onto the pavement again. Martha rolled her window back up and so did the men. She took the polyester blanket and spread it across her lap and tried to tuck the ends behind her shoulders but it was more like a piece of sponge than a blanket and it kept coming loose.

"Mexico is okay," she offered after a while, in response to Harlan, who was surprised to hear her try to make conversation. "In the country, in the desert, it's pretty, if there's enough rain. And the best thing is that people leave you alone."

Harlan didn't say anything for a while and then, not turning to look at her, he asked: "Were you born in Mexico?"

"Yes. But my father was born in Manitoba, up in Canada, where the Mennonites lived after Russia. He was young when they went down to Chihuahua, so he doesn't remember much about the north."

Martha looked at the craggy side of Harlan's face in the shade of his hat.

"Where did your people come from?" she asked.

Harlan glanced back at her this time and seemed perplexed by the question. "English, I guess. Or Irish? Maybe German. Nobody I knew ever talked about remembering family coming over from anywhere. I don't know anybody who knows about a country before this one. Except the Mexicans in town. It all happened too long ago, I guess."

"Is it strange for you not knowing?"

"I never really thought about it," he said. "Maybe that is strange."

After a while he asked: "Is it true that some of you Mennonites live without electrical power?"

Martha pulled at the foam blanket. "I was five before I saw the first electrical light bulb of my lifetime. A man from Chihuahua drove through the campos in a demonstration truck one night trying to sell us generators, and in the bed of his truck he had one hooked up to a Christmas tree all covered in big red and green bulbs. One of my brothers told me that if I looked at electric lights I'd be blinded so I covered my eyes until I couldn't hear the truck anymore and everybody laughed at me so I threw a rock at my brother's head and my mother wore me out with a switch."

"Is it also true what they say about Mennonites, that you keep everything in common, like Jesus said to do?"

Martha considered the question carefully. "I don't think so. There were things in our house, on the farm, that I always thought of as ours, by ourselves. But if somebody really needed something you gave it to him. If somebody needed help, you helped him. To build his shed or kill his hog. When somebody died, the family didn't have to go out and dig the grave. Other people always came to do it. In German you say *Glassenheit*" — she said it with a heavy accent, and it sounded as if it had come from someone else's mouth. "My mother said there was no right word for it in English. She said it meant something like" — Martha closed her eyes to remember — "to hold on by letting go, to increase by diminishing, to win by losing."

"Mmm, that's got a pretty sound," Harlan said. "You sure speak English real well."

"My mother was born here, in Texas."

"Where's your mama now?"

"She's still in Mexico, in the campo, with my brothers and sisters."

"Why are you up here, then? How did your daddy end up in jail?"

Martha fell silent for a while.

"My papa and I left the way of life."

A couple miles later, she said: "I think I'm tired of talking now."

She stared ahead between the two brothers as the car passed under a line of soaring electric transmission towers that carried power at a right angle to the road and into the distance on either side on the rolling grassland. At the wires' lowest ebb hung dozens of bright orange aircraft orbs, silhouetted against the sky so that they looked like flocks of spherical birds flying toward Martha in a line.

The land ahead began to look more rugged now. Low reddish limestone cliffs jutted up from sandy scrubland to which they seemed to have no geological relation. Past the towers, through a line of these cliffs, the road dropped sharply into an immense basin that swept toward the Chisos Mountains, the land between scattered with dark volcanic palisades like embodied shadows. Beyond the mountains segments of the river could be seen and past the river Mexico, visible for the first time.

Troy reached up and adjusted the rearview mirror so that he couldn't see Martha anymore. He thought about how much time he had spent in his adult life looking into rearview mirrors, usually the mirrors closest at hand, giving himself a good going over, rehearsing expressions to make sure they came off as natural, unremarkable. He found rearview mirrors extraordinarily useful, but for what seemed like days now the only thing he'd seen in one was the washed-out face of this sullen Mennonite girl and the treacherous road behind her and all the parts of Texas he knew best receding into the past.

"When we get to the border we'll take you to the bus station and give you fare to El Paso."

"I don't need fare from you," Martha said. "Just leave me at a bus station. I can take care of myself."

"You're going to get a little money and what you do with it and yourself from there on is your own business."

At the edge of the town of Lajitas, not really a town but a momentary confluence of trailer houses and telephone transformer poles, they passed a small aluminum-sided café whose lights were on. Troy doubled back on dirt town roads and drove briefly north again on the highway to a rest stop he had seen, with a circular aluminum table attached to a circular bench, under an aluminum replica of an umbrella that had probably once been covered with festive pink and blue stripes but was mostly bare metal now, flecked with paint chips. Troy told Harlan and Martha to wait while he went for food and to sit facing away from the road in case a car came by.

It was biting cold out now — colder than it ever was in this part of Texas in the fall. Under the heavy sky the sotol grassland looked gray and burnt. Martha pulled the hunting coat around her and walked twenty yards out into the brush to pee. When she came back, she saw Harlan sitting as his brother had instructed him to, with his back to the road, looking out onto a blankness of earth, and she thought about what someone would think if they drove by and saw a man sitting that way at a rest stop, in this kind of weather. They would probably slow down to see what he was looking at and when they saw it was nothing they would go tell somebody in town about the strange man at the rest stop. But Martha joined him on the narrow curve of bench facing the same way, east, toward where the sun might have been if they could have seen it. The light seemed to emanate equally and ineffectually from all parts of the sky.

She was getting tired of sitting in silence.

"How old were you when you started?"

"Started what?"

"Thieving."

"Little girl, I never stole a thing in my life. If you were paying attention, you'd notice my brother has stolen everything that's been stolen so far. I'm just along for the ride, same as you are."

"You stole that blanket and that bucket back at the motel."

"I'd say that sorry excuse for a motel owed us that, wouldn't you?"

Martha got up and walked to the road and looked one way and then the other. The Texas Panhandle had felt emptied of people but this part of the state, the closer it got to the river, seemed almost devoid of human presence, as if mankind wasn't supposed to be here at all.

Harlan looked at the girl as she stood near the road and thought that if it weren't for her hair, she would probably be able to pass for a boy. She had no breasts yet, or figure. The only parts of her that looked feminine in the least were her slender wrists and hands, with long, delicately tapered fingers whose nails had been chewed down to the quick. She looked like she didn't eat enough and never had — her pale blue eyes were striking and her face was pretty but her features were angled and hard-lined in ways that made her appear much older than she was. She seemed wizened in her mind, too, aware of things she shouldn't be yet — of what would happen soon when her body changed and boys her age and men much older began to look at her. She seemed to resent the burden of it before it even arrived.

Harlan took a wad from his pouch and felt the nicotine warmth spread slowly from his mouth down into his chest.

"I read in the paper once how a couple of those Apollo astronauts got sent down here to this part of the Big Bend to study the land, so they'd be ready to deal with the craters up on the moon. Can you believe that?"

"One night on a little TV my papa and I had, we watched an astronaut play golf on the moon and it made my papa laugh . . . he doesn't laugh very much," Martha said. "Do you think those men really went up there?"

"I don't know. I don't suppose I have a

reason to think they didn't."

"I think it was probably just a good TV show. To make people want to believe it, to make them feel better."

Martha looked at the ground and bent and picked up a beige rubber band nearly invisible amid the pebbles. She tested it, stretching it out with her fingers. She came back to the bench and sat down beside Harlan again and reached behind her head and began to braid her hair into a long rope that hung over her right shoulder. When she was done she wound the rubber band tightly around the end and sat very still again. The breeze had picked up now, causing the metal rest stop umbrella to creak like an old windmill. Martha took her arms up into her coat and wrapped them around her and Harlan pulled the brim of his hat down over his face.

"How old are you, girl?"

"Eleven. But I'll be twelve next January."

"You need to go back to your mama and your family in Mexico."

"I can't go back there anymore. I'm going to go with my papa."

"You're no more than a child. How are you going to get to El Paso to find your daddy? And him locked up besides."

She thought about how to tell the lie.

"He's getting out soon. He'll find me."

Martha watched a V of geese fly overhead, so high she couldn't hear any sound they made.

"Where were you headed with your brother? Before this happened?"

"We were going to try to find someone I knew. A woman. I was married to her. She left me and took all my money."

"Why did she do that?"

"I wish I knew."

"Do you know where she is?"

"I married her in Del Rio. She said something about Presidio once. But she could be plum across the country for all I know. What Troy was planning to do if we found her I don't know. I don't think he knew, either."

Harlan got up and spat past the edge of the rest stop's concrete slab and sat back down. "I hadn't seen Troy in years. I didn't have no expectation of seeing him again. I don't know how I let him talk me into going with him. Or why he came back, either. I think maybe he just ran out of road. You can't go on living that kind of life forever. But you can't leave it so easy."

A light rain began to fall. Martha climbed up on the metal table and sat with her legs folded under her, to get the cover of the umbrella. Harlan pulled up the collar of his work shirt and put his hands in his pants pockets and sat where he was, letting the water drip off the brim of his hat between his knees.

EIGHT

Nov. 15, 1972

Sometimes a man's face doesn't look like who he is — it's just an accident of the bones. The brow is too severe and the jawline is too sharp. The mouth is pulled down fighting into a semblance of anger even when none is intended.

By the time he was thirteen or fourteen, Harlan already looked like someone to be avoided in certain situations. His size contributed to the effect and he fell into the habit of hiding behind it, watching silently as boys he'd never even met gave him a wide berth. He wouldn't have known how to defend himself if he'd had to, but he discovered that just looking straight ahead and emptying all expression from his face did the trick. As he grew older, he knew that people talked about him and that they tried to avoid talking to him if they came across him in the grocery store or the post office. And yet he never left town, never seemed to think about leaving, even after Bill Ray was gone. He was one of the most alone people I ever knew, even when I was living with him. And then I left.

In the end this is what you need to know about Harlan, my younger brother:

On a Saturday morning in January of 1943 he woke up at dawn, before anyone else, and got out of his bed quietly.

He could have come across anything shiny and metallic and picked it up to play with it — a pocketknife or a money clip or a silver dollar. He was a three-year-old boy. But that morning he saw a Zippo sitting where Bill Ray had left it on the coffee table, next to a half-empty pack of cigarettes. Harlan took the lighter into the coat closet in the front hall and pulled the door closed to hide with it. He probably flipped up the top and ran his thumb over the flint wheel the way he had seen Bill Ray do, to watch it spark out into the darkness. Then, as little boys do, he grew bored and left the lighter on the closet floor and went to play with the knobs on the radio before anyone was up to stop him.

The winter coats acted as wicks, conveying the flames into the attic, where they snaked along the joists and into the paper insulation and dropped through the thin sheetrock ceilings into the rooms. Through the heavy smoke Bill Ray carried me out of bed in his bathrobe and put me in the neighbor's yard and then he went back in and found Harlan, hiding in the bathtub. He went back a third time screaming for Ruby and I saw him emerge without her from the smoke billowing through the front door, gasping for breath, his face blackened around his mouth and nose. He turned to go in again but two neighbor men grabbed him and held him back and he fought them and they had to take him to the ground and drag him across the street because the heat became too much to bear.

The volunteer fire department truck came, mostly just to contain the fire so that it didn't spread and to get Ruby's remains out. Most of the roof came down and when we went back the next day to see if there was anything we could salvage, it was so cold that the water from the fire hoses had frozen into solid ice over the blackness of the charred wall studs and the furniture and the exposed bedsprings. Everything glistened like crystal in the sun. People I knew and people I had never seen before came by and walked through the wreckage as if it hadn't just been somebody's home and Bill Ray watched them with empty eyes and let them. After an hour or so of picking through things, he put his arm around me and we left empty-handed to go to a house where someone was keeping my brother.

Harlan's life from that time forward was grounded in guilt he felt for a sin he couldn't remember, a sin of neither omission nor commission. As much as Bill Ray tried to shield him from it, he grew up a boy whose earliest memory was that he had killed his mother. He couldn't mourn her because he barely remembered her. He didn't remember her because he had killed her. And so on and so on, down to the bottom of his soul.

Aron woke before dawn, quietly pushed up the screen from the window next to his bed, and climbed out of it fully dressed onto a patch of grassless yard behind the boardinghouse.

Beneath his jacket was a buttoned leather holster with a shoulder strap he had stolen during the night from an American down the hall.

He looked up and down the street, presided over by one city streetlight on a telephone pole. He walked past houses fronted with ornate, white-painted metal fencing, behind which identical white metalwork covered the lower windows and the upper windows. It was unclear whether all this trellising existed to deter thieves — a job it looked poorly suited for — or whether it stood for some colonial architectural tradition. One of the houses appeared to be a makeshift clothing store; the metalwork was festooned with dozens of cheap American sports T-shirts and pajama tops, pinned side by side, above and below, undulating in the breeze like headless, legless bodies, a sight that momentarily spooked Aron in the clear moonlight. A few houses down was an abarrotes that sold milk and beer, next door to a narrow pulquería with an adobe front painted turquoise. On the curb in front of the pulquería a very old man sat hunched beneath an umbrella, though it wasn't raining. The man looked up, frightened, and then smiled as Aron walked past without seeming to notice him.

Aron walked to the end of the block and turned right onto a small, darkened side street and glanced behind him and then walked to the nearest parked car and checked its driver's-side door. It opened. He got in but got back out, leaving the door open. He went to the next car and then the next two, all unlocked, before coming to a beaten, unpainted Chevy Apache pickup that rested too low on its suspension. He got in and this time found the key in the ignition. He shut the door and started the pickup and put it into gear and pulled out, heading toward Calle Arroyo de las Víboras and the bridge over the river into Texas.

Nov. 17, 1972

I'm headed back now, driving east out of Fort Sumner, back up onto the llano. I've stopped in Clovis, N.M., at this little café to get a cup of coffee and a sandwich, to gather my thoughts and prepare myself.

It's been more than three years since I've been anywhere close to town, three more since the last time I was back at the house. I'd hoped to be wearing a better suit, but the suit comes with the room and the room comes with the car and I needed one that wouldn't attract attention. I open the wallet in the jacket pocket and look at the face and the name on the driver's license: Baldwin "Buster" Parker, Jr., 54, of Cache, Oklahoma. Southwestern Livestock Association membership card: Senior Judge — Equine — Since 1952. Every man I'd ever known with a connection to horses drove a pickup. The fact that Buster Parker was making the circuit in a car, a Nova no less, made me wonder if he had run into some problems.

The car was in such bad shape I had to pull off at a wrecking yard outside of Portales for a new fan belt. Some years before, I had passed this yard and made a mental note. It sat off a county road that ran by a small New Mexico state park called Oasis, named for a small seasonal pond that RV people frequented and tried to fish in, mostly for the novelty of it, catching nothing but an occasional ghost-white carp.

The wrecking yard, in a shallow caliche pit, lay only a few hundred feet down the road but it was completely hidden from the campers by rolling sand dunes and low cottonwoods. Over the gate hung a weathered wooden sign that said *COWBOY GRAVEYARD.* I didn't know whether this was the legal name or a joke or maybe both. I was frankly surprised to find the yard still there, a spread of maybe a hundred smashed, twisted, rusted, burned, gutted, gunshot, sun-bleached, wheel-less automobiles — cars, pickups, trucks — manufactured over the last half century, never to be driven again.

A couple of miles on the other side of the pit stretched a different kind of graveyard, a place called Blackwater Draw, a gravel quarry in a dry streambed where a group of archaeologists in the twenties had come across evidence of prehistoric human habitation on the plains. They called the kind of human who lived there — the earliest known human in North America — Clovis Man. This had always sounded funny to me, having once known a man from Clovis, this small New Mexico town where I was now, a town without much to recommend it, least of all the man I knew. The archaeologists dug up spear points, stone hammers, various other caveman things. They also found fossils of the big animals that the cavemen hunted, or maybe the animals that had hunted them — mammoths, saber-toothed tigers. I'd never been able to comprehend what this land must have looked like when animals like tigers and elephants roamed it. Could this flat, dry, treeless part of the earth have been that different? Jungle and swamp? Did actual bona fide bodies of water cover it? Driving by the draw always reminded me how little I really knew about anything, even the things I thought I knew best.

In the scrap heap the sun shot rays in every direction off splintered windshields. The wind sounded mournful through the open chassis of door-less cars. Some of the vehicles were flattened whole, piled on top of each other into high, multicolored cliffs of faded blues, greens, pinks. Some were hacked up, grouped into pieces — rear ends, trunks, and tailfins in a heap; front axles, hoods, and grilles in another. Hundreds of old tires, cut in half, laced inside with spiderwebs, grinned black grins into the bright daylight.

I looked to see if anyone was around, but there never is in such places — when a part is needed someone drives out from town to find it, and if parts walk off by themselves nobody much cares. There will always be more wrecks.

I stepped through the shadows, watching for rattlers and copperheads, and went to the corner where the mostly intact vehicles sat, lined up nose to tail. The stripped ones piled two high looked funny, like skeletons humping. Seeing the damage to each of the cars it was impossible to keep from imagining what had happened to the people riding in them at the time of the calamity. With some wrecks, there was no denying that death had come, decades before or maybe just a few months. In others, the passengers might have survived, but they didn't walk away and they were never going to be the same again.

I took off my jacket and put it on the roof of the cleanest car. I found a belt that seemed pliable enough but I hunted down a spare in case. Then I walked around looking at the least damaged cars, admiring the gracious lines of the older models, lines that seemed to go on and on for no other reason than beauty.

On my way out, I passed one that stopped me, a 1961 Lincoln Continental convertible, midnight-blue four-door. It had once been a magnificent automobile but now rested on its axles, sun-blasted, the body partially severed between the doors as if someone had tried to cut it in half with a band saw. Before I was working for myself I stole a car like this south of Dallas, a big score. But the reason the car stuck in my mind was what we found in the trunk when we opened it, the strangest thing I ever came across in a car: a library. Or what looked for all the world like one, dozens of hardback books almost completely filling the width of the trunk, arranged in five rows of wooden racks, spines up, alphabetized by title. At first we theorized that the man who owned the car might be a teacher or librarian, though the books had no markings. Maybe he was some kind of eccentric, we thought, and just got off on driving around with a trunkful of bookshelves.

My partner, a man named Dale, always on the lookout for an extra score, said: "Maybe he's a goddamned rare book dealer, did you ever think of that?"

He extracted some books from the shelves and examined them, thumbing intently through the first few pages as if he had some actual expertise. But he took two of the oldest-looking books to a dealer and it turned out that he was right: The man looked the volumes over carefully and then looked Dale over carefully and offered him a hundred on the spot.

I sold my half except for three I kept for a while, mostly because I found them so beautiful, bound in tan polished calf hide with gilt cords across the spine. They were a trilogy of Westerns from the twenties by a writer I'd never heard of, named Thornton Woods, and the title of the first book, **The World Beneath the Moon**, had such a nice ring that I started to read it. It told the story of a Tennessee fur trapper named

Daniel T. L. Geary who ends up in Texas after the Civil War, wounded and lost, and makes his way through a hellish landscape of Indians, mercenaries, and carpetbaggers. Relying more on his wits than his guns he builds a cattle business and starts a family that comes to control most of the Texas Panhandle. The second book, **Place of Passage**, about the patriarch's only son, Durant, picks up the story as the cattle empire comes under siege from settlers and a range war breaks out and the son's loyalties are divided after he falls in love with the daughter of a cotton farmer trying to fence off the ranchland. The books were pretty good, written by a man who clearly knew the territory and the time. But the last volume, **The Unsullied Country**, was something altogether different and strange, so unlike its predecessors it was hard to understand how it ever got published. The story took place almost entirely in the mind of Durant, now an old man living on the little that remained of his family land, in a Texas he barely recognized anymore. Through the whole book Durant never leaves the bed where doctors have confined him, his memory the only part of him still able to wander, spooling out over the years he spent with his wife, Vie, the woman for whom he had given up everything. The main part of the story concerns a journey the two take together by wagon as newlyweds, from Amarillo to Austin, to spend their honeymoon in the Driskill Hotel. At first it all seems like a believable enough memory. But the further along you go the more you suspect it's just a dream Durant is having, about a trip he wished he had taken with Vie, who was frail and unable to bear him children, ending the family line. As the two ride down off the plains and into the greenness of the Hill Country, the landscape gradually becomes more unreal. Durant develops the ability to speak the language of the Indians he comes across — Apaches and Tonkawas, hostile Comanches — and to converse with birds and his own horses. The newlyweds find that they no longer need to eat or drink. When they arrive at the state capital, the city is described as a paradise vision of the future, with domed alabaster buildings and dirigibles crisscrossing the sky, a place so magnificent they decide to stay for good. But once they do, the story more or less peters out because they're perfectly happy, and paradise ends up being an uneventful place.

It was the craziest damned book I'd ever read, but for the longest time I couldn't get it out of my head. I felt I knew Durant as well I'd known anyone in my life, and there were times when I fantasized he was an ancestor of mine. The fact that he was a character in an obscure Western novel didn't make thinking about this any less pleasing. If anything, it made it seem like a world existed where it could be possible. Just because a story isn't real doesn't mean it isn't true.

The black canvas top on the Lincoln convertible was up. The windows were so dirt-caked I couldn't see inside. I put the fan belts on my shoulder and reached out with both hands and grabbed the front and back handles — these were the first Lincolns with suicide doors. They came open with surprising ease, parting like castle gates. The pent-up heat inside boiled over me and I peered into the dim interior, which looked oddly preserved: all the seats intact, covered with a thin layer of dust, dash and steering wheel untouched, even the radio still in place. At the risk of getting my suit dirty, I climbed in and sat on the broad rear seat and stretched out my arms. I thought about closing the doors and staying inside for a while, hiding out, shutting out the world. But it was too hot, and I had to get the car fixed if I was going to make town by nightfall. So I got out and closed the doors and walked back to the road.

Nine

When Troy returned to the rest stop it was not in the Biscayne but another car, an apple-red Plymouth Valiant four-door that looked to be only a few years old, well kept. From a distance Harlan and Martha saw the car slowing alongside the shoulder and had no idea Troy was inside. Standing up, Harlan took Martha by the arm and the two began to walk slowly together up the road in the opposite direction, hunched against the rain, a mismatched pair against the immense landscape melting into the gray sky.

Troy eased the car beside them and rolled down his window.

"Hurry up and get in before somebody drives by and sees you," he said.

Harlan didn't stop immediately but slowed his pace and let go of Martha's arm and looked over at Troy in the driver's seat.

"You scared the hell out of us. Where'd this come from?"

"The same place they all come from. Parked somewhere and nobody paying attention. We can't risk keeping one too long now. We're almost there."

Martha's wet hair was plastered to her head like gauze. Before she walked around the wide square front of the car and got into the backseat she squeezed her ponytail with both hands over her shoulder. Harlan continued to stand in the rain looking at the car with water sluicing off the brim of his hat. "It's an improvement, I'd say."

"It's as red as a monkey's ass, and it's another cop make," Troy said. "But it'll get us the rest of the way. Get in. I got us food."

Harlan beat his hat against his knee and rounded the front and got in and Troy turned around in the middle of the road back toward Presidio. Three Styrofoam containers sat in the middle of the bench seat between Troy and Harlan. Troy handed the top one back to Martha.

"I got you a burrito this time, since you're from Mexico," he said. "I don't really know what Mennonites like to eat."

Martha took the still-warm container and put it on her lap and opened it but didn't begin to eat, waiting for Harlan and Troy.

"Thank you."

Harlan took one of the containers and

opened it and said nothing.

"What?" said Troy, taking his eyes off the road and glancing over to see what was wrong with the food.

"You know I don't like eggs. And you get me bacon and eggs."

Troy looked back down the road, which had become hilly and sinuous, twisting along the course of the Rio Grande's ragged line.

"You used to eat eggs. What's the matter with eggs?"

"Chickens are dirty animals, and stupid. I raised and sold chickens for ten years. I drove around with 'em cooped up behind me, shitloads of chickens and their shit for me to smell. So I don't like to eat their embryos, which is what you damn well might be eating when you eat an egg — the embryo of a dirty animal."

"Did you ever think what would happen if we let all those eggs become chickens?" Troy asked. "There'd be so many chickens we wouldn't be able to walk for stepping on them or drive for running them over. It would be terrible. A daily slaughter. In fact, Harlan, it's our moral duty to eat eggs to prevent so much needless chicken suffering."

Harlan snorted and began to pick at his

breakfast with a plastic fork. "You're full of shit. You hold the world record for being full of shit. Next time don't get me no eggs."

In the backseat Martha had already finished eating her burrito with her hands and put the container on the floorboard and stretched out on the wide seat with her ponytail hanging over the edge. The rain sounded heavier, like sleet, and the windshield wipers labored against it. The car passed a cluster of white wooden crosses where an accident had happened along a sharp curve, and then several miles later a couple of far more elaborate memorials, the kind often seen in Mexico, built like ornate birdhouses from painted wood and plastic glass, filled with crosses and rosaries and sometimes laminated photographs of the dead. In Texas the highway department didn't allow such big markers, but these probably remained because so little traffic passed along this road; nobody official had bothered to clear them away.

Through the veil of rain Martha saw the thin serpentine branches of ocotillo coiling up into the air alongside the road, another sign of the border and the nearness of Chihuahua. The narrow, intermittently paved road, Farm-to-Market 170, was known as the River Road and it ran through half of

Big Bend National Park, meaning that almost no one lived along it. Troy had driven it years before, and it looked exactly as he remembered it, a road that seemed not to have been plotted and cleared but etched over thousands of years by the passage of animals and people following the course of the water. On a curve along a low crest the river suddenly became visible beneath them for a few seconds, a narrow slab of gray flanked by a ragged oxbow lake. The land on the other side was almost too obscured by mist to perceive and looked more like a continuity of water than the terrain of another country.

Between Lajitas and Presidio they passed only one other vehicle, a huge white RV with an elderly couple up front, both wearing the same kind of transparent green golf visors. The man and the woman, perched in their seats fifteen feet above the road, waved down enthusiastically, as if from a different reality, where it was a nicer day and the bleak landscape through which they were all passing in the rain looked far different. Martha instinctively returned the wave before remembering that she shouldn't and withdrew her hand.

They came into Presidio in the early afternoon, past a billboard bearing a faded image of a mustachioed cowboy riding a bronco out of the middle of what seemed to be the sun, except that the core of the sun was jet black and ringed with a lariat. Around the circle of the sun and the lariat were written the words: WELCOME TO THE REAL FRONTIER. PRESIDIO, TEX. EST. 1683.

"Is it true that it's that old — older than the United States?" Martha asked.

Troy turned and shot a look out of the corner of his eye. "You need to get down out of sight now. We're nearly into town."

She sunk into the footwell, which felt as big as a bathtub, and could hear Harlan's voice:

"It wasn't called Presidio back when it was founded. It was a mission then, with some long Spanish name, something to do with a burning cross, some miracle some Indian saw one night, if I remember. The U.S. of A. was still a long time in coming. Back then, this whole country was a frontier. You could call any of it anything you wanted as long as you had more guns than the next cowhand that came along."

Troy slowed the car when the road began to look more like a street, running past tangled telephone-wire junctions and trailer houses and a John Deere outlet that should have been surrounded by pickups on a

Monday afternoon but was dark. When signs began to appear at the intersections he rolled his window down and up again to clear the water and tried to read the street names. Before they had arrived anywhere that seemed like a proper town, he turned right onto an unpaved road and took it to its end, past tiny adobe-walled houses with corrugated metal roofs and chain-link fences. Thin trees straggled between them, with leaves twirling off like little dying helicopters. Troy crawled past a few houses before stopping in front of one that looked much like the rest. He reached into his inside jacket pocket and pulled out a piece of paper and looked at it.

"What're we stopping here for?" Harlan asked, trying to see the house outside the car through the scrim of water running down his window. "Who lives here?"

Troy sat silently with the engine running, looking at the house and the houses around it and the few cars parked close to them. "Don't do anything, I'll be back in a second," he said, and he wrestled his arms out of his jacket and pulled it over his head before opening the door and trotting to the mailbox at the edge of the driveway alongside the house. Nearby, a dog set up a culpatory howl. Troy stood by the mailbox for a moment and waited, then opened it and pulled out all the mail and jogged back to the car. With water running off him onto the seats he shut the door and shuffled through the dozen or so envelopes in his hands, looking closely at the handwritten names and the typed ones behind the cellophane windows. Then he opened the door again and dropped all the letters into the mud and put the Plymouth into drive and pulled away.

Harlan turned his body on the seat to face Troy directly.

"Is that where she lives?"

Troy glanced several times into the rearview mirror before turning onto another dirt road and settling back into his seat, wiping the water from his face with his sleeve.

"Does she live there, Troy? Who told you to look there?"

"Somebody who knew her."

"Did she come here after me or was this where she lived before?"

"I don't know any of that."

Harlan leaned closer. *"Did you ever talk to her? Did she talk to you?"*

Troy lifted his foot off the gas and let the car coast along a row of houses facing a barbed wire fence, along which three coyote carcasses were strung to the top wire, hanging like old fur coats.

"No, Harlan. I don't even know her. You're the one who knew her. She was *your* wife."

"You seem to know people who know things about her I never did."

"Well I guess they didn't know anything, did they? Or she's not getting mail under her name. But I highly doubt that. I don't think she's there. She probably never was."

Harlan turned to look over his shoulder, back toward the street they had left, wanting to see now what the houses looked like.

The car began moving again, sluggishly in the mud, swimming from one side of the road to the other. The rain picked up and the wipers made a hard, muffled sound like a bass drum playing outside.

From the backseat came Martha's voice again:

"We're here in town now. Can you please take me to the bus station and let me off? Thank you very much for the ride."

Troy turned onto a paved street and the car felt solid beneath them again.

"First we're going to the bridge to see if there's a line. I don't want to get stuck on this side of the river with you around to be seen. Just stay down and we'll all say our goodbyes before you know it."

He continued driving west for several blocks toward the milky sun, which seemed to be at least halfway down the sky. For a city as old as Presidio, it was remarkable how undeveloped the city blocks still seemed, half-formed, with more dirt roads than paved, houses scattered off the roads at odd angles. Lots were filled with old cars and leaning telephone poles with wires loping low to the ground, like a tethering system designed to keep everything from drifting into the river. The frontier drive that had pushed westward toward every inch of American border seemed to have lost its way here, or never arrived.

Troy turned south onto Highway 67, a broad, well-paved road, the only one in the city that felt like a stretch of government pavement, bordered with tall streetlights. Though palm trees weren't seen in any quantity at this latitude, the highway, as it neared the international bridge, was lined at regular intervals with tall elegant Mexican palmettos. They seemed to have been planted there with United States transportation funds to usher drivers into a more exotic clime, except that when the road became Mexican Federal Highway 16 through the Chihuahuan desert a palm tree wasn't seen again for hundreds of miles.

The bridge, a two-lane wooden trestle from the thirties, was not the property of either government but belonged to a local businessman who occasionally made the newspaper because he had managed for years to prevent a federal bridge from being built upriver, leaving him the only private owner of an international crossing in Texas; his bridge was the sole means of passage into Mexico for six hundred miles between Laredo and El Paso.

As Troy approached it, he could feel the nearness of the border almost physically, in his chest. The rain had let up but the soil, drought-hardened, struggled to take in so much water at once and the excess pooled in the ditches and ran downhill to the river. It had grown so cold outside that ice slicks began to form on the pavement and Troy slowed, looking for them. Only a few cars moved on the road as they got closer, and Troy hoped the rain would keep the crossing traffic at home. But when they rounded the final bend before the road descended to the river he saw a line of cars and trucks stretching for several hundred yards toward a place he could not see but assumed was the toll shack and the Border Patrol checkpoint.

He drove closer but began to fear getting

pinned into a lane, so he pulled the Plymouth over to the shoulder and flipped on the emergency flashers and told Martha to stay as far out of sight as she could. He got out and walked briskly along the side of the road toward the bridge, looking straight ahead, as if none of the vehicles he was passing were there. Harlan watched him until he could no longer make out his form in the water that thickened into the distance. Pickup trucks with beds full of Mexican men and families holding coats and tarpaulins over their heads inched by; the occupants stared out with eyes that looked stunned by what nature had allowed, a kind of cold never experienced this far south even in the depths of winter. When the people passed the pulled-over Plymouth they slowed and glared at Harlan inside it, as if he was the cause of the backup that had forced them into such misery.

Next to where Troy had pulled the car, on a concrete expanse, a huge bronze statue of a man carrying a gavel in one hand and his hat in the other stood between two widely spaced palm trees. Looking up, Harlan didn't recognize the figure, who had a big round face and a sullen glare, but he was able to make out the words on the plinth, which named the honoree as Anson Jones, the final president of the Republic of Texas before it dissolved in 1845, ending Jones's dream of independent nationhood. The gilded words on the plinth said: "The Revered of Senates and the Light of Cabinets! The echo of his words lingers in the Councils of his Country, alone unheard by ears deaf to the claims of merit, dull to the voice of Honor, and dead to the calls of Justice. To them the sand; to Thee the Marble!" But then after such praise the eulogy ended strangely, concluding with no explanation: "Departed 9th of January, 1858, by his own hand. May he rest in Peace, Safe in the arms of the one Disposing Power, Or in the Natal or Mortal hour."

After several minutes, Martha's voice, deep and hollow from her position down in the footwell, broke Harlan's reverie.

"Do you think he'll come back? Maybe he's just going to walk across."

Harlan turned to speak but remembered the audience passing outside the windows and looked ahead as if he was alone in the car.

"He'll come back."

"How do you know?"

"I don't know how I know. Leaving's about the only reliable thing Troy's done his whole life. But this ain't the way he'd do it."

The inside of the car seemed to shut out all sound from the world.

"I'm cold," Martha said finally.

Harlan fiddled with the Plymouth's heater controls and put his hands against the vents but felt no warmth coming out. The traffic alongside them had ground to a stop, but occasionally groups of slow-moving, hunched-down people passed on foot, passengers who had also gotten out of their vehicles to walk to the bridge and find out what was wrong.

Moving through one of these groups in the opposite direction, threading his way through cars, Troy reappeared. He got in soaking wet, shivering, and put his hands under his armpits inside his suit jacket.

"The rain's got the river too high and the bridge is nearly swamped," he said. "The goddamned thing's made out of wood, like a bridge in some old Western movie. They're afraid for it, with that much water pushing at it. They're letting just a few cars over at a time. The rate they're going we won't get across before nightfall." He looked through the watery windows at the people straggling along the road, more now, some carrying bags and boxes, hoping to be allowed to walk across if they couldn't drive. "We can't sit like this waiting with her in here."

He put the car in reverse and began backing up carefully along the shoulder past the long line of unmoving vehicles piled up behind them. At points people blocked the way and took their time stepping off the pavement to let them pass. A couple of kids slapped the side of the Plymouth and said things in Spanish that only Martha, balled up under her coat, could understand. When they finally came into the clear, Troy put it in drive and arced across the road into the opposite lanes, passing two brown sheriff's cars that seemed to be headed in to handle the mounting crowd.

He pulled into the nearest gas station, wondering how long it would be before the Plymouth was reported stolen. To appear normal, he asked for a fill-up and stood under the canopy as the attendant pumped, watching a pair of sparrows defy the cold to peck insects from the car's grille. He went inside and asked the clerk for the location of the bus station.

"There ain't no bus station in this town," the clerk, an elderly white man, said, looking Troy over closely, failing to place him. "There's a place where the bus stops, if that's what you mean. The afternoon bus to

El Paso comes through about five-thirty if it's running in this kind of weather."

"Where's the stop?"

"At the café."

"Where's the café? Does it have a name?"

"It don't need no name. There's only one. Head down O'Reilly that way to Erma, then left up to Bledsoe."

Troy found the place, designated as the bus stop by a small Greyhound sticker in the front window next to a Texas flag sticker and another of Our Lady of Guadalupe. By its colors, teal-blue trim with cream cinder-brick walls, the café seemed to be affiliated with a motel just across a service road, the Three Palms, with the same paint job and three feeble-looking palm trees growing near a sign depicting three palms in silhouette. Troy parked on the gravel stretch alongside the café and got out, glancing at the cars he could see in the motel parking lot. "Just stay in here for a minute, stay down," he said as he shut his door. "I'm going in to figure out about the tickets."

Martha opened the back door and stepped out.

"I'm getting out now," she said. "I'm staying here."

She stood where she was, waiting for him to say something or grab her.

He looked her over thoroughly for the first time, in her faded pinkish flower-print shirt, with her thin bare arms.

"Put your coat on," he said.

She reached inside and got it and Harlan opened his door and got out, too.

"I need a cup of coffee," he said.

Troy looked at Harlan and the girl, who both stared back at him.

"Come on, Troy. For God's sake. What's the use of sitting out here now?"

The interior of the café was bare-bones — no booths, only a few tables with clear plastic coverings and metal-legged turquoise chairs pushed beneath. The high horizontal windows were completely covered with short dusty curtains so that no light from outside entered and the fluorescent lighting was almost painfully bright. A woman stood behind the counter, a big Mexican-looking woman, and a solitary patron, an elderly Mexican-looking man wearing an old cowboy hat, sat slumped near her in a chair facing away from the tables, staring at a black-and-white television above the counter showing a football game with the sound off. Harlan and Martha stood near the door as Troy approached the woman and nodded cordially down at the man, who seemed not to be a customer but connected somehow to the establishment. Troy asked to buy a ticket for the bus.

"No, sir," the woman said. "You buy it on the bus from the driver. It's cash only. It's twelve dollars."

The man in the chair — who upon closer inspection looked profoundly old, his cheeks covered in rough gray stubble that someone probably shaved for him — laughed and Troy thought it had something to do with the ticket situation. But when he looked at him, he saw the man wasn't paying any attention to him. He was staring at the silent football game and mouthing words at it, winking and chuckling at the screen. He turned his deeply wrinkled face up to Troy and looked into his eyes for an uncomfortably long time and then back at the television and pointed to it with an outstretched arm and nodded gravely, as if something was happening on the screen that Troy should know.

Troy turned to the woman, who might have been the man's daughter or granddaughter.

"Is he trying to say something to me?"

"No, no. He can't talk."

"Is he all right?"

"He's fine. We like to say he just got lost in thought one day and never found his way back out again."

She smiled in a way that suggested she delivered this line to all out-of-town customers, though there was also something about the café that made it seem as if this woman and old man were the only ones who ever passed through its doors. Troy looked down again and the man stared back at him with a baleful glare, the way old people who have lost their minds sometimes do, a face that said: You probably know who I am but I don't anymore, and that's not fair.

Troy thanked her and glanced toward Harlan and Martha, who stood uncertainly near a table by the door. Troy went into the bathroom and locked the door behind him and looked at himself for a long time in the rust-pocked mirror. He had the acrid taste of fear in his mouth — it had been there for days — and he could feel his heartbeat surging behind his ears. But the face he saw in the mirror was that of a man who looked perfectly normal, absolutely calm and composed, the face of somebody else, the way it had looked his whole life but even more so today. He went to one of the urinals, a tall ornate old-fashioned model that seemed to be a relic from a prior establishment or a prior century. It resembled a marble sculpture, and while he peed into it he lowered his forehead slowly onto the broad top, which was cool and damp to the touch. Despite the cold outside it felt soothing against his skin, consoling, like a gift, the closest thing to a religious feeling he had had in years.

When he opened the bathroom door his line of sight ran directly behind the lunch counter and he saw the woman — the waitress, or possibly the owner — squatted down on her big thighs in her pink uniform dress, the way someone would squat to look for something. But she didn't look like she was looking for anything. The way her head was inclined he thought maybe she was getting sick. She suddenly noticed Troy standing there, just a few feet away, and she stared at him and made a motion with her hand that he was unable to interpret. Did she need his help to get up? Had she lost something? The expression on her face was one of distress, but a distress she might have experienced before, a problem she had some practice in. He stepped forward toward her but before he could take a second step, the expression on her face turned to one of actual terror and she went all the way to her knees and put her head near the ground.

It was only then that Troy felt a draft of cold air on his face and realized too late that someone had come through the front door of the café and the woman had been telling him to remain out of view, to go back into the bathroom. But he was already almost past the corner of the corridor and whoever had come in would have been able to see him or his shadow by now. The old man hadn't moved from his chair and still stared at the television, as if the woman hadn't disappeared beneath the counter. Troy took a half step forward and saw Harlan midway inside the dining room, facing the door, standing very still, his hat on one of the tables, his hands held slightly away from his body with his palms facing the floor as if he was practicing a dance step. He didn't seem to see Troy behind him. The girl was sitting, with her chair turned so that she faced sideways from a table, half toward the door and half toward him. Her mouth was moving and she was saying words in a high, agitated, barely audible whisper that sounded like neither English nor Spanish, and Troy knew that if he took another step he would be able to see the person she was addressing.

He held his breath and tried to remember if he had seen a window in the bathroom or an exit door down the hallway. As he stepped backward, the old man slowly turned his head in his direction and put one of his gnarled fingers up to his grinning face, underneath his right eye, and pointed the finger toward the television and said something that sounded like "Buffalo!" Then another voice, raspy, from the front of the café, said loudly, *"¡No te muevas!"* and a rail-thin man appeared in Troy's vision, walking sideways toward the left side of the café, holding a pistol straight-armed in front of him, swinging its aim rapidly from Harlan to Troy.

Troy knew the instant he saw the man. Not just from the resemblance — a narrow face with high cheekbones and pale eyes set just too widely apart — but from the child-like way Martha held her body and the expression he could see on her half-turned face. The man was so ragged it was impossible to tell how old he was. He looked like someone who hadn't slept in months and hadn't been outside for longer than that. His short-chopped blond hair was darker than his skin and his whiskers were like ash spread aimlessly over his cheeks and chin. He was dressed in what looked like pajamas but was probably some type of Mexican field garb, a loose white jacket and tunic that hung down over baggy pants of the same thin material. The pants, stained brownish yellow at the crotch and knees, were far too short and didn't seem to belong to him, and on his feet were the kind of huaraches with car-tire soles, above which the leather weavework was busted, barely covering his bony feet. Troy had never seen anyone outside of a hospital look so deathly sick and broken down. Trembling, the man shone with a strange dignity, the dignity of the thoroughly defeated.

The pistol in his right hand was small and decorative-looking, with a snub barrel covered in scroll engraving like a woman's purse gun. But as small as it was, it seemed to require a great deal of effort for him to hold it at the end of his straightened arm, and the tight way he gripped it suggested he had never handled a pistol before. Troy looked at Harlan, who was still holding out his hands but no longer looking at the man. He was looking down instead at Martha, who was crying, quietly, saying something over and over again in German. The man held out his left hand sternly toward the girl and she obeyed him, not budging from the chair where she sat, looking much younger than Troy had seen her to be.

Troy took a slow sideways step into the room while raising his hands, too, not above his head but in front of him with palms out in a calming gesture. From the corner of his vision, he could still just see the old man of the café, who had not turned to witness any of what was happening but had fallen silent and sat very still in his chair, breathing heavily and audibly. The waitress was nowhere to be seen, concealed fully behind the counter.

Troy tried to look Martha's father directly in the eyes, the way he had heard you should in a situation like this, but the man's eyes seemed to stare right through him, through the cinder-block wall behind him, out into the alley. Troy thought that if he didn't start talking soon he would never get the chance.

"I know who you are," he said, speaking slowly. "I know you. You're Martha's daddy. Do you speak any English?"

The man's face didn't show any awareness that he had heard Troy's voice and he moved the gun off Troy back to Harlan and looked hard at Harlan and then down at Martha.

Troy raised his hands higher, trying to draw the man's attention back to him.

"Listen, this is all just a big misunderstanding! There's no need for a gun in here. No one's going to hurt your little girl and no one's going to hurt you. She's been looking all over Texas for you and here you are! She can go with you now and my brother and I can go on our way. Your girl is just fine. Everything's fine. Todo está bien. Do you understand me?"

The man looked back at Troy as if the sound coming from his mouth wasn't language but just a noise that made it difficult for him to concentrate. He kept the gun on Harlan, leveled at his chest, and then he turned his eyes back down to his daughter. He opened his mouth and made a horrible noise like a cry and a retching cough at the same time and he spoke again, this time in English that seemed comprised of the few words he knew.

"What did you do?" he said.

He looked at Harlan and his eyes were wide and flashing now and he trembled so that the gun moved in circles at the end of his arm.

"What did you do?" he said again.

Harlan looked up from the girl and stared at Aron and Martha's voice rose in a howl from below.

"He did nothing, they did nothing!" she screamed in English. "I told you. They just drove me, Papa. I was in the car and they drove me here because I made them take me to you. They did nothing! *Don't hurt anybody! I don't want you to hurt anybody!"*

His eyes seemed to register only a partial understanding of what she had said and whatever he comprehended changed nothing in his bearing. He shifted his eyes quickly to Troy and then back to Harlan and tears began to roll down his cheeks as he said again, his voice rising:

"What did you do?"

Troy took a full step forward now and said: "Tell him in Spanish, Martha. Tell him in Dutch, that you're okay. If we don't leave here right now somebody's going to walk through that door and it's all going to be over. Tell him I know he doesn't want to go back to jail. Tell him they'll take you back to Tahoka and you and your daddy will never see each other again. *Do you know how many people are looking for you right now?* Your picture's probably going to come up on that TV screen any minute."

Martha turned her head toward the picture on the small set, which showed a close-up of a man's face inside a football helmet and heavy snow coming down in front of him, though it was hard to tell whether it was snow or static in the reception. A picture of herself appearing on the same screen seemed inconceivable, something that could not happen in the world as she knew it. She tried to remember the last picture taken of her and how old she would have been but she was too scared to think.

Her father was still pointing the pistol at Harlan, shaking badly now in his knees and shoulders. But he took in a deep breath and steadied himself and said the words in English again — *"What did you do!"* This time it didn't sound like a question but like a statement, made in the high keening voice of a child. Then he clamped his eyes shut and leaned his head back at an odd angle.

Troy propelled himself through the open space between two tables, across a stretch of dirty linoleum floor that seemed to go on for eternity. The walls gave a hollow-sounding clap too weak for a real gun to have made. But in the quarter second before the sound echoed, Troy's outstretched right hand burst into a bright-red flare that splattered onto the plastic covering of the café tables nearby. And time, which had been compressed to the density of a diamond, suddenly opened up, making what happened next seem to happen inside an enormous space where everything could be seen clearly but nothing could be changed.

Troy's body spun through a revolution and slapped into the cinder-block wall on the other side of the café and Harlan reached out for the pistol, which made its small clap a second time, and Martha screamed and the old man at the back of the café, his eyes still fixed on the TV, put his hands over his ears and began to howl like a dog. Troy slumped against the wall and grabbed at its shiny painted surface with his left hand and looked down at his suit jacket. His head came up and he looked surprised and his legs gave way underneath him, sliding out along the floor and knocking over a chair. He sank all the way to the linoleum with his back to the wall, and blood streamed from his right hand as he placed his left palm carefully over the gabardine of his jacket near the top button.

Aron staggered back out of Harlan's reach and raised his other hand to the pistol to hold it in both, making the gun tremble even more violently. Martha crawled toward her father on the floor, screaming. Aron swung the gun in Harlan's direction but he was no longer looking where it was aimed. He was looking in horror at his hands, at the tiny thing in them and the film of smoke that hung around it, and he suddenly let the pistol go and it bounced on its grip and landed near the threshold to the front door. He looked down and seemed to see his daughter for the first time below him.

Thinking she had been hit, he fell to his knees and lifted her up by the shoulders and struggled to get them both to their feet and looked wildly into her eyes and up and down her body to see if there was any blood on her. Martha made a sound just short of a scream, and grabbed at him violently but he held her away and then seized her in both of his arms and held her tightly against him until she stopped struggling. He looked wild-eyed over the top of Martha's head at Harlan and began to inch himself and his daughter slowly backward toward the inside glass door to the café. Still facing Harlan, he pushed the door open with his body and reached into the vestibule and opened the front door and pulled Martha with him out into the rain, and a cold damp air rolled into the dining room before the glass doors gradually closed themselves. The sound of Martha's cries fell away, and the old man grew quieter until he, too, no longer made any noise. The inside of the café was suddenly silent and completely still except for the images flickering on the television and the haze from the gun gathering into a membrane between the floor and ceiling.

Harlan turned and straddled Troy with his body. He bent over him and brought his face close to his brother's.

"Jesus God, Troy. *Oh, Jesus God in heaven.* How bad are you hit?"

Troy looked down and tried to unbutton his jacket with his good hand but couldn't manage it. "I can't feel it," he said. "I can see it but I can't feel it. It couldn't have been much." Harlan opened the jacket and saw the small, clean hole — no more than a .22 — through the white shirt just below the ribs. And he saw the pool of darkness beginning to form around Troy's legs on the floor.

"Help me! Help me up, Harl! We've got to get out of here!"

The voice of the woman called out sharply from behind the counter: *"¡Hector! Hector! ¿Estás herido? Hector!"* But Hector, sitting in the same position with his back to the front door, was watching the television set again and didn't answer her.

Harlan leaned his right shoulder down and hooked his arm under Troy's and slowly hoisted him off the floor. Troy cried out in pain and his body went slack and Harlan slung Troy's limp right arm all the way over his shoulder and steadied him against his hip to keep him from falling. He looked toward the back of the café and caught sight of the black-haired woman almost against the floor, peeking around the edge of the counter to figure out whether she was still in danger and what kind of damage had been done to her business. "Hector! Hector! No puedo verte! *¡Háblame, Hector!*"

She inched forward until she could see Hector sitting untroubled in his chair, then she scooted back behind the counter and her head disappeared entirely again.

"Do you want me to call the police?" she called out.

Harlan struggled backward along the floor holding Troy's weight and slowly bent his knees and picked up the pistol near the door and kept it in his hand.

"Not unless you think you have to."

He dragged Troy into the vestibule and looked through the side windows into the heavy gray of the parking lot to see if Martha and her father were out there. Then he pushed through the open door into the rain, leaving two thick boot trails of blood along the narrow sidewalk that led around the café to the parking lot. He had no thought about whether anyone was outside to see him, but no one was and no one drove by as he wrestled to get the passenger door of the Valiant open and his brother into the seat. He dug in Troy's pants pockets for the keys and Troy grabbed his arm and looked in his eyes as if he wanted to tell him something but nothing came out of his open mouth. Harlan closed the passenger door and ran around the front of the car and got in. The front of his khaki shirt was soaked in blood. Troy had slumped over onto the driver's seat and Harlan lifted him up and pushed him over and used both hands to lay Troy's head carefully against the window on the passenger side.

Harlan started the engine and put on the wipers and was about to pull the stick down into reverse but then he didn't. He sat staring into the rain, listening to the low sound of the motor and the thump of the wipers and then he turned the key and killed it and the wipers stopped in the middle of the windshield.

He took off his hat and set it on the dash and leaned his big body against Troy's and laid his right ear against his chest, on the damp white shirt where the jacket had fallen away. He stayed this way for a long time, his head resting on his brother's body, the inside of the car silent except for the falling rain. Finally, he sat up and took his hat and put it on his lap. The windshield had filled with water again and the rain streaked down the side windows and when the cars finally pulled up he could see nothing of them but their lights splintered into a million red and blue pieces.

Nov. 18, 1972

I write this sitting at the kitchen table at home, at what used to be my home, the only place I ever really thought of as such. I don't remember much about the first house anymore, other than what it looked like on that cold February day after the fire when Bill Ray took me to see it, when the burnt walls and roof beams were glittering with ice formed by the water the firefighters had poured on them.

This house is so much smaller than I remembered it. It's hard to understand how we all lived here together for so many years in a collection of such little boxes. But we did okay, at least when Harlan and I were young. More or less my whole conception of the world and of myself was formed right here, at this table, in this kitchen, back down that little hallway into that bedroom that's no more than thirty feet away, inside these thin painted sheetrock walls that you could hear through and that let in so much of the cold in winter.

Breaking into your own home — a home that's not yours anymore but in some ways always will be — is a funny thing. You feel like a stranger to yourself, as if you're somebody else paying a visit to your life. But it helps you get perspective you might not otherwise be able to get on what some small things and places mean, even if you don't always want them to.

Sitting here brings back a dream I used to have when I was young, a dream that seemed very real even though almost nothing happened in it.

It was nighttime and I was driving up and down the main street like we all did on weekend nights when we were young, waiting for somebody to come along and relieve the boredom, waiting for something to happen that never did. Up and back and up and back again, past the courthouse, past the school and the grocery to the blinking yellow light and down again to the west side, past the motel to the old grain elevator parking lot where we made the loop. But when I got to that end of town for the hundredth time I decided not to make the loop. I decided to keep driving past the streetlights into the darkness on the other side of the grain silos, and I found a part of town there that I'd never seen before, a part that I'd never even known about.

There wasn't anything special about this

other part of town. It wasn't a dream about something better. It was just a street that was new to me out west of the motel, with a little coffee shop and a couple of glass-fronted stores.

I couldn't understand how I'd never known about it, living here my whole life, but I was so happy to find it. I drove past the lighted window of the café and even at that late hour I saw a few people sitting in the booths, drinking coffee. It looked nice. I thought: Now, sometimes, I can come out here.

ACKNOWLEDGMENTS

I would like to acknowledge my debt to Jack Black's 1926 memoir *You Can't Win,* to the writings of Robert Smithson, the photographs of Stephen Shore, William Eggleston, and Alec Soth, and the movies *Two-Lane Blacktop, Wanda, The Last Picture Show,* and *Stranger Than Paradise.* My understanding of Mennonite life was deepened immeasurably by Harry Leonard Sawatzky's 1971 history *They Sought a Country: Mennonite Colonization in Mexico.* I would also like to express my gratitude to the late, great Chris Burden, from whose video piece "Big Wrench" I have lovingly borrowed the name Jim Quaintance.

PERMISSIONS

The author acknowledges permission to quote from "Mr. Fool," words and music by Darrell Edwards, George Jones, and Herbie Treece, copyright © 1959 (renewed 1987) Trio Music Company, Fort Knox Music, Inc., Pappy Daily Music LP, and Glad Music Publishing & Recording LP. All rights for Trio Music Company administered by BMG Rights Management (US) LLC. All rights reserved. And from "I Must Be Somebody Else," words and music by Merle Haggard, copyright © 1966 Sony/ATV Music Publishing LLC. Copyright renewed. All rights administered by Sony/ATV Music Publishing LLC. International copyright secured. All rights reserved. Lyrics for both songs are reprinted by permission of Hal Leonard LLC.

Also included are lyrics from "My Horses Ain't Hungry" and "The Butcher's Boy," traditional, and from "Little Rosewood

Casket," published by Louis P. Goullaud and Charles A. White, 1870.

ABOUT THE AUTHOR

Randy Kennedy was born in San Antonio and raised in Plains, a farming town in the Texas Panhandle, where his father worked as a telephone lineman and his mother as a teachers' aide. He moved to New York City in 1991 and worked for twenty-five years at the *New York Times,* first as a city reporter, then for many years writing about the art world. A collection of city columns, *Subwayland: Adventures in the World Beneath New York,* was published in 2004. He is now the director of special projects for the art gallery Hauser & Wirth. He lives in Brooklyn with his wife, Janet Krone Kennedy, a clinical psychologist, and their children, Leo and Iris.

The employees of Thorndike Press hope you have enjoyed this Large Print book. All our Thorndike, Wheeler, and Kennebec Large Print titles are designed for easy reading, and all our books are made to last. Other Thorndike Press Large Print books are available at your library, through selected bookstores, or directly from us.

For information about titles, please call:
(800) 223-1244

or visit our website at:
gale.com/thorndike

To share your comments, please write:

Publisher
Thorndike Press
10 Water St., Suite 310
Waterville, ME 04901